# Death of a Ghostwriter

ALSO BY GAYNOR TORRANCE

JEMIMA HUXLEY SERIES
Book 1: The Cardiff Killings
Book 2: The Briarmarsh Close Killings
Book 3: The Caerphilly Mountain Killings
Book 4: The Leighton Meadow Killings
Book 5: The Marquess Club Killings
Book 6: The Rhymney Valley Killings
Book 7: The Boy in the Reeds

WYE VALLEY WIDOWS
Book 1: Death of a Ghostwriter

# DEATH
## of a
# Ghostwriter

# GAYNOR TORRANCE

JOFFE BOOKS

Joffe Books, London
www.joffebooks.com

First published in Great Britain in 2025

Cover art by Cherie Chapman

ISBN: 978-1-83526-974-9

*For Steve, the best husband, friend, soulmate, homemaker,*
*baker and barista I could ever wish for. Always . . .*

# CHAPTER 1

Since taking his first steps, it seemed that Albert had made it his mission to live life to the full. Throughout childhood, from the moment he woke up to the second his head touched the pillow at night, his waking moments were filled with mischief and activity. His active imagination, boundless energy, sense of fun and enthusiasm for life proved infectious, and people of all ages gravitated towards him.

As a small child, Albert enjoyed the nightly ritual of bedtime stories. For those fifteen minutes or so before he fell asleep, he'd snuggle beneath the covers, feeling warm, comfortable and safe. He'd close his eyes as he listened to his mother's soothing voice transporting him to different worlds, where anything seemed possible.

Learning to read had a profound effect on him, as it expanded Albert's horizons. Though, never satisfied with the books he read, he'd embellish the original, until he began to create original characters and stories and record his ideas on the page.

It seemed that he was always destined to be a writer, and eventually he became one of the fortunate few who managed to build a career around their passion. But, as every author knows, being a good writer didn't guarantee success. And despite Albert's books having attained worldwide sales in the millions, he did not take the credit for them. For Albert was a highly paid, and exceptionally successful ghostwriter.

As an adult, his love of life remained apparent. Though there was another side to him too. A side he was keen to explore. A side he was determined to keep hidden. But secrets rarely stay hidden for ever. And it turned out that some of those who thought they knew Albert best knew very little about him at all. There was no denying that he was dependable, hard-working, conscientious. A devoted husband. A loving father. An all-round good guy and family man. But people were about to realise that there was more to him than met the eye.

On what began as a typical morning in late spring, Albert woke to the sound of birdsong. He yawned and stretched as dawn's first rays filtered through the flimsy bedroom curtains. For someone who usually woke at the slightest sound, he'd slept unusually heavily and felt groggy and slightly disorientated. Though he thought it was nothing a hot shower followed by a two-minute blast of icy water wouldn't cure. It was a routine he always followed. No matter the time of year. The sudden drop in temperature was shocking. Sometimes unwelcome. But invigorating, nevertheless.

He glanced across at his still-sleeping wife and smiled contentedly. It was almost two years since a chance encounter had drawn them into each other's orbit, and there wasn't a day that went by when he didn't thank his lucky stars for that fateful moment.

Albert felt as though he was the luckiest man alive. He still experienced a fluttering in the pit of his stomach whenever he looked at her and had to pinch himself to believe that this drop-dead gorgeous woman had agreed to marry him. He saw the way other men looked at her and knew that she could have her pick of the best. Yet for some inexplicable reason she'd chosen him.

He sighed, sad in the knowledge that they'd be parted for the next two weeks. It was a pattern they were both accustomed to, but heart-wrenching, all the same. One week together. Two weeks apart. Still, needs must. And there was no denying that it had the benefit of keeping their relationship fresh. After a quick shower and breakfast, he would soon be loading his bags into the car. It was an established routine.

Albert slipped out of bed and crept downstairs, determined not to disturb his sleeping beauty. For some reason he found himself humming 'Luck Be a Lady'. And even though there was no music playing, he could hear Frank Sinatra's voice singing it as clearly as if he were standing only a few feet away. Once in the kitchen, he set about scooping coffee into the filter machine. It would be freshly brewed by the time he'd finished showering.

It was a ritual of his to sing in the shower. It was something he'd done for as long as he could remember. And as powerful jets of water rained down on him, he belted out the lyrics of 'Mack the Knife', followed by a soulful rendition of 'Moon River'.

Later, as he emerged from the en suite, he could smell the freshly brewed coffee, and it made his mouth water. As far as he was concerned it was the best part of breakfast. Gave him the kick he needed to start the day properly.

The bed was empty, with the duvet scrunched in a messy heap, and there was no mistaking the sound of the radio, blaring from the kitchen. Albert dressed and headed downstairs. It wouldn't be long now before he was on the road.

'Good morning, darling,' she said. 'I've made your breakfast.' Whenever they were together, she insisted that he start the day with smashed avocado on a slice of sourdough, lightly sprinkled with chilli flakes. It was nice enough, but he'd much prefer to have a full English.

Albert pulled her close. 'My perfect wife.' He smiled and feathered her upturned face with kisses.

'I try my best. But I hate the mornings when I know that once you've finished your breakfast, you're going to walk out

the door, and I won't see you again for another two weeks.'
Her voice faltered and tears welled in her eyes.

'I know it's hard for you. Believe me, I find it hard too.
I hate that it must be this way, but there's nothing I can do
about it. I've worked my way up in that company and proven
my worth. They value my contribution, which is why I get
paid so much.'

'Surely you could find another job. One where you didn't
have to spend two out of every three weeks away from home?
It can't be that difficult. Not for someone of your calibre.' She
gripped his arms and looked at him imploringly.

'I wish it was that simple but it's not. I know this company inside out. If I went anywhere else, I'd have to start far
lower down the chain and eventually work my way up. Our
finances would take such a hit. We'd most likely have to rent
somewhere smaller, and I'm sure you wouldn't want that?

'And let's face it,' Albert continued, 'I'm not exactly
young. No one is going to want to take a chance on a fifty-
two-year-old guy. Not when there are so many younger people
out there who have a realistic chance of giving so many more
years to a business. Believe me, since we found each other, I've
thought about walking away from the job. But I'm a realist.
If I hand in my notice, it'd be as good as saying that I'd given
up. I wouldn't get a comparable job anywhere else.'

Almost half an hour later, having loaded his bags into the
car, Albert was on his way out of the house. 'I should have a
gap in my schedule at about four o'clock. I'll do my best to
call you then.' He opened the passenger door and slung his
briefcase on the front seat. The car had been serviced the previous day. An arrangement with the garage meant that they
collected and returned it to their home address. They also
provided Albert with a courtesy car for the day, which meant
he could go about his routine. It cost a little extra, but it was
worth it. After all, time was money, and with a deadline loom-
ing for the return of the first round of edits, it had allowed
Albert to rework the final scene of the latest book in the Harry

Blake PI series. And even he was impressed with the result. It was a doozy.

Once in the driver's seat, it took a few minutes for Albert to readjust the seat and mirrors, as the mechanic must have been shorter than him. Eventually satisfied that everything was as it should be, Albert started the engine, turned, and waved goodbye to his wife as he pulled off the drive.

Whenever he was on the road, he liked to turn the music up and feel the beat pulse all around him. He found it helped alleviate the boredom of driving. This morning, there was no choice to be made. It had to be Ol' Blue Eyes himself. He'd just accelerated onto a section of dual carriageway when 'My Way' began to play. Oh, how he loved that song. It was one of his favourites. Reaching out with his left hand, he turned the volume up even further and began to sing along to the lyrics he knew so well. He was doing seventy when a Vauxhall Corsa overtook and cut in front of him, braking sharply. It was apparent that the driver intended to pull off at an exit point that was almost upon them. The sensible thing would have been to stay in the inside lane — there had been no need to make such a reckless manoeuvre.

Cursing, Albert sounded the horn and slammed his foot on the brake. But nothing happened. His car kept going at seventy miles an hour. It hit the back of the Corsa, spun out of control and overturned.

The last words Albert ever heard were 'I did it my way'. He was dead before help arrived.

# CHAPTER 2

*Sylvie's morning*

Sylvie Franklynn lived in the picturesque village of Monksworthy. In fact, she still lived in the house where she was born. She co-owned and worked in the Delicious Desserts Tearoom with her best friend Liz Morgan, who was also a lifelong Monksworthian, and neither woman had any desire to live anywhere else.

When Sylvie had got married almost thirty-five years earlier, it had been to someone who was not a villager. She had persuaded him to move to Monksworthy. Not that it had taken much cajoling. After all, what was there not to like? The house was comfortable. The locals friendly. And the village even had a decent pub.

After a few years of marriage, they'd had a daughter, whom they'd named Annabel. When she reached adulthood, she spread her wings and moved to a nearby town. However, she still had close ties to the village as she worked as a wedding planner at the nearby Cavendish-Mortimer Estate.

Monksworthy had been awarded the accolade of Best Village in the Wye Valley on no fewer than seven occasions. It was a hotly contested annual competition, which was viewed as a matter of pride. As such, it wasn't unusual for villagers to put a great deal of time and effort into ensuring that their local area was in tip-top condition. Casual observers could mistake it for friendly rivalry whereas those in the know acknowledged that beneath the surface it was open warfare, often with no holds barred.

It was common for spies to be sent out to snoop on the competition by spending time in pubs and tea rooms throughout the valley. A favoured tactic was to have someone walk their dogs in far-flung villages, as dog walkers were generally a friendly lot, and prone to let their guard down, especially if a stranger was enjoying the fresh air with their adorable canine family member. Useful snippets of information were casually revealed by the unwary. In recent times, however, there had been a spate of misinformation which had led to some villages adopting ridiculous ideas. Thankfully that had not happened in Monksworthy, as their residents prided themselves on an ability to sift the so-called wheat from the chaff.

The Wye Valley was an area steeped in history, myths and legends. It had been awarded the status of an Area of Outstanding Natural Beauty, and that fact meant that come rain or shine, tourists flocked to the area. There were regular bus tours with agreed stopping points, of which Monksworthy was one. Only the very worst weather prevented visitors travelling from far and wide to immerse themselves in the magical offerings of the Wye Valley. As groups wandered around, it was a common occurrence for residents to hear visitors oohing and aahing, as they marvelled at the aesthetic perfection.

It was one of those places where the demand for properties inevitably outstripped availability. After all, if you were one of the few fortunate enough to live in Monksworthy, why would you want to live anywhere else?

A Monksworthy property becoming available on the open market was as rare as hen's teeth. And no matter how rundown the property, there would be a queue of people

7

waiting to snap it up. Very rarely did a property remain on the market for more than a few days and the price-tags reflected the fact that it was desirable place to live.

Estate agents described Monksworthy as having 'Goldilocks' proportions, being neither too large nor too small, but in fact, just right. It was a close-knit community. A place where neighbours talked to each other. A village where everyone knew everyone else — or at least thought they did.

It had quaint thatched cottages alongside dwellings of a more traditional construction. There was a village hall located on the edge of a substantial village green, a cricket pitch, a duck-pond, a garden centre and a village shop. Not forgetting the tearoom and the local pub.

All in all, it was a great place to live.

* * *

Having recently celebrated her fifty-seventh birthday, Sylvie could easily have passed for ten years younger. Naturally, she had a few grey hairs and a couple of laughter lines, but then again so did many people. Perhaps what had helped her most was that she had maintained a positive mental attitude and habitually looked for the good in people. She had worked throughout her adult life, made a home for herself, her husband, and their now grown-up daughter. She was also active in village life.

Sylvie had an enquiring mind, and knew she was as sharp as a tack. Yet she'd noticed how, since refusing to colour the grey strands, a significant number of people seemed content to treat her as though she was losing her faculties. It was irritating and disrespectful. After all, no one would dream of treating a man differently just because their hairline was receding. And as for those men with a full head of grey hair . . . well, they were frequently referred to as a 'silver fox', whereas a grey-haired woman was viewed as either someone who didn't care about their appearance, or else an old woman who offered little of value to society.

It was a double standard and Sylvie, for one, had had enough of it. So what if she chose to allow her hair to go grey, dyed it blue, pink, green, yellow, or even shaved it off completely. It was her hair. Her body. Her choice. And she was not prepared to allow anyone to force her to conform to their idea of how she should look.

She wasn't one to pester the doctor for no reason at all. She'd coped stoically with the menopause, though had struggled with night sweats for at least six years, which in turn affected her sleep. Her energy levels were flagging which resulted in her often feeling tired. And in the last year or so she had gained a little weight, so she had been forced to buy new clothes.

A few months ago, Sylvie had had a doctor's appointment. She was poked, prodded and had blood samples taken. When the results of the blood tests came back, she was shocked to discover that she was classed as being pre-diabetic. She'd not even heard of the term before. But when the doctor informed her that she needed to ideally lose a stone in weight, and exercise more in order to fend off diabetes, Sylvie accepted that the time had come for her to make a concerted effort to turn things around. This wouldn't be easy, especially since she spent her working life at the village tearoom, where Liz was for ever baking delicious treats to tempt their clientele.

One Monday, when the tearoom was closed, she'd gone shopping with Liz, and together they'd chosen a whole new wardrobe for Sylvie, including a fancy pair of trainers, with eye-catching patterns and colours. Being kitted out to enable her to exercise, Sylvie began a new health-focused regime. Only a couple of weeks in, it was proving easier said than done.

\* \* \*

That Monday morning, Sylvie woke to the sound of the radio. She yawned and opened her eyes, realising that she was alone in the house. In the last two years, her husband seemed to spend more time away on business than he did at home. It was ridiculous, really, as he was at an age when he should be winding down too. But oh no . . . he seemed to thrive on going hell for leather, giving everything he had to his mysterious job. A career he refused to speak about as he claimed to want to keep his work and home life separate. It had frustrated her at first, but she trusted him and had eventually learned to accept it. He'd occasionally mentioned someone named Harry, but only in the vaguest of terms. And even after almost forty years of marriage, she still hadn't met this Harry, or anyone else he worked with for that matter.

Having finished her breakfast, Sylvie was getting ready for the weekly exercise session on the village green, when the doorbell sounded as someone kept their finger on it. Being only partially dressed, she grabbed her robe from the hook on the bedroom door. 'All right! Hold on! I'm coming!' she shouted. As she clattered down the stairs she could see Liz's outline in the door's glass panel.

'What's the rush?' she asked, as she opened the door.

Liz's face was flushed with excitement. 'Just been speaking to Gwen. Did you know that Barney's got the hots for some hoity-toity fancy piece he met at his spa?'

'Seriously?' Sylvie's eyes widened in surprise. 'But only last week he swore to all of us that he'd had it with romance.'

'Oh, you know what he's like.'

'Sure do. Barney's in love with the idea of being in love.' Sylvie shook her head and smiled.

'Precisely. It's all about the fantasy with him. When reality kicks in he runs for the hills. Give it a few months and he'll be looking to end things.'

'Glad I'm not on the dating merry-go-round, though Bertie's far from perfect.'

'I suppose you've got the best of both worlds, with his working patterns,' said Liz. 'One week at home. Two away. It must help to keep things fresh, as you've still got your freedom.'

'I suppose it has its advantages, but if I'm honest, I'd like him to be around a bit more. It'd be nice to spend a bit more time together. I must admit, though, sometimes when he's here, I get the impression that his mind's elsewhere.'

'If you ask me, he works too hard. He needs to ease his foot off the gas. Take things easy once in a while. You've only got to look at my poor Vince. Literally worked himself into an early grave.' Liz sighed. 'It's been over three years, and I miss him every day.'

'Oh, come here.' Sylvie pulled her friend close and hugged her tightly. 'Your Vince was one of the best.'

'He certainly was,' she sighed. 'Anyway, c'mon, Sylve. You need to get ready. You know what Rowena's like. She'll give us hell if we're late. She's a sadist at the best of times and tardiness brings out the sergeant major in her. You weren't there to see it, but I still have visions of Ethel Brinkley being bullied into doing twenty sit-ups.'

'Seriously? But she's seventy-something!'

'Precisely. It wasn't a pretty sight. She turned a funny colour. I thought she was going to have a coronary. She dropped out of the group after that. I'm telling you straight, you don't want to mess with Rowena.'

Rowena Evans was another Monksworthy resident. She was also a personal trainer, and an effective one at that. Being young, attractive, and a fitness fanatic ensured that she always had plenty of clients, and it wasn't unusual for her to turn potential customers away as she often had no spare capacity in her busy schedule.

'Get a move on, ladies! C'mon, pick up the pace,' she called and clapped her hands rapidly as Sylvie and Liz strolled towards the village green. In good weather they exercised outside, relocating to the village hall if conditions were less than optimal. This was the weekly class held exclusively for female villagers aged fifty and over. Rowena held a similar one for the men. They were the only group sessions she did, preferring instead to work with people on a one-to-one basis.

11

Half a dozen villagers were already being put through their paces. They were all following the well-known routine designed to promote flexibility and loosen the muscles before they got down to some of the more challenging aspects of the workout.

'Whatever you do, don't stand behind Doreen,' whispered Liz, as she nudged Sylvie sideways. 'I dread to think what her diet's like. She toots whenever we bend or squat, and the smell is dreadful.'

Sylvie laughed and shook her head.

They were well into the main exercise routine when a police patrol car pulled up on the edge of the green. Sylvie glanced across and saw Sergeant Simon Porter get out of the vehicle. He was Liz's younger brother and had always had a soft spot for Sylvie.

'What's up with your Simon?' asked Sylvie, as the sergeant headed in their direction. Even from a distance, it was obvious that he looked troubled.

'No idea,' puffed Liz.

'Ladies! Ladies! You're out of step! Concentrate, please!' shouted Rowena, as she glared disapprovingly at Sylvie and Liz.

'Sorry,' apologised Liz, as she tried to get back to the correct movements and rhythm. Seconds later, as everyone lunged forward, Doreen's bottom trumpeted loudly, causing Liz and Sylvie to giggle uncontrollably.

As Simon closed the distance between them it looked as though he was carrying the weight of the world upon his shoulders. He stopped about ten yards away from the group of women. When he caught his sister's eye once more, he gestured to Liz. It was clear that he had something he needed to talk to her about.

Liz had a bad feeling as she broke away from the group. Simon rarely came to the village when he was on duty, which must mean that something was awry. But she had no idea what it could be.

'What's up?' she asked.

Simon glanced furtively across at Sylvie, before telling Liz the news.

12

# CHAPTER 3

*Harriet's morning*

Despite living in a large town only thirty or so miles from Monksworthy, Harriet Joyce was completely unaware of the village's existence. As usual, her life was busy, busy, busy, which was just the way she liked it.

If anyone were to ask Harriet to list her favourite things, she'd most likely say that they were spreadsheets, deadlines and to-do lists. In fact, she was a fan of anything that helped to improve her productivity level.

Everyone who knew Harriet joked that it was exhausting to be around her. Through childhood and beyond, she'd been a bundle of energy. Keen to learn. Desperate to achieve. She wasn't happy unless she was busy. It had been a long-standing joke in her family that she was such a livewire she could help power the national grid. She was always on the go. If not physically, then mentally, as her mind was in overdrive, looking for things to do. Problems to solve. People to help. Causes to further. Her work ethic was phenomenal. The woman was a human dynamo driven by the desire to succeed in whatever task she undertook.

For Harriet, that Monday morning began the same way as every other. She woke ten minutes before her alarm which was set for six a.m. regardless of the day of the week. It was a tough regime to adhere to but one she firmly believed in as she thought that lying in bed was a waste of time. By six thirty each morning, no matter the weather, she'd be out of the house to begin a five-mile run. For many years she'd taken the same route every day and initially ran it alone. Then, as time went by, she was joined by another woman, then another. And as word spread, their numbers increased until there were eventually twelve of them. They'd somehow set up their very own unofficial running club. It was a satisfying start to the day, enjoying the camaraderie with like-minded people, while having the feeling of safety in numbers.

Once back home, Harriet completed her warm-down routine before hitting the shower for precisely four minutes. She turned the temperature down for the final thirty seconds and stood beneath a stream of water so cold that it made her teeth chatter. It was a brutal yet exhilarating feeling. Something she believed fired up the synapses, setting her up for the day ahead. Having selected and laid out her outfit the night before, all she needed to do was blow dry her hair, apply her make-up, and get dressed.

Fashion was important to Harriet. It wasn't as though she was a shopaholic. Far from it. She prided herself on the fact that she offered sound advice to people with various addictions. And she certainly wasn't going to allow herself to be labelled as anything *-aholic*. No. Her passion for clothes and matching accessories was just that — a passion.

She loved window shopping, enjoyed browsing boutiques, and trying on clothes and buying things that suited her. Such a passion might seem strange for someone who was obsessed with time management, but Harriet factored it into the week, allowing herself two and a half hours each Tuesday morning, between nine and eleven thirty. She also factored in a five-minute walk to the train station, a ten-minute journey into the city centre, and the same on the way home. This allowed her a whole two hours in which to indulge her passion of shopping. She even took the extra precaution of setting an alarm on her phone to ensure that she did not lose track of time.

Harriet swore she would never forget the 'Tuesday morning from hell', as she invariably referred to it. The occasion when all her carefully made plans for the day went out of the window. Indeed, the catastrophe of that shopping trip had resulted in her policy of setting an alarm on her phone. For one reason or another she'd lost track of time which resulted in her arriving on the platform as the train was pulling out. To make matters worse, the next one wasn't due to arrive for an hour. It had been such a colossal waste of time. Time Harriet knew she would never be able to make up unless she juggled things around and worked into the early hours. It was a series of unfortunate events she was unprepared to repeat.

Harriet worked hard for her money and certainly had no intention of frivolously wasting it. In her opinion, that would have been abhorrent. No, she was a woman with standards. And it just so happened that those standards were high. Always buy new. Only quality items. And always stick to shades of blue, with the odd black or grey item interspersed among her purchases. If she kept to those rules she couldn't go wrong. Oh, and most importantly, always ensure you accessorise appropriately. In Harriet's case, that meant a suitably sized Radley handbag and shoes of the same colour with heels no lower than two and a half inches.

Being a Monday, it was not a designated shopping morning. And as the eight o'clock news came on the radio Harriet was already tucking into her breakfast, having first put a wash on. With a full day ahead of her she was conscious of the fact that she needed to keep to the self-imposed schedule she had sorted.

At one o'clock she was due to meet a friend for coffee and a light lunch. Unsurprisingly, it was scheduled in for the same time each week. This meant that she needed to leave the house no later than twelve forty-five. It would allow her sufficient time to arrive at the café with a minute to spare. If there was a glut of pedestrians which prevented her from walking at her usual speed, the additional minute she had allowed should theoretically enable her to still arrive at the venue by one o'clock.

It sounded sad, to plan your life to such a fine extent. Some might say it was obsessive-compulsive behaviour. But as far as Harriet was concerned, it was merely common sense. If you had a lot to accomplish and limited time, then good planning was the key to achieving your goals. She wholeheartedly believed in the adage, 'If you fail to plan, you are planning to fail.' And Harriet had no intention of willingly allowing herself to become a failure.

As soon as she finished her tasks for the day, she would set about making a list of everything she needed to achieve for the following day. Taking the time to order them by importance, and allotting times for each task. It was a big ask to keep to the timetable. But she'd learned over the years that grit, determination, and an absolute sense of self-belief enabled her to achieve so much when most people would have given up.

Harriet worked from home, frequently putting in ten-hour days, five days a week. Being self-employed she could manage her workload as she saw fit. This helped, as today she was going to take ninety minutes out from her work schedule. With a pot of coffee freshly brewed, she switched on her laptop.

The next four hours would be intense, interesting and inevitably frustrating as she replied to twenty emails. It was a big ask for anyone, but especially so for someone like Harriet, whose alter ego was known and trusted by many. Though only a handful of confidants knew her true identity. For Harriet Joyce was widely known as Aunt Aggie, an agony aunt who dispensed impartial common-sense advice to the masses. Well, at least to readers of either the glossy monthly magazines or the popular daily newspaper that paid her for her services.

Harriet placed her phone on silent, then clicked on the folder containing the emails she intended to answer during this session. Having already sifted through them and familiarised herself with the contents yesterday afternoon, she was confident that she had all the necessary information to hand to offer appropriate advice. What sometimes took longer was if some troubled person was seeking moral rather than practical advice. Harriet was reluctant to tell people what they should do, as emotions and relationships were complicated, and things could quite easily go wrong.

She was aware that those seeking advice were only giving her a brief snapshot of their problems — scenarios seen only from their point of view. Each had been submitted by a magazine reader. Four of them would feature in both the physical and online edition of the publication. But Harriet had adopted a policy of responding to everyone who sought her advice.

First off, there was a student with an eating disorder. The pressure of exams was becoming too much, and the young woman had resorted to binge eating. The immediate sense of gratification quickly turned to self-loathing, which resulted in her purposely making herself sick. Her behaviour had gone unnoticed for a while. But recently it seemed as though her younger sister had discovered what she was up to and had attempted to blackmail her so that their parents wouldn't find out.

Second, a young man was at the end of his tether. Having recently moved in with his girlfriend he'd discovered that she wasn't the woman he thought she was. His rose-tinted view of their relationship had changed in recent weeks when he began to realise that she was controlling and sometimes violent if she didn't get her own way. Things had started to go wrong when he had needed to work late for the best part of a week, as the company he worked for was under pressure to meet a deadline for a lucrative contract. He'd explained the situation to his girlfriend, but it seemed that she didn't believe him. She accused him of cheating on her. When he tried to reassure her that this wasn't the case she called him a liar. And the more he tried to convince her that he was telling her the truth, the more she disbelieved him. They had argued until she threw a plate at his head, narrowly missing him. Things continued to get worse until it reached a point where he felt there was no going back. He wanted advice on how best to end their relationship in an amicable fashion.

Then there was the woman whose husband of fifteen years had walked out on her. She claimed that until the day it happened, she hadn't realised that anything was wrong within their relationship. He'd cleared out their bank account, leaving her with debts. And if that wasn't bad enough, she had found a handwritten note slotted beneath her pillow. In it, her husband had gone into detail about how he had never loved her, how he had only married her for her parents' money. But now that their financial legacy was all gone, he had no reason to stay with her. He'd used her up and spat her out. She was completely broken to discover that the marriage had been a lie and didn't feel able to talk to anyone about it.

This woman had suffered the most awful humiliation possible. It was no wonder that she didn't feel capable of turning to her friends. To do that, she would have to admit to everyone who knew her that she was gullible. To be taken in by somebody for such a long period of time without suspecting that they were up to no good suggested that you were not a good judge of character. This woman might find it easier for people to think that her husband had walked out on her because he was fed up with their marriage rather than tell them what he had really done. At least that way, she'd have their sympathy instead of them thinking she was such an idiot to be taken in by his lies.

Harriet was busily replying to the woman when the doorbell sounded. At first, she considered ignoring it. After all, she was in full flow. She knew precisely what she wanted to say, and appreciated that any distraction, no matter how minor, might result in her losing her train of thought. As she was on a tight deadline, it wasn't a risk she was prepared to take. But

18

whoever was at the door wasn't prepared to take no for an answer as they kept a finger on the buzzer. Finally accepting the fact that they weren't going to just walk away, Harriet huffed in frustration as she pushed back her seat and headed to the front door.

'Hold your horses,' she shouted. As she unlocked the door, she readied herself to give whoever was making that awful racket a piece of her mind. They might very well be impatient, but she was annoyed. They had interrupted her thoughts at an important juncture, and she already sensed that she would not remember everything she wanted to say to that poor woman who deserved the very best of advice to enable her to see a way forward.

She opened the door and began to speak before she had time to see who had been so insistent on getting her attention. 'What's so urgent?' There was no attempt to mask her obvious annoyance.

# CHAPTER 4

*Thea's morning*

That same morning, Thea Robinson was up and out early. The day was her own, and she intended on making the most of it. After all, what was a thirty-three-year-old lady of leisure to do with her time, if not indulge herself with some pampering?

She loved her spa days. Not that she'd found a favourite venue yet. A couple had been downright awful. Most were mediocre. There were a few, however, that stood out among the competition. But Thea still wasn't completely satisfied that she had found the perfect spa to meet her exacting standards.

It was becoming an obsession with her. And as such, she was working her way around various spas located within a hundred-mile radius of her home. She was amazed at how many of them there were. And if by the end of her market research she still hadn't come across what she considered to be perfection, well . . . she'd just have to extend the search area.

There were inevitable traffic queues as Thea negotiated the roads around Bath, but once free of the city she made good time. She was heading for an unfamiliar area. The Forest of

20

Dean. The word 'forest' evoked images of greenery and tranquillity, of getting in touch with nature and distancing herself from the stresses and strains of everyday life. This gave her hope that it would be a good place to relax.

Thea didn't have a conventional job, or even any recognisable career. That said, she was a woman with big plans and was prepared to do whatever it took to achieve her goals. She'd already accomplished so much through planning, hard work and dedication. She was someone with her eyes on the prize and was going to claim it, come what may. She had learned a valuable lesson at a very early age. Life was full of choices. And making the right decision at the right time could often be the difference between success and failure.

Over the years, Thea hadn't had any close female friends. This was most likely because she was wary of other women, especially if she sensed they were a threat. She was astute enough not to let this show and kept her insecurities hidden. She took pains to be exceptionally polite and superficially friendly.

As an ambitious woman, she set her sights high. She had no intention of settling for a life of mediocrity or partial success. She had always dreamed of living the high life. Of mingling with the rich and famous. But for that she needed money, so she set herself goals.

For a girl brought up in the care system she had already come a long way. There was no denying that she'd battled the odds and made something of herself along the way. There were many people out there with far more advantages than Thea. She wasn't the cleverest. She wasn't hard-working. She didn't have an entrepreneurial bone in her body. That said, she did have an idea of how to get what she wanted, and it was an idea as old as time itself.

Thea had set out to 'Eliza Doolittle' herself. She had taken elocution lessons. Studied fashion magazines. Learned about interior design trends. Practised making small talk. Perfected her smile. And she was selective about every aspect of her life.

21

She was choosy about the food she ate. Choosy about the wine she drank. Choosy about the clothes she wore. Choosy about the gym she used. Choosy about the car she drove. Choosy about the hotels she stayed at. Choosy about those she socialised with. But most of all, choosy about finding the right sort of husband.

In her late teens Thea's ambition had been to find a man who would love her. Cherish her. Treat her like the princess she dreamed of being. In return, she would take her marriage vows seriously, because as far as she was concerned, marriage was for life. She was an old-fashioned girl at heart. If treated right, she would honour. Obey. And without a shadow of doubt, she believed in the part of the vows she would commit to, which said, 'till death do us part'. She would be the best wife she could possibly be, doing everything to make her husband happy.

The spa to which Thea was heading was located on the Cavendish-Mortimer Estate. This meant nothing to her, but upon further investigation she had learned that this was not any ordinary housing estate. Instead, it was set in the expansive grounds of a stately home, owned by Sir Barnaby Cavendish-Mortimer. The package she had purchased was eye-wateringly expensive. But this was a much-needed treat to soothe away the stresses and strains of recent months. And, oh boy, did she deserve a bit of pampering.

As she manoeuvred her Mini convertible into a space outside the spa's entrance, Thea's heart sank as she took note of the three other cars parked alongside. She'd been quite happy with her car until now. But having spotted these she suddenly realised that it just didn't cut the mustard. It was a cheap alternative, when parked alongside a Porsche 911 Cabriolet, a Lexus LC convertible, and a Mazda MX-5.

As Thea took her imitation Louis Vuitton carry-all out of the boot she sighed. She'd always thought it was a good fake — good enough to fool most people. But the owners of these cars weren't the sort of women who would be duped by her knock-off luggage. They'd see straight through her. The only viable option she had was to check in as quickly as possible. Head to the changing rooms and hastily stow her carry-all in a locker. With a bit of luck, she might still get away without anyone spotting it.

'Remember, lady, you've gotta fake it till you make it,' Thea muttered to herself. 'Shoulders back, chin up, chest out. You're as good as anyone else. Better even, considering how far you've come. And at least these Loubishark sneakers are the real deal.' The trainers were a recent birthday present from her husband, and she appreciated his generosity. With a deep breath she lowered the straps of her bag onto the crook of her elbow. Pointing the key fob to lock the car, she turned to face the entrance of the spa. 'You are the mistress of your own destiny,' she said. It was a mantra she lived by.

'Good morning.' The young man at the reception desk smiled, his teeth perfectly aligned and gleaming.

'Hi there. I'm booked in for a full-day package.' Thea gave her name.

The young man scanned the list. 'Yes, and I see it's your first time as a guest.' He then spent a few minutes explaining what she should expect from her visit. 'Now, if you'd like to head through to the changing room, Chantelle will be with you shortly. Enjoy your time with us, and don't forget to let a member of staff know if there's anything you require.'

Having enjoyed a full body massage, a swim in the pool and twenty minutes in the sauna, Thea readied herself for a leisurely lunch. Later that afternoon she had a facial, manicure and pedicure booked. It would be heavenly.

As she entered the facility's restaurant, Thea spotted three other women seated at a table. Until now she hadn't encountered any other guests. The group all seemed to know each other and were no doubt the owners of the fancy cars. As she headed to a table at the far side of the room, she noted that none of the women made any attempt to acknowledge her.

While waiting for her lunch to arrive she glanced at her phone. She had switched it off and placed it in the locker along with her other belongings as she'd enjoyed the morning session. Seeing that she had seven missed calls from the same unidentified caller, she decided to wait until she'd eaten to call them back. After all, another half an hour or so wouldn't make much difference, and she'd worked up quite an appetite.

When Thea eventually spoke to the person who was obviously so keen to make contact, her plans for the afternoon changed.

# CHAPTER 5

Earlier that morning on Monksworthy's village green, Sylvie kept glancing across at Liz and Simon. She was so distracted that she was unable to follow the exercise routine. Her friends had walked far enough away that they were out of earshot and were huddled together in a conspiratorial fashion. Despite not being able to hear what they were saying, Sylvie could tell that they were discussing something important. Liz's back was to her, so there was no knowing what her facial expression was like. However, every so often, Simon stole a glance at Sylvie, and even at this distance she couldn't fail to spot concern etched across his face.

There was no doubt in Sylvie's mind that whatever he was telling his sister, it wasn't good. But she couldn't for the life of her think what it could possibly be.

'Sylvie!' yelled Rowena. The younger woman clapped her hands in annoyance. She'd already switched the music off, and everyone was looking around to see what was going on. When Sylvie ignored her, Rowena's expression darkened. Being a personal trainer meant that she expected her clients to listen and do as they were told. Especially this lot. After all, she was doing them a favour.

'Hey, if you're participating in this exercise session then get with the programme and concentrate. You can catch up on the latest gossip after class.

'That goes for you too, Liz!' Rowena shouted even louder. 'If chatting to your brother is more important to you, then take it somewhere else.'

Simon shot the younger woman an angry look but didn't respond.

Suddenly realising that she might have overstepped the mark, Rowena backtracked a little. 'No disrespect, Sergeant Porter, but you're kinda ruining the vibe I've got going on. These group sessions are like herding cats. They're difficult to motivate and get distracted at the best of times.' When Rowena eventually realised that the people she was annoyed with weren't taking the slightest notice of her complaints, she switched the music back on and cranked up the volume to maximum. It was so loud that all present could feel the beat pounding inside them.

Sylvie couldn't wait any longer. Even if whatever was going down between Liz and her brother had nothing to do with her, she wanted to reassure herself that this was the case. Her thoughts were all over the place as she tried to guess what was going on, and it didn't help that the damned music was so loud.

She'd taken no more than a couple of steps towards them when she saw Simon touch his sister's arm. His nod was almost imperceptible, and the siblings stopped mid-conversation. As Liz turned to face Sylvie, her stomach lurched. Her expression said it all. There was no denying that there was something terribly wrong. Liz swiftly closed the distance between them. Simon was only a step behind.

Sylvie's first thought was that something awful must have happened to Annabel. 'What is it? What's the matter?' Even to her own ears, Sylvie's voice was almost unrecognisable. She looked from one to the other, her vision blurred with tears as panic took hold.

'Syl—' Liz wrapped her arms around her friend and held her close.

Sylvie felt her strength drain from her body in anticipation of what she was about to learn. 'Not Anna! Tell me it's not Anna.' She was sobbing now. Pleading with them to tell her whatever it was they were about to say but not wanting to hear it all the same.

'It's not Anna. Sylvie, look at me. Look . . . At . . . Me.' Simon's voice was calm and reassuring, which helped Sylvie focus on what he was saying. 'It's not Anna. There's no reason to think that there's anything wrong with Anna.'

'Oh, thank God.' Sylvie felt a wave of relief wash over her, only to quickly realise that if Anna was all right, there was only one other person who could have made them react this way.

'Sylvie, earlier this morning, there was a fatal traffic collision. I was one of the first officers at the scene, and I'm sorry to have to tell you that Albert was the driver. There was nothing that could be done to save him.'

'B-Bertie? M-my B-Bertie?' As she said her husband's name, it was as though she was suddenly too weak to stand. But fortunately, Liz still had a firm hold on her and somehow managed to keep her from collapsing to the ground.

'C'mon, let's get you inside,' said Simon, as he helped his sister support Sylvie's weight. They made their way slowly towards Sylvie's house, took her inside and sat her down. 'Make Syl some tea, will you, Liz? Put in plenty of sugar. She needs something for the shock.'

Liz did as her brother asked. The news of Albert's death had shocked her to the core. It had momentarily transported her back to that awful moment when she had learned of her own husband's death. When the words were out there, there was no taking them back. It had felt like a knife to the heart, and in that moment something inside her had died too. It had taken such a long time before she had felt as though she had a reason to get up in the morning. And, if it hadn't been for

Sylvie supporting her every step of the way, she knew that she most likely wouldn't have got through those darkest of times. But Sylvie's friendship and kindness had never wavered. She had gone above and beyond.

Now the roles were reversed, and the time had come for Liz to return the favour. To stand by her friend, and naturally, Annabel, too, should the young woman need her support.

# CHAPTER 6

Despite being seated, Sylvie felt as though the room was spinning. As she tried to steady herself, she gripped the edge of table so forcefully that her knuckles turned white. It was as though she had entered an alternative universe. One where time slowed down, and nothing made sense. A place that was familiar yet alien at the same time. She needed to ground herself before she completely lost it.

Sylvie knew that Simon was speaking to her. She could see his lips moving. But his voice had slowed to a low drawl. Sounding like a 45-rpm vinyl being played at 33-rpm. It had been a fun thing to do in the days before CDs and, more recently, streaming. God . . . how the world had changed. Often not for the better. Things were different, that's all. People were different. Life was different. And Bertie was . . . Bertie was . . . Bertie . . . was . . . dead.

Sylvie flinched as Liz placed a reassuring hand on her shoulder. That simple touch broke the spell and returned her to the here and now.

'Drink your tea while it's hot, Sylve.' Liz held a half-full mug towards her friend. She hadn't wanted to risk filling it, as Sylvie was trembling.

Sylvie did as she was told and sipped the liquid, wincing at the overly sweet taste. She had to force herself to swallow it, as she hadn't taken sugar in her tea for many years. Bertie was the one who liked things sweet. Two sugars in tea. Three in coffee. And a generous sprinkling over his Weetabix. She'd often joked that it was a wonder he had any teeth left.

And there it was again. Bertie . . . was . . . dead.

'Can I see him? Will you take me to Bertie?' It was the first coherent words to come out of her mouth since they'd taken her back to the house.

'Of course you can. But first, I'll need to make a few calls. Make sure everyone's ready for you.'

'But you're sure it's him? This isn't just a wind-up?' Sylvie's attention was focused upon Simon.

'I'm positive, Sylvie. I've known Bertie for a long time. It was definitely him.'

'Oh . . . I need to get organised. There're things to do.' Sylvie went to stand up, but Liz stood behind her and kept a firm grip on her shoulders.

'You stay where you are, my lovely. I'm here for you. I'll come with you to see Bertie, if that's all right with you?'

Sylvie nodded and reached up to place a hand over Liz's. 'Thank you.' She squeezed it to emphasise her gratitude.

'And when the time's right I'll contact Dave Pritchard. He'll see Bertie right. Give him a good send-off, and I'll make sure he does it at cost. Don't you worry about that. But that's for later. Let's get today over with first. One step at a time, eh?'

A few hours later, Liz and Sylvie travelled in the back of the car as Simon took them to identify the body. As they sat in silence, Sylvie stared blankly out of the window. Lost in thought. While Liz held her friend's hand in a show of support.

After forty minutes, Simon and Liz guided Sylvie towards an external hospital doorway. It was one that once you knew of its existence you hoped you'd never need to use. Situated away from the main entrance, it was tucked out of sight from those who were not in the know. A buzzer and intercom ensured that visits to this department were strictly by appointment only.

The two women stood aside to allow Simon to see to the formalities. He pressed the buzzer and identified himself. They had clearly been expecting him, as following a short conversation, the door's locking mechanism clicked.

Sylvie tensed. The moment of truth was fast approaching, and there was no going back. Deep down she knew that Bertie was dead. But until she saw his body, there was always a glimmer of hope that Simon had got it wrong and that this had been a horrible mistake. And she'd forgive him if he had got it wrong. She'd forgive anyone anything if only it turned out not to be her Bertie.

Simon held the door open as he allowed both women to enter the building. He was about to follow them when he sensed movement in his peripheral vision. As he glanced around to get a better look he saw another police officer. He was too far away to see her clearly, but Simon vaguely recognised her as being from the same station, though she was not someone he knew. This other officer was escorting another woman towards the building, who, just like Sylvie, appeared to be shell-shocked. The only difference was that this other woman had no one with her to offer some much-needed support.

A mortuary technician was there to greet them. Her voice was calm. Devoid of emotion. 'If you'd take a seat until we're ready for you. It shouldn't take long.' She indicated to a room with an open door. The sign on it read, *WAITING ROOM.*

The buzzer sounded once more as the three of them headed inside. Simon hung back, allowing Sylvie and Liz some space. He was finding this entire experience far more difficult than usual. He'd brought other bereaved family members here during the course of his career. It was a difficult but necessary part of the job. Any officer tasked with informing relatives that their loved ones were recently deceased found the experience stressful. But this was far more so. Knowing everyone involved made it personal. Which inevitably increased the feeling of pressure, as he wouldn't be able to just walk away and do his best to forget about it at the end of his shift.

The mortuary technician was speaking to the other officer now, and the woman she was accompanying was directed to the waiting room too. When the technician eventually left, the two officers struck up a muted conversation.

Inside the waiting room, Liz looked up as the other woman entered. Noticing that she was unaccompanied, and recognising the bewildered expression, Liz couldn't help but take pity on her. As there were only two seats in the room, she stood up and moved towards the stranger.

'Please, take this seat. You look as though you need to sit down.' The woman glanced at her blankly, and Liz decided it was best just to take charge. Placing an arm gently around the woman's shoulder she led her towards the vacant seat. The woman offered no resistance. 'Please, sit.'

She did as she was told.

'This is a dreadful time,' said Liz. She couldn't think of what else to say. This woman was a stranger. But despite Liz being there to support Sylvie, she couldn't ignore the other woman's obvious distress.

'M-my h-husband,' muttered the stranger. She was immaculately turned out, with matching shoes and handbag. Her hair was just so. It was as though she had just stepped off the cover of a glossy magazine.

'Mine too,' said Sylvie. Her gaze remained focused on some elusive spot on the far wall. And without looking she did a surprising thing and reached out to take the other woman's hand.

The stranger welcomed the physical contact and grasped Sylvie's hand tightly. These two women, who had never met until now, were united in their grief. Both taking strength from a common understanding of having their world suddenly ripped apart.

Liz decided it was best to give them some space. After all, there was nothing she could do or say, and it appeared as though, at least for the moment, Sylvie was bearing up. She turned without saying anything and headed back out of the room, fully expecting to find Simon waiting to be told when they could take Sylvie to identify Bertie's body. But there was no sign of her brother.

Stepping further into the corridor she looked about and spotted him about fifty yards away. He appeared to be having a heated conversation with another police officer. Their voices were low, and she was unable to hear what was being said, but both of them were gesticulating, and it was apparent even from this distance that all was not well.

Hearing a sound from the opposite end of the corridor, Liz saw a man approach. Sensing that he was there to tell Sylvie that they were ready for her, she headed back into the waiting room. It was immediately apparent that neither woman had moved. They remained as they had been — still holding hands. It was a touching scene.

'Albert's ready now,' said the man. 'Which one of you is his wife?'

Sylvie and the other woman both looked up and spoke in unison. 'I am.'

Liz swallowed hard and forced her lips together so that she did not say the wrong thing. She suddenly wished that she was anywhere other than in that room.

# CHAPTER 7

It was immediately apparent to Liz that of the four of them in the room, only she fully grasped the potential implication of what had just been said. Neither Sylvie nor the other woman was thinking clearly. As being so wrapped up in their own grief neither seemed to have heard the other say that they were Albert's wife.

Liz appreciated that it wasn't beyond the bounds of possibility that two people named Albert had been brought into this facility that day, with both unfortunate souls now awaiting identification by their next of kin. After all, Albert was not an entirely uncommon name. Then again, it wasn't the most popular of names either. And Liz wasn't inclined to believe in coincidence.

If truth be told, Liz had occasionally wondered what Albert was up to during the regular intervals he spent apart from Sylvie. Throughout the time she had known him, he'd been evasive about what he did for a living, and why he needed to spend so much time away from Sylvie. But she had never voiced that concern, as she knew Sylvie wouldn't have appreciated it. After all, it was just a feeling. Nothing she could put her finger on. A Spidey sense that perhaps all might not be as it seemed. He was affable, charming, even. Had the ability to make people feel good about themselves. Though, in retrospect perhaps too keen to make people like him? After all, if he convinced everyone that he was an up-front good guy, then why would anyone question his regular absences?

Liz had enjoyed Albert's company, as they shared an obsession with all things crime fiction. He had always been happy to chat about books in that genre. He'd even introduced her to the works of some authors whose creations had passed her by, but once alerted to them had gone on to become firm favourites. It was thanks to Albert that she'd become aware of the author Veronica Dumont, and her compelling protagonist Tilly Taylor. Not to mention her other highly successful series featuring PI Harry Blake. They were on-the edge-of-your-seat reads. And the way Harry Blake was described made her heart flutter. The man was an absolute dreamboat.

Liz had considered Albert to be well-read, interesting and erudite. She looked forward to their discussions, as he was the only other person in their friendship circle with a penchant for Liz's favoured genre. Though, on reflection she realised that perhaps she'd allowed their shared interest to cloud her judgement and quash any niggling doubts before they had a chance to grow into worrying theories.

Albert had also bonded with Simon, despite the police officer being younger than the rest of them. Their friendship flourished around Albert's interest in police procedures. He occasionally sought Simon's opinion on whether details in various police procedurals seemed credible and was keen to learn how things were done in real-life police work.

Almost right from the start, Albert had routinely spent a significant amount of time away from the village, leaving Sylvie alone, even when Annabel was born. Bertie would play the doting dad for a week at a time, but he'd still up sticks for the next seven days as his job, which he was always very cagey about, apparently required him to travel for one week in two. Though in the last few years, he'd claimed his work commitments had increased, which meant that he spent even more time away from home. Liz hadn't said anything to Sylvie at the time, but she'd thought it strange, as most men of Albert's age were content to wind down, not take on more responsibilities.

Liz swallowed hard and her mind raced as she tried to come up with a logical explanation for what had just happened. The possibility that Bertie had been a bigamist was so out of left field that on the only occasion when it had entered her mind, she'd brushed the idea away as a flight of fancy brought about by an overactive imagination. One occasionally heard about such occurrences. But in relationships of strangers. Not your best friend, someone you saw day in, day out for much of your life. The thought was sheer lunacy. A ridiculous and abhorrent idea, no doubt brought about by the combination of shock and stress.

Sylvie and Liz had shared so much throughout their lives. Knew each other inside out. Been each other's Maid of Honour. Went into business together and were closer than some married couples. Over the years Sylvie had never once given Liz cause to think that her marriage to Bertie was anything other than a fully committed, genuinely loving relationship. They'd always seemed so happy together. Which meant there had to be some other rational explanation for this other woman claiming that she was his wife too.

Liz knew that despite any misgivings she might have had about the man, Bertie had been devoted to Sylvie and Annabel, and they both idolised him in return. It was inconceivable he would jeopardise that. The very thought of what it would do to Sylvie should he have lived a double life was something Liz didn't want to think about.

There was the sound of approaching footsteps rapidly ricocheting across the floor of the corridor. Liz hoped it was Simon as she didn't want to be the one to voice her fears to Sylvie and the other grieving woman. If it did turn out to be the case that they were both married to the same man, then there was no telling how they'd react. They could faint. They could fight. They could . . . Liz's thoughts were racing, and each scenario that played out in her mind's eye didn't have a good outcome. Then again, since when was someone's death ever a good outcome?

Simon was the first of the two officers to appear in the doorway. He quickly assessed the scene in front of him and realised that all wasn't well. Liz had never been so pleased to see her brother. She stared at him, raised her eyebrows, and discreetly nodded towards the others in the room. The mortuary technician was about to say something when Simon interjected:

'I'd like a word.'

The technician glanced across. 'I'm sorry, it'll have to wait.'

'Now,' said Simon. His usually friendly tone was replaced with an assertiveness which left no doubt that this was an order, not a request.

'Liz, I'll be back in a second,' Simon added.

Her brother's expression confirmed her fears. There was only one Albert. Bertie. Or whatever else this other woman had called him. Sylvie and this stranger were both married to the same man. How could Albert have done such a thing?

'Won't be long now. Simon's just got a few things to sort out,' said Liz. She was relieved that neither woman appeared to have picked up on the awful mess they were about to find themselves in the middle of. Then again, if you hadn't suspected that anything was amiss in your marriage, why would you expect that your husband was a bigamist? Though it was somewhat disconcerting to see that Sylvie and the other woman were still holding hands.

Liz breathed a sigh of relief when Simon appeared in the doorway once more. At least now he could take charge, and she wouldn't have to deal with the inevitable fallout on her own. His reappearance went unnoticed by Sylvie and the other woman. Simon gestured for Liz to join him in the corridor. They walked away until Simon was sure they were out of earshot.

'Was Albert a bigamist?' she asked.

'Not exactly. But it's best that we get Sylvie in there to identify the body. We need to get her out of here as soon as possible.'

'Well, if he wasn't a bigamist, what the hell was he?' From the look on Simon's face, she knew that he was keeping something awful from her, but Liz couldn't imagine what could possibly be worse than Sylvie having to find out that her husband was married to another woman.

'It's looking as though two wasn't enough for him.'

'You mean there are more?' Liz's voice squeaked in surprise.

'Keep it down, Liz. There's one more. At least we think there's only one more. It appears that Albert might have been a polygamist. Obviously, we need each of them to formally identify him as their husband before we can be certain. But it's looking that way. Poor Sylvie, this is going to devastate her.'

'And there's Annabel to think of,' added Liz. 'She adored her father.'

'I know. It's such a mess. The fallout from this will be horrendous.'

'So, are you going to tell them? Sylvie deserves to know.'

'Not yet. As I said, we need formal identifications from each of them.' Simon was about to say something else when the other police officer appeared and headed in their direction.

'They've managed to contact her and she's on her way. How do you want to play this? We don't want them to find out while they're here.'

'I agree. As we arrived first, we'll take Sylvie in straight away. Once we're out of the building I'll give you a bell to let you know that the coast's clear. As far as I'm concerned, this is just a formality. I've known the guy for years so I'm positive it's him. Give me a ring later and let me know what happens with yours. What did you say her name is?'

'Harriet. Harriet Joyce.'

'Did you get a name for the other woman?'

'I believe it's Tess. I just hope we've gone before she arrives.'

38

# CHAPTER 8

Liz struggled to get her head around what she had just been told. It appeared that everything pointed to Albert Franklynn having been married to three women. She appreciated that they wouldn't know for sure until the other two women had identified him as their husband too. But her heart ached for Sylvie, to know that her world, which only a few hours earlier had been broken, was soon about to be smashed to smithereens.

Sylvie was one of the kindest people she knew. Someone whom Liz would turn to if she ever needed help. Apart from Simon, Sylvie was the only person she trusted implicitly. As Sylvie would drop whatever she was doing and go above and beyond. No questions asked.

Liz was finding it impossible to come to terms with this shocking turn of events. Especially since she had just met one of Albert's other wives, and the woman had seemed so completely normal. She appeared to be just as broken and bewildered as Sylvie. There was no doubt in Liz's mind that her grief was genuine, and there was nothing to suggest that this other woman had any inkling that Albert had been up to no good. The man had a lot to answer for. But like the snake he'd been he'd managed to slither away from the consequences of his actions. Leaving others to pick up the pieces.

But for now, Liz knew that she had to put these thoughts out of her mind. It didn't matter how angry she felt. Her priority was to support Sylvie. At this precise moment, her friend didn't need to know what Albert had done. That would be down to Simon to address.

Sylvie was remarkably calm and dignified as she identified the body. Simon and Liz stood either side of her, holding her tightly to support their friend throughout this part of the ordeal. The siblings were aware that she needed them more than ever as it was inevitable there were more shocks to come.

They were travelling back to Monksworthy when Sylvie spoke. They were the first words she'd uttered since confirming that it was Bertie's body. 'Will you ring David Pritchard for me?'

'Absolutely. You can leave it to me. But there'll be plenty of time for that,' reassured Liz. She squeezed her friend's hand in a show of support, all the while thinking about the problems Sylvie and the other wives were about to face. If they all truly believed they were married to the love rat, then they would each demand the right to organise his funeral.

'It'll take a while before arrangements can be made. There'll have to be a post-mortem before they'll release Albert's body,' said Simon. He couldn't quite bring himself to refer to him as Bertie. Not after what that man had done. It seemed far too informal and friendly. 'There's no way around it.'

They sat in silence for the remainder of the journey. Each was lost in their own thoughts. When Simon's phone pinged to announce the arrival of a message, it sounded excessively loud. Liz flinched but said nothing, all the time wondering if it was confirmation that the other poor woman had identified Albert as being her husband.

Having returned to the village, Liz set about taking charge. Simon remained in the car, as he had some calls to make, and needed to speak out of earshot of the women.

'I'll stay here with you tonight, Syl.'

'You don't need to. I'll not be much company.'

'I don't want you being on your own. When's Annabel due back?' Sylvie's daughter was on holiday in Brazil. 'Do you want me to try to get a message to her?'

'No. There's no point upsetting her. It's not as if there's anything she can do. She's due back on the fifteenth.' That was two days away. 'It won't be easy to rearrange flights. So best leave her. She'll know soon enough.'

'In that case, I'll move in until she returns. Take care of you, like you did for me. You mustn't be on your own.'

'Thanks, you're a good friend.' Sylvie gave a weak smile. 'Liz, can I ask you something?'

'Anything, you know that.'

'I'm not sure if I imagined it, but that other poor woman in the waiting room — was her husband called Albert too?'

Liz suddenly wished she was anywhere other than here. She had hoped that Sylvie would not have noticed that awful moment in the waiting room. Hoped she'd been too consumed with grief to have picked up on it. There wasn't anything she could do but answer the question honestly. After all, it was only a matter of time before this seemingly rotten mess all came out, and Liz didn't want Sylvie to look back on this conversation and realise that she'd been hiding something from her. Such an epiphany could destroy their friendship, and it was a relationship that meant a lot to both women.

'I believe she did,' said Liz. She decided for the moment that it was best to say as little as possible. Simon, in his professional role, should be the one to break the news. 'Would you like a cuppa?' Deflection seemed like a good option for the moment, and when Albert's reprehensible shenanigans were confirmed, it would be time for plausible deniability as far as having learned about what he'd done only hours before Sylvie.

Liz was filling the kettle when Simon walked into the room. The expression on his face said everything she needed to know.

'Sylvie, I need to tell you something,' he said.

Liz stopped what she was doing and moved to her friend's side. Sitting next to her, she put her arm around Sylvie.

'This is going to be difficult for you to hear, but you must listen carefully to what I'm about to tell you.' Simon pulled up a seat and sat down directly opposite Sylvie. Leaning forward he took her hands in his. 'It seems that Albert had more than one family.' He paused to allow the words to sink in. When Sylvie didn't say anything, he continued. 'Do you understand what I'm saying?'

Sylvie nodded. 'That woman in the waiting room?' She sounded surprisingly calm.

'Yes. But there's another woman too.'

'Three of us? Oh, Bertie, what have you done?' Sylvie's voice faltered when she next spoke. 'What are their names?'

'The lady you've already met is Harriet Joyce. I haven't met the other one, but I believe her name is Tess Harris.'

'You said that Bertie had more than one family,' said Sylvie. She was remarkably lucid given the circumstances.

Simon sighed. 'I did. Are you sure you want me to go into this now?'

'Absolutely. I can't possibly feel any worse. And by the sound of it there's been far too many secrets. So, it's best to get everything out in the open once and for all. I'll have to face it at some stage, and I'd like to do it now.'

Liz squeezed Sylvie's shoulder. 'We're both here for you, Sylve. No matter what, you can rely on us.'

Simon's cheeks flushed. He hated to be the one to stick the knife in further, but Sylvie had asked, and she deserved to know. It was better that she heard it from him, than from some heartless gossip further down the line. Once people got to know what Albert had done, everyone would be talking about it. Something like this was newsworthy, and it wasn't beyond the realms of possibility that a reporter could turn up on the doorstep wanting to get her side of the story. It was better all round for Sylvie to be prepared, not risk being blindsided and publicly humiliated if that were to happen.

42

'It seems that Harriet and Albert had two children. A daughter, Zara. And a son, Leo.'

'Oh.' The word was no more than a squeak. Sylvie let out a long, trembling breath before she spoke again. 'So Annabel has a half-sister and brother. When I think back to the number of times she pleaded for us to let her have a brother or sister . . .' She pulled her hands from Simon's and distractedly wiped away a tear. 'And she had both all along. How old are they?'

'I've no idea. All I know is that they're old enough not to be living at home,' said Simon.

'And what about the other woman? I know you've only just told me, but I can't recall her name.'

'It's Tess, but no, I don't have any details on her.'

'Umm . . . Would I be able to speak to them?'

'Do you think that's a good idea, Sylve? You're in shock. Take a few days to allow the dust to settle,' said Liz. 'You've done nothing wrong. You don't need to torture yourself by getting in touch with them.'

'But I have to speak to them. I need answers, and I'm sure that Harriet and Tess will need them too. I thought Bertie and I had a happy marriage. But he couldn't have loved me. Not the way I lov—' Unable to finish the sentence, Sylvie's shoulders shook as she sobbed uncontrollably.

All Liz could do was hold her friend tightly until the sobs subsided. Eventually, Sylvie regained her composure, and Liz spoke. 'Forget about the other women, Sylve. They're not important. Just concentrate on yourself and Annabel. And if further down the line there needs to be a conversation with Harriet or Tess, then I can speak to them on your behalf. You really don't need to have anything to do with them.'

'Th-thanks, Liz. But as painful as this is, it's something I need to do for myself. You see, if I'm going to move on from this, I have to face it head on. I don't want to. But I must. For my own sanity. I can't begin to understand why Bertie did what he did. But perhaps between us we can begin to make sense of this dreadful mess.'

Liz continued to cradle her best friend. All the while thinking that if Albert hadn't died in that crash, she'd happily have killed him herself, for putting Sylvie through so much heartache.

'And when they release his body, we'll have to sort out funeral arrangements,' Sylvie continued. 'It's best that we do it together. After all, it's not as though we can split him into three and each hold a funeral. No, as much as I don't want to, we need to put our feelings aside and do what's best for all of Bertie's children.

'I never thought I'd feel like this, but finding out what he's done makes me hate him. I trusted him. I believed that he had our best interests at heart. But he didn't. It turns out he was a liar and a fraud.'

'Some people have affairs for years on end,' said Liz. 'It doesn't mean that he didn't love you.'

'But they weren't affairs, Liz. That obviously wasn't enough for him. He had to take things further and married two other women. And he fathered two more children.' Sylvie began to cry again. 'It's just one almighty mess, and we're left to pick up the pieces.'

'First thing tomorrow, I'll have a word with the other Family Liaison Officers and ask them to broach the subject with Harriet and Tess. But for now, you need to rest. It's not the time to make any decisions. You might feel differently in the morning,' said Simon.

# CHAPTER 9

The following morning, Liz came downstairs at six o'clock to find Sylvie sorting through paperwork on the kitchen table. A Tina Turner CD was playing and there was a pot of coffee on the go.

'You're up early. Guess you couldn't sleep?'

'Took me a while to get off, you know, with things going round in my head.'

'I'm not surprised. You've had the stuffing knocked out of you.'

'Well, when I finished crying, I realised there's no point feeling sorry for myself. It's not going to change anything. It's obvious now that Bertie's made a pig's ear of everything. But no matter how angry and humiliated I feel, there are things to be done, and it's down to me to do them. So, I'm using Tina's energy to inspire me. Let's face it, that woman had more than her fair share of marital problems. But she picked herself up, dusted herself down and showed everyone what she was made of. And that's exactly what I intend to do. When we first got together, Bertie used to call me his "little pocket rocket" because I wouldn't allow anything to stand in my way. And that's precisely how I intend to behave now.'

'Good for you.' Liz felt a sudden burst of pride. Her friend was clearly made of strong stuff. 'And I'll be with you every step of the way. You've only got to ask. But Sylvie, you do realise that when this all comes out, people will start to gossip?'

'Of course I do. It's human nature. But I've done nothing wrong. So, I've nothing to be ashamed of. I've no intention of allowing people's opinions to get me down. I'm going to hold my head up high and ride it out, and I'll do my best to ensure that Annabel doesn't suffer because of her idiot father. People will move on to other things soon enough. Once we've got the funeral out of the way, we can start to look to the future. You want a coffee?'

'Oh, yes, please.' Liz was amazed at how well her friend seemed to be coping, although she sensed that it would only be a matter of time before her bravado gave way, and the reality of the situation hit home.

'Let's face it, Liz, it wasn't as if Bertie was ever here full time. In the last year or so he only ever spent one week in three at home. And now I know why. It wasn't that his so-called work commitments were so full-on. It was because he was shacked up with two other women.'

'But I think deep down that he loved you, Sylve. I don't think he could have faked that for all those years.'

'I'm sure you're right. Bertie loved me and Annabel. Let's face it, I had no idea that we had anything other than a normal marriage.'

'Apart from the fact that he spent a great deal of time away from home,' interjected Liz.

'I agree. But while he was here our relationship just seemed normal. I had no cause to doubt that he was anything other than a faithful husband, and a kind and doting father. Though it's evident from what's just come to light that Bertie loved himself more than anyone else. Otherwise, he wouldn't have kept three of us on the go. It makes my blood boil to think of how he treated us. Annabel and I deserved better.'

A knock on the door interrupted their conversation. 'I'll get it,' said Liz. She returned moments later with her brother in tow.

'How're you doing, Sylvie?' asked Simon. He shuffled his feet and avoided eye contact. His cheeks were flushed. He always looked that way whenever he was around her. It had been like that ever since his teenage crush, which he hadn't got over, despite both of them having gone on to marry other people. Though Simon's marriage hadn't worked out and he was long since divorced. He knew that he would always have a soft spot for Sylvie. Which in turn made him feel awkward in her presence, though thankfully Sylvie either chose to ignore it or else she was unaware of his feelings towards her.

'Oh, you know . . .'

'Simon's got something to tell you,' interjected Liz. She despaired at her brother. He wasn't like this with anyone else. But whenever he was around Sylvie, he almost invariably reverted to being an embarrassed teenager. She waited for a few seconds, and when he failed to say anything, she nudged him.

'Er, yes. That's right, I have. I've spoken to Harriet Joyce's FLO.'

'FLO?' Sylvie's brow furrowed and she shook her head. 'I've no idea what that is.'

'Sorry, Sylvie. I'm so used to the jargon I forget that people outside the force might not understand the acronyms.'

Liz shot her brother a look of annoyance. 'Just get on with it, Si.'

'A FLO is a Family Liaison Officer. I'm acting as yours. Anyway, Harriet Joyce said that she wants to meet you too. And given the circumstances I think it's best if I accompany you. Her FLO will be there too.'

'And I'll come along for moral support,' said Liz.

'No, you won't. Not on this occasion.' Sensing his sister was about to argue, Simon gave her a hard stare before continuing. 'The meeting will take place as part of the force's responsibility for the investigation into Albert's death. Which means that it's not appropriate for you to tag along.'

'I'd like to speak to Harriet alone,' said Sylvie. 'We've things to discuss. Personal matters which won't have any bearing on Bertie's accident.'

'That's as may be,' said Simon. 'But given the fact that both you and Harriet have only just learned of Albert's deception, it's a sensible precaution for your respective FLOs to be on hand. Given the nature of what's happened, it's possible tempers could flare. And once news of what Albert was up to breaks, the spotlight is well and truly going to be on you. So, believe me when I say that you do not want to risk giving the media any more fodder.'

'Where and when will we meet?' asked Sylvie.

'We thought that the police station would be the best place. Keep you away from prying eyes. Would eleven o'clock suit you?'

'That's fine. Set it up. Will the other woman be there too?'

'Apparently not. I was informed that Tess Harris identified Albert as being her husband. Though, when she learned that there were two other wives, she made it clear that she wanted nothing to do with either of you.'

'Can't say that I blame her,' said Sylvie. 'Learning that your husband's died is bad enough. But to learn that he was still married to another two women takes it to a whole new level. She'll probably need more time to come to terms with what's happened. Perhaps she'll change her mind later, when she's had a chance to process things.'

# CHAPTER 10

The journey to the police station was a complete blur. Sylvie had no sooner sat in the back of the car than Simon was telling her that they had arrived.

As she stepped out of the vehicle she looked up and saw the station. Suddenly it hit her that she might have made a mistake. Perhaps it wasn't a good idea to meet Harriet. Yesterday, as they'd sat together in the cramped waiting room, readying themselves to be called to identify their dead husbands, she had thought that Harriet, whose identity she had been unaware of at the time, seemed like a nice sort of woman. Bizarrely, they'd even ended up holding hands in an unconscious show of unity. Each took strength from the other, knowing only that they were both facing the same ordeal — the death of a loved one.

At the time, Sylvie hadn't given Harriet more than a superficial thought. The only thing they'd had in common throughout that short period was that they were both newly bereaved widows, trying to come to terms with how their day had gone from ordinary to horrendous. They were somehow united in their new-found grief.

Now, as the moment was almost upon her to come face to face with one of Albert's other wives, Sylvie was beginning to think that Liz had been right. She was taking things too quickly. She needed time to grieve, to allow Albert's passing to sink in before she took such a radical step. For, suddenly, there was no doubt in her mind that that was precisely what this was. After all, how much more of a radical step could you take than meeting another of your husband's wives?

It wasn't as if this woman was Albert's ex-wife. She was still married to him. Just as Sylvie was. In a country where polygamy was unlawful, did that mean that she, Sylvie, was unwittingly guilty of the crime? It wasn't as if she had been complicit in her husband's infidelity. She was too moral a person to ever condone what he had done. But in the eyes of the law was it possible that she could be charged with having been in a polygamous relationship? Most people were aware of the phrase that 'ignorance of the law is no defence'. Sylvie had never broken the law in her life and had done her utmost to instil those values in Annabel. The very thought that she might be charged with and subsequently face trial for being an accomplice in Albert's crime made her sick to the stomach.

Sylvie had to ask the question, no matter what answer she would receive. 'Simon, will I be charged with polygamy?'

'Absolutely not.' He reached out and grabbed both of her hands without thinking about it. 'How could you even think that? You've done nothing wrong. Sylvie, you've been married to the same man for thirty-five years. You're not the one who went on to marry other people. That was down to Albert, and you're not answerable for his crimes.'

Sylvie breathed a sigh of relief. Simon's reassurance meant that it was one less thing for her to worry about. 'That's good. This meeting today, how's it going to work?'

'Both FLOs will be present throughout. Just let me know if it all gets too much for you, and I'll take you home. You're under no obligation to talk to each other. But as you said that you wanted to, and she was amenable, this seemed like the best way to set up the meeting.'

Sylvie and Simon had been in the room for a short while when the door opened. Sylvie swallowed hard as a lump rose in her throat. Now that the moment was upon her it suddenly seemed far worse than yesterday's ordeal of having to identify Albert's body. At that time, she had felt very little. The news of his death had been a shock, and the unexpectedness of it had left her numb. She had just gone through the motions of what she needed to do, but it had been as though it was happening to someone else. Whereas now, she was thinking more clearly.

Sylvie instinctively stood up. It was a subconscious action, not wanting to put herself at the immediate disadvantage of having to look up into the other woman's face. When Harriet Joyce entered the room, Sylvie saw that the woman was a good six inches taller than her and much slimmer too. Not only that, but she also looked well turned out. Dressed immaculately, not a hair out of place. She was obviously feeling the strain, however, as her face looked drawn, and from the puffiness around her eyes it was apparent that she had recently been crying.

Both women eyed each other, unsure of what to say or how to behave. Simon was the first to speak. 'I suggest we all take a seat as I'm sure you both have a lot of questions.'

51

# CHAPTER 11

With everyone eventually seated, both officers were aware that you could cut the atmosphere in the room with a knife. This was such an unusual set of circumstances that there was no rule book to follow. With no sign of either woman wanting to strike up a conversation, Simon dived straight in.

'Ladies, I sympathise with your loss and can only begin to imagine how distressing this meeting must be for both of you. But as you both wanted the opportunity to talk to each other, I feel that we should make a start as there will undoubtedly be a lot of questions. I would respectfully ask that, despite the possible difficulties, you try to keep in mind that neither of you is to blame for the predicament you have found yourself in. As hard as it is, it might be better for both of you to try to work through this together. After all, Albert is the only person at fault.'

Sylvie stared blankly at him. Simon sounded so detached. So formal. She knew he was speaking in his role as a police officer. Yet she was so used to thinking of him as merely a friend.

'But before we begin, there are some things you need to know.'

'Bertie gave me his dead mother's engagement ring,' interrupted Sylvie, succumbing to a sudden urge to demonstrate how much she had meant to her husband. For someone who spent her life trying to be kind, she suddenly didn't care if this upset Albert's other wife. All that mattered in that moment was that Sylvie was hurting and needed to feel superior. If only for a few seconds. She sniffed haughtily as she held out her hand, with fingers splayed to show everyone the ring. 'He said it was a family heirloom, and he wanted me to have it.'

Harriet studied the ring for a few moments, then shook her head and chuckled. Realising that everyone was staring at her caused her to laugh even harder.

'What's so funny?' snapped Sylvie. Her cheeks had reddened with indignation, in the knowledge that Albert's other woman was laughing at her. 'Albert gave it to me, not you.'

Sylvie's protestation caused Harriet to laugh even more, until tears ran down her cheeks. 'Sorry, sorry,' she eventually said, as she regained her composure. 'That's so funny. I guess it shouldn't be, but it is. He's played us again.'

'What do you mean?' asked Sylvie. She looked at Harriet as though the woman had gone mad.

'Take a look at this.' Harriet held out her left hand to display her own engagement ring. 'This was his dead mother's engagement ring too.'

As Sylvie leaned forward to get a better look, she realised why Harriet had reacted the way she had. And in that moment, the animosity she had felt towards Harriet dissipated. Sylvie took a deep breath. 'Truce?' It seemed an odd word to use, but she couldn't think of anything else to say.

'Truce.' Harriet held out her hand and Sylvie shook it.

'What have I missed?' asked Simon. He looked and sounded confused.

The other FLO shrugged her shoulders.

'Harriet's right. He played both of us. He gave us identical rings.'

'This proves we're not rivals,' said Harriet. 'We're just two gullible women who fell for his lies.'

'I'd say it makes us allies. I bet if we took the rings to be valued, we'd probably find that he bought them from the same jeweller at the same time,' said Sylvie.

'Most likely got a discount. Buy one, get one free. The stone probably isn't even a diamond.'

'Ever the cheapskate.'

'Oh, he was certainly that all right. Always on the lookout for a bargain.'

The atmosphere in the room had thawed, as both women accepted that through no fault of their own, they were in this mess together.

Simon cleared his throat. 'This is what we've established so far. First, Albert used different names. Harriet, you believed your husband to be Albert Joyce. Sylvie, your husband was known as Albert Franklynn. There is also another widow, who knew her husband as Albert Harris.'

'So that's how Albie got away with it?' Harriet's voice was shrill. 'He created different identities.'

'It appears so,' said Simon. 'One can only presume that it was a safer option for Albert to keep the same first name as it lessened the chances of him slipping up and raising suspicion.'

'How did you find out about the other names?' asked Sylvie.

'I was first at the scene, and as I knew Albert it was easy for me to identify him,' said Simon. 'As I wasn't on duty at the time, it was down to the attending officers to deal with the case. My understanding is that a briefcase was found in the passenger footwell of the car. Inside that case were a selection of mobile phones and inside each of their cases was a driving licence. The photographs were all of Albert. But subsequent enquiries revealed that he used a different date of birth for each.'

'Are you saying that you think he stole people's identities?' Harriet's eyes widened. She looked and sounded incredulous.

'It's something we're looking into,' said the other FLO. 'As things stand, we've no idea of his real age or identity.'

'You said that apart from us, he had another wife. Where's the other woman? Why isn't she here?' asked Harriet.

'When Tess Harris identified Albert as being her husband, she was informed of the fact that he was also married to the two of you. From what I've been told she took the news badly.'

'As did we all, I'm sure,' said Sylvie.

Harriet nodded in agreement. 'It was devastating to discover his deception. But it doesn't explain why she hasn't attended this meeting. No matter how much he's hurt us, we still have things to discuss. And we'll only get answers by speaking to each other.'

'It's a given that everyone reacts differently. It's laudable that you both agreed to speak to each other so soon. Not only are you grieving, but I'm sure you both must feel raw and resentful towards Albert, and no doubt towards each other. But as you both had children with Albert, it's sensible that you—'

'You have a child?' interjected Harriet. Her tone was accusatory, as though Sylvie had no right to have had a child. As she stared in disbelief, Harriet's immediate thought was to wonder if things could possibly get any worse. Since learning of Albie's death, she had become aware of betrayal upon betrayal he had unknowingly heaped upon her. She felt stupid. Humiliated. Having spent years helping people navigate their way through seemingly insurmountable problems, some of which were a result of their own actions, it was a slap in the face to discover that her own life had been a sham. She had sometimes pitied others. On occasion, despaired at their naivety. Yet here she was, the go-to person for doling out sound advice, completely floored. Pathetic. Clueless.

'Yes. Bertie and I have a daughter. Her name's Annabel. I wanted more children. Annabel wanted siblings, but Bertie was dead against it. Whenever I'd bring it up, he insisted it would be selfish to have more than one. It caused no end of arguments.'

'Annabel, that's a lovely name.' Harriet breathed deeply as she did her utmost to ground herself. When she spoke again, her voice was more controlled. 'Well, I guess Annabel's now got herself a half-sister and brother. After all, Albie's seen to it that they're family, whether we like it or not.'

'I guess you're right.' Sylvie sighed in resignation. 'Our children make it impossible for us to walk away from this once everything's died down. They're Albert's legacy. Ours too. What are your kids' names?' She'd already forgotten that Simon had told her their names when he broke the news to her yesterday.

'Leo's the youngest. He's twenty, and Zara's thirty.'

'Zara's thirty?' Sylvie covered her mouth and swallowed hard.

'Why is that important?' asked Harriet.

Appreciating how upsetting this was to Sylvie, Simon answered for her. 'Annabel's also thirty. She was born in May.'

Harriet's voice dropped to little more than a whisper. 'So was Zara . . . We must've been pregnant at the same time.'

The revelations came thick and fast after that, as the two women pieced together certain elements of Albert's duplicity. It was established that he had married Sylvie seventeen months before his marriage to Harriet. They also learned that his marriage to Tess had occurred less than two years ago.

The initial frostiness evident at the start of the meeting had all but disappeared as Sylvie and Harriet began to accept that they had a lot in common. It would have been easy to despise each other. But the very fact that they both acknowledged that the way they dealt with this situation would have a direct impact on their children made them determined that, as far as possible, they would put their pride and resentment aside and do what was best for Albert's children.

Indeed, they were so deep in conversation that both women failed to notice a knock on the door which resulted in both FLOs subsequently leaving the room. Simon was the first to return. As he sat down and cleared his throat, there was no doubt that he was about to impart some unwelcome news.

'Oh, don't say that you've just discovered there's another wife,' sighed Sylvie, voicing her concern before Simon had a chance to deliver yet another blow.

'No, but you both need to brace yourselves for what I'm about to tell you.'

Harriet and Sylvie looked at each other. In the relatively short amount of time spent together that morning, they had clearly started to form a bond. They simultaneously reached out to take the other's hand.

'I've just been informed that during an examination of Albert's car, it was found that the brakes had been tampered with. Which almost certainly led to the collision.'

'You're saying that someone tried to kill him?' Sylvie suddenly felt light-headed. 'Simon?'

'I'm afraid so. Following this discovery, Albert's death is now being treated as murder, which means that you'll both be questioned.'

'You think one of us is responsible?' Harriet's eyes widened.

'It's standard procedure at this stage. Tess Harris will be questioned too.'

57

# CHAPTER 12

For Harriet and Sylvie, the morning was becoming more surreal by the second. Learning that Albert's death was now being treated as murder meant that in the blink of an eye, both women had gone from being grieving widows wronged by an unfaithful husband to potential suspects in his murder. Could things possibly get any worse?

In the blink of an eye, so many lives had been upended. After spending decades living what they had each believed to be a normal married life, they had learned upon Albert's death that they had shared the same husband throughout that time. Having to come to terms with so many unpalatable facts in such a short space of time was a huge ask. Yet the shocks just kept on coming. Moments after they'd learned that Albert's death was being treated as a potential murder, they were both taken off to separate interview rooms where they were to be questioned under caution about every aspect of their lives.

As she walked along yet another dimly lit corridor, it suddenly hit Sylvie that unless she could convince the police that she had been unaware of Albert's deceptions and could account for her movements in the hours leading up to the crash, there was a possibility she could find herself in serious trouble. After all, it wasn't unusual to hear of people who had been convicted of serious crimes and imprisoned, only to have their sentences quashed years later, when evidence came to light to prove their innocence.

As a sense of panic took hold, Sylvie's heart began to race. Stopping abruptly in her tracks she reached out and touched Simon's arm. Her voice was unnaturally high and tremulous as she spoke. 'Si, be honest with me. Do I need a solicitor?'

He stopped and turned to face her, aware that she needed some reassurance. On a personal level he felt wretched, as putting someone he cared about through such an ordeal seemed unnecessarily brutal. But as a police officer he knew he had to follow the rules without fear or favour. 'It's up to you, Sylve. But I don't for one moment think you've got anything to worry about. I know you haven't done anything wrong.'

'But you're not going to be the one interviewing me. That officer doesn't know me.' Sensing tears roll down her cheeks she turned away and hastily wiped them.

'Here, take this.' Simon fished in his pocket and removed a carefully folded tissue. 'Don't go upsetting yourself. This is nothing more than following procedure. Ticking the boxes as they say.'

'A-are y-you sure?'

'Absolutely. I'll sit in with you, but it'll be a formal interview, and everything will be recorded. So don't get spooked by that. Just be yourself.'

As Sylvie sat and answered the questions put to her, she suddenly felt old and tired. Stress and exhaustion were catching up with her as she had not slept properly since learning of Albert's death.

'Are you all right, Sylvie?' asked Simon who up till then had been sitting quietly.

'Umm?' At the sound of his voice, she turned and looked quizzically at him.

'Are you OK?'

59

She nodded half-heartedly. 'Just tired, and my head's banging.'

'It's just that Sergeant Jones asked you a question, and she's waiting for an answer.'

'I can see this is getting too much for you,' said the sergeant. 'But it's the last question I'll ask and then this interview will be over.'

Sylvie nodded her understanding.

'I'd like an account of your whereabouts from five o'clock on the afternoon before your husband's death, until eight o'clock the following morning.'

There was a slight pause as Sylvie gathered her thoughts. 'I was with my friend Liz the day before. We run a business together. A tearoom. I work front of house so all of our customers that day would have seen me. We closed for the day at about six o'clock. I popped home for about half an hour. Then Liz and I went to the local pub for dinner. Simon was there too.' She nodded in his direction.

'I was,' he confirmed. 'We were there until closing time.'

'And after that?' pressed the sergeant.

'I went home to bed.'

'Can anyone confirm that?'

Sylvie's shoulders slumped even further, as she realised she had no alibi. 'No. I was alone.'

Sergeant Jones made a note of something. 'And the morning of the accident?'

'I got up at my usual time, had breakfast and got ready for an exercise class. That's where I was when Simon came to tell me what had happened.'

'Thank you,' said the sergeant. 'You're free to go.'

Before being interviewed, Sylvie and Harriet had swapped numbers and agreed to meet on the following morning. If each was honest about it, there had been the briefest of moments when both women wondered about the possible guilt of the other. But no sooner had the seed of doubt entered their respective minds than they chose to dismiss it. There was no rational reason for either of them to do this. No empirical evidence at this stage to prove innocence or guilt. Yet being treated as suspects when they were shocked and grieving, bonded the two women in a way which might not otherwise have happened.

The truth was that, before coming together that morning, both women had had the same thought — that they would undoubtedly dislike the other. But surprisingly this turned out not to be the case. The more they spoke about their respective family lives with Albert, the more they realised that they had a lot in common. After all, they had been married to the same man at the same time. A man who had betrayed them both throughout that time. And whose actions had resulted in them both having to act as a single parent throughout much of their married lives. It was also apparent that Albert had loved them both, along with all of his children too.

As strange as it might seem, Harriet and Sylvie realised that far from being rivals for Albert's affection, their husband had treated them with parity. His wives had never been a threat to his other relationships as they had not been aware of the existence of his other families.

Their frank discussion had given them both food for thought. Though neither of them had been prepared for the most shocking revelation of all. Albert's death hadn't been caused by a vehicle malfunction, a momentary lapse of concentration or because of the reckless behaviour of another road user. Instead, there had been a deliberate act of sabotage which had resulted in his death. However badly he had behaved towards them, he hadn't deserved to die like that.

They both returned to their homes that day having learned that someone had murdered their husband and deprived their now adult children of their father. And this act of violence bonded Harriet and Sylvie. Neither woman was the sort of person to sit back and allow whoever was responsible to get away with it.

Sylvie's mind raced as Simon drove her home. She felt so different from the blubbery mess she had been less than twenty-four hours earlier. The shock of Albert's death coming out of the blue, and shortly afterwards learning that he had been a polygamist, had been too much to cope with. But this morning, the things she had learned about Harriet, a woman she should have disliked, had unexpectedly caused her to feel closer to her than to any of her friends. After all, Harriet was the one person who understood precisely how Sylvie felt. And that was because she was being forced to come to terms with the inevitable repercussions of Albert's actions too.

'How are you doing back there, Sylvie?' asked Simon, as he glanced at her in the rear-view mirror. When she didn't respond, he sighed and spoke again. 'Look Sylve, I know it must have seemed awful being questioned like that.'

'Oh, you think?' Sylvie couldn't help but snap.

'Like I said at the time, it wasn't personal. Since Albert's death is now being treated as a potential murder, the three of you must be questioned. It's procedure. But I don't believe you had anything to do with it.'

'I should think not,' she interjected. 'And since no one spent the night with me, does that mean that I'll be treated as a suspect? Let's face it, I had the entire night when I could have driven to wherever Albert was staying, sabotaged the brakes of his car, and returned home without anyone being any the wiser.'

'Don't be like that, Sylve. Yes, they will check things out. It'd be remiss of them not too. But I take it your car was parked outside your cottage as usual?'

'Of course it was.'

'In that case you've nothing to worry about. There're a couple of properties with CCTV. If you'd taken your car, it would be picked up by one of those. But as you didn't, you've nothing to worry about. Give it another twenty-four hours and you'll be ruled out of the investigation.'

'Thank goodness for that.' Sylvie's sigh was both audible and protracted. 'Perhaps then, your lot will get on with finding out what happened and why.'

'I understand your anger, and if I could have spared you that indignity, I would have. But it was out of my hands. So, I'll ask again, how're you doing?'

'Better than I anticipated,' she replied.

'I hope you appreciate that back at the station I had my policeman's hat on. Which meant I had to demonstrate a professional detachment and not act in the manner of a friend.'

'I know that, Si. I had a momentary wobble, that's all. I'm having to face one shock after another. It's relentless, cruel and before you say anything, I know that it's unavoidable. But knowing that doesn't make it hurt any less. I feel as though I'm in a metaphorical boxing ring, pitted against a prizefighter. I'm not capable of defending myself, so I just have to take the blows. Each time I get knocked down I struggle to get up, but I'm hit again, and again, and again. It's awful. I'm scared, confused, and I don't deserve this.'

'You're right, you don't.'

'It's only yesterday that I learned that my husband died. Yet despite being married to Albert for thirty-five years, I didn't really know him at all. It's all such a mess.'

'That's the first time I've ever heard you call him Albert.'

'Right now, I haven't got it in me to call him Bertie. It's too familiar and just doesn't seem right. Not for the man I put my trust in and shared a life with. I laid myself bare to him. Physically and mentally. He knew everything there was to know about me, and I thought I knew everything about him. We even swore that there would be no secrets between us. But I've learned now that he was a cheat and a liar. As things stand, I'm angry with him, and I'm angry with myself too. But, who knows, perhaps when things aren't so raw, I might be able to think of him as my Bertie again.'

'I guess it's understandable you feel that way.'

'Umm.' Sylvie shrugged. 'In a strange way it's helped meeting Harriet. When you initially told me what Albert had done, I despised her. My first thought was that that woman had stolen my husband. But when you said that as well as being married to him, they'd had kids, too, it somehow made things better, not worse.'

63

'How's that?' Simon's brow furrowed as he puzzled over this statement.

'Well, I realised that she's just like me. She and her kids had a life going on with him. Albert was her husband and their father. Just like he was with us. He lied to all of us, and we never suspected a thing.'

'Not quite like you, Sylvie. As far as we can ascertain you were legally his wife. Harriet didn't marry him until later. And as he was already married to you, it nullifies their marriage.'

'It might very well be seen like that in the eyes of the law, but I don't think of it that way. And I doubt Harriet will either. We're in this together. At least until we've had the funeral. Albert's seen to that. It makes sense for us to meet up again to get to know each other better and possibly make some plans.'

'Tread carefully, Sylvie. You've had a hell of a shock and you've no idea how Annabel will take things. We all know that she idolised her father when she was a kid.'

'Precisely, but the key factor there is when she was a kid. She left home years ago, Simon. She's got her own life now. I know she'll be upset and angry. But I've a feeling she'll eventually come to terms with it.'

'You're probably right. But you also need to keep in mind that someone sabotaged Albert's car and whoever did that, meant to harm, if not kill him. Now I know you, and I'm certain that you had nothing to do with Albert's death. But Harriet . . . Well, until we've thoroughly checked her out, she's an unknown quantity. So, all I'm saying is keep your wits about you. Don't be too trusting. At least until we're certain that she wasn't the one who killed him.'

'Wow! I can't believe you just said that.' Sylvie experienced a sudden flash of anger. 'And I bet the officer taking Harriet home is saying precisely the same thing to her, but about me.'

'It's just precautionary, Sylvie. At least until we have a clearer idea about who might have done this. Just let us check this Harriet woman out first. The bottom line is that I don't want you unnecessarily putting yourself in danger.'

# CHAPTER 13

The following morning, Sylvie was up and out early. She'd managed to convince Liz that she didn't need babysitting. And as Liz had spent the last two days ignoring their business, she was glad to spend time in her own bed to catch up on her sleep, before making an early start at the tearoom. It was all well and good leaving one of their part-time staff to run the place in an emergency, but there were baked goods to prepare, stock to be ordered, takings to check, daily accounts to be compiled and cash to be banked. The list of tasks was growing by the minute.

Sylvie had already thrown Simon off the scent by leaving him a voicemail message on the previous evening, to say that she was planning on sleeping in, so there would be no need for him to call around until at least midday. The last thing she needed was for him to follow her around like an obedient dog, getting in the way of her and Harriet discussing a way forward from the dreadful predicament that Albert had left them both in.

Having entered a postcode into her car's satnav, Sylvie set off on the twenty-mile journey. They'd agreed on a venue far enough from their respective homes to be reasonably certain of no one knowing them. It wasn't that either woman felt they had anything to hide. It was just that if word had leaked out about what Albert had been up to, people, especially journalists, would be unable to help themselves. It was inevitable that everyone would be curious, which would put Albert's families centre stage, and right now that was something they could all do without.

At that time of day, Sylvie found a parking space quite easily and walked towards the pub where they'd agreed to meet. It was part of a large chain, which served breakfast and remained open until late into the night. Suddenly realising that in her eagerness to make a quick getaway she'd forgotten to have breakfast, Sylvie decided to throw caution to the wind and treat herself to a full English washed down with the establishment's policy of unlimited coffee. She'd not eaten much since learning of Albert's death, and it seemed like an opportunity to put her own needs first without feeling guilty about every calorie she consumed.

It was barely eight thirty when Sylvie walked into the pub. Glancing around, she saw that it was empty apart from an old codger sat alone nursing a pint, which didn't seem like a good idea given the early hour. As the smell of bacon and grease hit her nostrils, her stomach growled, and her mouth watered in anticipation of a large portion of what under any normal circumstance she would consider to be forbidden food.

'What'll it be, my love?' The young man behind the bar seemed barely old enough to shave. Sylvie suppressed a smile, appreciating that thinking everyone else was exceptionally young was a sign of getting old. She placed her order, and after telling him which table she intended to sit at, he handed her a mug and pointed out the self-service coffee machine. 'Does all sorts at a press of the button, so help yourself. Refills included. I'll be over shortly with a serviette and cutlery. The food should be with you in about fifteen minutes. Just give me a shout if there's anything else you want,' he announced with a smile.

There was still no sign of Harriet when the food arrived, and Sylvie occupied herself by tucking in. She hadn't had a fry-up in such a long time. It was something Albert had frowned upon, and as Sylvie chewed that first mouthful of bacon and sausage, it occurred to her that there were so many things she had either done, or not done, over the years to keep her husband happy.

If he'd been there now, he wouldn't have allowed her to enjoy this breakfast. He'd have made little comments to guilt-trip her into making what he believed was a sensible choice. Things like, 'That'll raise your cholesterol level.' Or 'You could feed a family of four with that.' He'd chuckle away as he made the comments, and she would have thought he was saying these things because he cared about her and wanted her to be more health conscious. But now that she was aware of his dark secret, she realised another important thing about their marriage. Albert had been a controlling man, and she'd allowed him to get away it.

Sylvie was on her third forkful when the door opened, and Harriet entered the pub. There were dark patches beneath her eyes, and she looked as tired as Sylvie felt. She scanned the room, then held up a hand in greeting when she spotted Sylvie. 'Sorry I'm late. There were five lots of roadworks. Traffic was a nightmare.' She folded her coat as she spoke and placed it on one of the empty seats. 'Are you sure we should be doing this?' Her tone was serious.

'What? Having breakfast?' asked Sylvie, as she put her knife and fork down.

'No. Spending time together. To be honest, it feels a bit weird. We know nothing about each other, apart from the fact that we were both married to the same man at the same time. Which you'd think would naturally make us enemies,' said Harriet.

'I agree. But what are we supposed to do? We're slap bang in the middle of an awful situation. Something that nine-ty-nine per cent of the population will never experience. No one but us can understand what we're going though. And as for being enemies, I'll admit that when I learned what Albert did, and who you are, I hated you for a while. But the more I thought about it, I realised that we're not enemies. You didn't steal him from me. I didn't take him from you. Neither of us had a clue about what he was up to.

'You're right. We didn't. Under normal circumstances it's possible we could become friends.'

'Who knows, it might end up that way. But for now, I need your support, and I think you need mine.'

Harriet nodded. 'I do.'

'So, to hell with what anyone thinks. Once word gets out, we'll have enough people judging us,' said Sylvie.

'It'll be easier if we put on a united front.'

'Another reason we should stick together. At least for the time being.'

Harriet's stomach growled. 'I can't remember the last time I ate, and right now that looks and smells delicious.'

'Go and treat yourself. Tastes even better knowing that Albert wouldn't have approved,' said Sylvie. When Harriet laughed, it was apparent to both women that he'd treated them in the same manner. It was something else they had in common.

With breakfast done and stomachs no longer growling, they set about things in earnest. 'How did your interview go yesterday?' Sylvie asked.

'It was harrowing,' Harriet replied. 'I was asked the most personal questions. It was as though they really thought that I had tampered with his car. In the end they seemed satisfied as I've got an alibi. Leo and a couple of his friends spent the night. Two of them slept downstairs, so there's no way I could have made it out of the house without being spotted.'

'Were you warned that I might have killed Albert?'

Harriet's posture changed, and it was immediately apparent that she was clearly uncomfortable with the question. She was initially silent, but when she realised that Sylvie genuinely expected an answer, she spoke. 'Yes, my FLO did mention it.

Numerous times, in fact. Though I don't believe you did, and I'm a pretty good judge of character.'

'Well, I hate to break it to you, but they tried the same tactic with me. I've known Simon, my FLO, since we were kids, and he did his best to warn me off meeting up with you. Said you were a suspect until they could prove otherwise.'

'The cheek of it.' Harriet sounded genuinely offended.

'I guess they're just trying to protect us. But a word to the wise, and don't take this the wrong way—'

'What?' interjected Harriet.

'Perhaps you should stop thinking that you're a good judge of character. I thought that about myself too. But Albert managed to hoodwink both of us throughout our entire relationship with him. Which suggests to me that we're both lousy judges of character.'

Harriet laughed so hard that tears rolled down her face. 'Fair point. We're obviously a couple of saps.'

'Seriously though, can you believe that they're treating us as suspects?' asked Sylvie.

'I know, it knocked me for six. As if we haven't got enough to contend with.' Harriet shook her head.

'Simon told me that they're still trying to establish if there are any more wives,' said Sylvie.

'There can't be. He was spreading himself thin with three of us. Surely there couldn't be more. He'd created a logistical nightmare for himself as it was. What was his pattern of being with you?'

'One week in three. Claimed he was travelling for work the rest of the time.'

'Same here. It used to be every other week until about two years ago.'

'Snap. I guess that's when Tess must've come into the picture.'

'Did Simon tell you anything about her?' asked Harriet.

'Nothing apart from what he said in front of you. It must've been a huge shock for her finding out about us. Let's face it, it's likely they've only been together for a couple of years. They'd probably still be all loved-up as there's hardly been time for the shine to go off things.'

'Guess we need to speak to her. Find out what she knows.'

'Definitely. Albert was due to come back to me the day of the accident. When was the last time you saw him?' asked Sylvie.

'He'd had one week away. So, I was due another week before he showed up again.'

'Which means he must've been with her. We need to find out where she lives and turn up on the doorstep if she doesn't voluntarily make contact.'

'I bet there's way more he kept from us,' said Harriet. 'Let's face it, he lived a lie for well over thirty-five years.'

'What else could he have hidden from us?' Sylvie was perplexed.

'Well, for starters, he used different names, so who the hell was he? It's possible that the three personas he created were just that — created. Could be he was someone else entirely. How do we know that he wasn't some criminal mastermind, creating these different lives to stay one step ahead of the law?'

'Surely not? Albert wasn't the brightest by any stretch of the imagination.'

'Or was that an act to fool everyone?' asked Harriet.

'But how would we even set about finding out who he really was? Surely the police would be doing that?'

'I would've thought they'll make some sort of effort. But do you really think they've got the time or the resources to carry out a thorough investigation? They're interested in his murder, but once they've figured out who was behind it, I wouldn't be surprised if they closed the case.

'We're the ones with the vested interest in getting to the bottom of who he was.'

'You're right,' said Sylvie. 'We owe it to ourselves and especially to the kids. You don't think that whoever did this to Albert could come after any of us?' Her voice rose to a squeak as a series of awful scenarios flashed before her.

'After everything that's happened in the last few days, I guess anything's possible. And don't forget that our FLOs have warned us not to put ourselves at risk. I don't know about you, but I don't want to spend the rest of my life living in fear of the unknown. We're better off establishing the threat, if there is any, and dealing with it. It's the only way we'll ever feel safe again.'

'So, what do we do? Do you have a plan?'

'Not as such. We need to speak to Tess. Get her take on things. It's possible she might know who was out to get him.'

'I suppose I could try to find out where she lives. I could butter Simon up, see if he lets something slip. Failing that, I could ask his sister if she could pump him for information.'

'His sister?' asked Harriet.

'Yes, her name's Liz. She's my best friend. You've already met her. She was with me when I came to identify Albert's body.'

'That's an excellent idea, but if that comes to nothing, we could also try to find her on social media, though we might have to wade our way through hundreds of Tess Harrises.'

'Even if she has various social media accounts it doesn't mean we'd find her that way. Chances are her surname wasn't Harris before she got married to Albert, and we'd be on a hiding to nothing searching every profile linked to the name Tess.'

'I suppose she could even be a technophobe like Albert. Did he have any social media accounts that you know of? Because he certainly didn't while he was with me. Come to think of it, he was camera-shy way before we routinely had mobile phones. Always insisted on being the one to take the photograph, but never wanted to be in it,' said Harriet.

'He was the same with me. Used to joke about having a face that would crack the lens. But it all makes sense now. He obviously didn't want to risk his photograph getting out there, as it might compromise him. What a snake.'

'Oh, he was that all right. Seems as though it was one lie after another with him. And as far as I'm concerned, I want to get to the truth, because you can be damn sure that once any journo gets wind of this, they'll sink their teeth in and won't let go. It's better we find out the truth before they do, as at least that way we can forewarn the kids of what's likely to come out. We won't be able to stop them reporting on it, but we can do some damage limitation.'

'There's so much to think about.'

'Certainly is. We should also check out his bank accounts. Did you have a joint one?'

'No. Albert was dead against it. Said we were better off keeping our finances separate,' said Sylvie.

'Same here. But he must've had a series of accounts as he had three different identities. Which makes me wonder about how he made his money.'

'You've lost me there.'

'Well, his employer was hardly likely to pay his wage to three different people. So, was it paid into one account and transferred from there into accounts he'd opened under his various identities?'

'Good question. I suppose if we both search through his things at our homes, we might find something which would enable us to track down what he was up to.'

'Come to think of it, was he really working for a living? I never met anyone he worked with. And whenever I questioned him, he'd only speak about his job in the vaguest of terms,' said Harriet. 'He told me that he worked in an office, but never said where, or gave any indication about which company he worked for. Whenever I pressed him for an answer, he just shut me down. Which inevitably led to an argument. In the end I gave up asking. The kids and I never went short, and apart from the fact that he was evasive about his job, I never had an inkling that there was anything dodgy about him.

'You're right. He used to say that he'd signed a confidentiality clause in his contract, which meant that everything was hush-hush. Like an idiot, I just accepted what he said and didn't push him on it.'

72

'He certainly did a number on both of us. But he must've been getting money from somewhere, because we never went short, and our outgoings exceeded my monthly salary.'

'Same here,' said Sylvie. 'You're right. It doesn't add up. I dread to think what he was doing to make his money. I just hope it wasn't anything dodgy, and now that he's gone, we're left to face the consequences.'

'Where did you and Albert meet?' asked Harriet.

'At the Cheltenham Literature Festival of all places.'

'Are you a big reader then?'

'Not especially. That's Liz's passion. I knew she wanted to go to the festival, so I got us tickets as a birthday present. Thought it would be a nice thing to do, and she loved it. I was a bit bored to be honest, until I bumped into Albert. He was carrying a pile of books, and I wasn't looking where I was going. I helped pick them up, and things went from there. He gave me one of the books. A crime novel about someone called Tilly Taylor. I didn't have the heart to tell him that it's not my sort of thing. I ended up giving it to Liz. She loved it.'

'I had no idea Albert was interested in literature. In all the years we were together I can't ever recall him picking up a book,' said Harriet.

'After that, whenever the author, Veronica something or other brought out a new book, he'd always give me a copy. I'd pretend to read it, then pass it to Liz. She kept all of them. She's quite the hoarder.

'What about you, where did you first meet?' asked Sylvie.

'I'd gone to see the Hallé Orchestra perform. Albert's seat was next to mine. We got talking in the interval and went for a drink afterwards.'

Sylvie's jaw dropped. 'He never showed the slightest interest in classical music when he was with me. It's almost as if he was two different people.'

'Perhaps that's how he managed to hide what he was doing. Different personas for different lives. It would minimise the chances of him slipping up and giving the game away.'

Sylvie's phone pinged. It was a text from Annabel to say that she had landed at Heathrow. Her stomach flipped at the thought of what was about to come. There would be no delaying the inevitable. That evening, she would have to call round and break the news to her daughter that Albert was dead.

'Is everything OK?' asked Harriet. Even though she didn't know her well, it was immediately apparent that whatever news Sylvie had just received had made her tense.

'It's my daughter. She's due back home today and doesn't know about Albert. I need to break the news to her this evening.'

Harriet reached out and squeezed her hand. It was a supportive gesture and much appreciated. 'I hope it's not too traumatic for her. I've already broken the news to my two. It was the hardest thing I've ever done.'

They left the pub as the lunchtime crowd began to arrive. Having more confidence in each other and a shared sense of purpose, they agreed to meet at the pub again on the following day.

# CHAPTER 14

Sylvie had asked Liz and Simon to help her break the news of Bertie's death to Annabel. Had it not been for the shocking revelations which had been uncovered about Bertie's dubious past, Sylvie would have done this alone. She was convinced that Annabel would be devastated to learn of her father's death. But given the fact that she idolised her father, it was conceivable that learning of the existence of his other families might push her over the edge. And as Sylvie was still trying to come to terms with Albert's betrayals, she didn't feel strong enough to deal with the potential fallout on her own.

Simon was keen for him and Liz to support Sylvie. As they were both close to Annabel, he thought it was for the best. She would undoubtedly have many questions when she learned about her father's deception. None of what Albert had done was in any way Sylvie's fault, but there was a realistic possibility that Annabel might give her mother a hard time.

Imagining how her daughter would take the news filled Sylvie with dread. Throughout Annabel's childhood she'd been a protective parent, and that tiger-like mentality didn't disappear just because your offspring was no longer dependent upon you. Without doubt, Sylvie would walk over hot coals rather than risk causing her daughter any pain.

As she counted down the hours until she saw her daughter, Sylvie did the only thing she could to stop herself from going mad with worry. She set about being busy. The tactic was helpful, as focusing on other things was a distraction. It gave her less time to obsess about how things might play out with Annabel.

As her husband had routinely spent weeks away from home, she'd become accustomed to him not always being there, which somehow made his passing seem less real, as a small part of her was unable to fully accept that he wasn't going to walk through the front door at any moment. Even though she had identified his body and knew without a shadow of doubt that he was never coming home again.

Sylvie found it strange sorting through Albert's things. In many ways, it was far too soon, as she was mourning the loss of the man she loved. Having spent her entire life in this house she knew every nook and cranny. If Albert had squirrelled anything away, she would inevitably find it. He'd moved in when they returned from their honeymoon. She'd practically begged him to move in sooner, but he had insisted he was a traditionalist and didn't want them to live together before they were married.

His firm stance had set the tone for their entire relationship. Sylvie, so blinded by love, wholeheartedly believed him to be a man of principle. On reflection, it was obvious that it had been an act. Faced with recent revelations, it was now blindingly obvious that he had manipulated her from the start, and she had fallen for it hook, line and sinker.

She'd always known that Albert had been a neat freak and had joked about his fastidiousness on many occasions. He disliked mess and clutter, insisting that a neat home was a happy home. In the early years she'd admired the way he'd endeavoured to lead by example, not being one for impulsive purchases, having only the essentials. His obsession with frugality soon began to wear thin, however, and she'd told him that if he wanted to live like that, then that was up to him, but she and Annabel wouldn't be following his example.

Despite knowing that Albert had very few possessions, going through them brought home to Sylvie just how little he had. Then again, now that she knew that he had been living three separate lives, it was hardly surprising. As she methodically sorted through his clothes, she quickly realised that there was no point in bagging any of them up to take to a charity shop. Everything had seen better days. It was impossible to imagine that anyone would want to buy them. For the time being, she was reluctant to throw any of them away — after all, Annabel didn't even know of her father's passing, and it was possible that she just might want a keepsake as a reminder of him.

She was about to get a few shoeboxes out of the bottom of Albert's wardrobe when the doorbell rang. The last thing she wanted right now was to break off from this task. There was a moment when she considered ignoring it, but the bell sounded again, and this time the visitor's finger remained firmly fixed in place. Whoever it was had no intention of giving up any time soon.

Sylvie huffed and stomped down the stairs to open the door. It was Simon.

'Just checking that you're all right,' he said.

She sighed. 'I'm fine.'

'I called around earlier, but you weren't here.'

Sylvie didn't want to tell him about meeting up with Harriet, as she sensed that he would disapprove and try to discourage her from doing it again. 'It was starting to feel a bit claustrophobic being cooped up here, so I went for a drive to clear my head.'

Simon nodded his approval. 'Fair enough. You've had a lot to come to terms with in the last few days.'

'Sorry, Simon, I don't mean to be rude, but was there anything you wanted? Only I'm in the middle of sorting through Albert's clothes, and I want to get it out of the way.'

'That's understandable. I won't take up much of your time. Of course, I'll be seeing you later when we head over to Annabel's, but I wanted to update you on things.'

'Has something happened?'

'Through the course of our enquiries we've learned that Albert's car was serviced less than twenty-four hours before the crash.'

'So, the crash could have been caused by negligence on the garage's part?'

'The investigating officers are looking into that possibility. They'll know more when they've concluded their enquiries.'

'So, it might not have been murder. Is there any update on wife number three?' asked Sylvie.

'If you mean, has she changed her mind about meeting you, then no, she hasn't. I haven't spoken to her, so I can only pass on what I've been told. And she can't be compelled to see you. You might want to speak to her, but she has the right to decline. She's being treated the same as you and Harriet. She attended the station and was questioned just like you. Someone will follow up on what she said and check her alibi. Apparently, she's distraught. As I've already told you, there were no children from that relationship, so she's got no reason to want to meet up with you or Harriet.'

'It's understandable, I suppose,' said Sylvie. She sighed. It looked like Simon wasn't going to help set up a meeting between them. 'Was Albert with her that morning?'

'I believe so.'

'So, I guess the accident must've happened close to wherever they lived?'

'That's right. Look, I appreciate that it's easier said than done, Sylvie, but it's best not to dwell on these things. The investigation is out of your hands, so leave it to us. I promise you, we'll get to the bottom of what happened. You've enough on your plate, with having to break the news to Annabel later today.'

Despite knowing that Simon had her best interests at heart, Sylvie was beginning to feel irritated. It was all very well for him to act the policeman. After all, it was his job. But she couldn't understand how he could possibly expect her to sit back and allow things to play out. Sylvie wanted answers, and she wanted them now. Not six months down the line. Or possibly never.

On a personal level, she thought a lot of Simon. He was Liz's brother, and they'd been friends for many years. But just because she knew he was a good guy, didn't mean he was capable of getting to the bottom of what Albert had been up to.

Recent revelations showed that her husband had been a conman. After all, he'd conned her and Harriet, too, for decades, without either of them having an inkling that he was up to anything. But what if there was more to it than that? What if he had other cons on the go? Things that were nothing to do with being married to three women at once.

If the problem with the car turned out not to be the fault of the garage, it could mean that someone had deliberately tampered with it to either scare, hurt or kill Albert. And if any of those scenarios were the case, it was also possible that they could come after Albert's family members too. Any, or all of them, could become victims through no fault of their own.

Sylvie said goodbye to Simon just as her phone rang. It was Harriet.

'I've just had the police around. Have they updated you yet?' Harriet sounded breathless as she spoke.

'If you're referring to the fact that he'd just had the car serviced, then yes. I've also had it confirmed that Albert was with Tess before he left for work that day, and the crash occurred shortly after he left home.'

'We need to speak to her. Find out if she knows anything.'

'Apparently she has no intention of speaking to us,' said Sylvie.

'I don't care whether she wants to or not. We're all in the same boat, and as far as I'm concerned, she can bloody well stump up for her share of the funeral costs.'

'We'd have to find her first,' said Sylvie.

'See if your friend Liz can get anything out of her brother. It might not seem so obvious if she's the one pumping him for information. In the meantime, I'll do a bit of digging, see what I can find.'

With a few hours still to go until Sylvie was due to break the news to Annabel, she continued with the task of going through Albert's things. The only items remaining in his wardrobe were the three shoeboxes, stacked neatly, one on top of the other. As she knelt to retrieve them, she decided to remove them all at once. As she grasped the bottom one, she was surprised to find how heavy they seemed. Dragging them from the back she removed the top one first which weighed next to nothing. The second of the boxes was the same. But when she lifted the final box, its weight suggested that it contained something other than shoes. Sylvie's heart rate increased as she lifted the lid, and her eyes widened when she discovered what looked like a small safe box hidden inside.

In all the years they'd been together, Sylvie hadn't known that Albert had hidden such a thing only a few feet away from the bed they shared. Then again, it appeared that there were many things she hadn't known about her husband. So she shouldn't be surprised at this latest revelation, should she?

# CHAPTER 15

The following morning, Sylvie was up before the sun had risen. Despite being used to sleeping alone, it had been a long and lonely night, as unwelcome thoughts refused to allow her some peace. Her eyes were puffy and sore from crying and tiredness. But splashes of cold water soothed her skin and helped her feel more awake. As she stared at the mirror, she barely recognised her reflection. She looked old. Tired. Ill.

It hadn't helped that she'd slept fitfully. Which was hardly surprising when shocks and indignities came thick and fast. In the last few days her life had been upended. Revelations had left her questioning the validity of everything she had taken for granted. It was too much to process. Especially when all she wanted to do was curl up into a ball and stop the world from turning.

Informing Annabel of Albert's death hadn't gone the way she expected. Annabel, who was jetlagged, had taken the news better than Sylvie had anticipated, though whether that was because she was too tired to fully appreciate what she was being told was uncertain.

Simon had explained about Albert's other families, and Annabel had sat in silence, supported by her partner, Damien.

When they had said what they needed to say and were about to leave, Damien assured Sylvie that he would take care of Annabel, and it was agreed that they would call at Sylvie's the following evening, once they had rested and were more attuned to the British time zone.

It bothered and puzzled Sylvie that her daughter had hardly reacted to any of the news. She knew that people dealt with situations in very different ways. But when Annabel had lived at home, she'd had a close relationship with her father. She'd idolised him, and he claimed that she was the apple of his eye. It made no sense that Annabel had taken the news so calmly, coping far better than she would have thought possible. Especially since she had been informed of so many awful things in such a short space of time.

It was still quite early, and Sylvie was already mentally drained, with another full-on day in front of her. Still, she was in no doubt that it was better to keep busy. Having reached rock bottom when she'd learned of what Albert was up to, she was determined that she wasn't going to allow it to define her. She'd always been a fighter and intended to hold her head up and rebuild her life. But before she could do that, she needed to put Albert to rest.

Sylvie slugged another mug of coffee which was already cooling.

In many households a safe box might have been an innocuous item. A locked fireproof container where passports and other important documents were stored. But given that until yesterday, Sylvie had been unaware of its existence, it seemed as though she had discovered Pandora's Box. She couldn't help but wonder what new, unwelcome revelations it might contain, as recent experience had taught her that Albert had been a man with many secrets, and none of them were good.

As Sylvie reached out and touched the smooth metal exterior, her hands trembled. Her mouth was suddenly dry, and she swallowed hard as a lump rose in her throat. She was suddenly so filled with dread at what she might find that she closed her eyes and took a deep breath to steady her nerves. What hellish information did this contraption contain? Intuition suggested that the contents of this box would most likely result in another stab to her heart. But no matter how dreadful it might be, or how upset it would leave her feeling, she needed to get the thing open.

The heartache she had felt since learning of Albert's passing would not go away until she had discovered all his secrets. And just like removing a plaster, it was best to do it quickly and without hesitation. But it was locked and required a six-digit key code to open it.

Sylvie set about using every date she knew that meant something to her family. She tried birthdays and anniversaries but had no luck. In desperation she rang Harriet, who picked up just as Sylvie's doorbell rang.

'I might have found something, but I need your help,' said Sylvie. She spoke as she headed to the door.

'You've got it, just tell me what you need,' said Harriet.

The doorbell sounded again. It seemed to Sylvie that since Albert died, everyone was becoming impatient. 'Hold on, Harriet, I need to get the door.' She opened it to find Liz standing there.

'I've arranged for cover at the tearoom. It'll be a quiet day. I've checked and there are no coach tours doing the rounds. So, I'm all yours.' She barged her way past Sylvie before her friend had a chance to object.

'I'm on the phone,' was all she had time to say, before Liz had made her way into the kitchen.

'Are you able to speak freely?' asked Harriet. She'd heard the conversation taking place in Sylvie's house.

'Yes, it's fine. It's only Liz. Anyway, I've come across a safe box, hidden inside a shoebox. It's locked with a six-digit key code. I've tried all the dates which mean something to me, but he hasn't used those.'

'And you want meaningful dates from my side of the family?'

'Precisely.'

'No problem, I'll text you a list of them. Don't forget that he might have tried to confuse things by Americanising the dates,' she added.

'I don't follow,' said Sylvie.

'Well, they display it, month, day, year. So, for example, 01 02 03 would be the second of January 2003 and not the first of February 2003.'

'That's a thought. I'll try doing that while I wait for your list.'

'You're still coming to the pub this morning?' asked Harriet.

'Absolutely. But since she's turned up, I'll have to bring Liz along too. I won't be able to fob her off. She'll stick to me like a shadow for the rest of the day.'

'No problem. Perhaps we can convince her to try to get the lowdown about Tess from her brother. Anyway, I'll send the list through in the next few minutes and see you both at nine o'clock.'

'Was that Annabel?' asked Liz, as Sylvie returned to the kitchen. Liz was already pouring herself a cup of coffee.

'No, it was Harriet.'

'Harriet? The other wife?' Liz's eyes widened in surprise.

'One of the other wives. You met her when I went to identify Albert.'

'Do you think it's a good idea for you two to be talking to each other?'

'Yes, I do. I wasn't sure at first. But the more I thought about what Albert had done, I began to realise that Harriet and I were never rivals. He did this to both of us, so Harriet and I have a lot in common. I know you'll think it's strange, but I quite like her. She's the only person who completely gets what I'm going through.'

'You've got me,' interjected Liz. 'I'm always here for you.'

'I know you are, and I appreciate it. But you don't really know what it's like. It wasn't as if your Vince had other wives on the go. He was faithful to you to the end.'

Liz's breath caught in her throat at the mention of her deceased husband.

'I'm sorry, Liz, I didn't mean to upset you. But Vince was a special man. Not like Albert. Turns out he was nothing but a snake, and from what Simon said, it seems as though someone might have tampered with his car. Harriet and I are just trying to make sense of everything. She seems like a decent woman.'

'You're vulnerable, Sylvie. You've only met her a couple of times. But you've no real idea what she's like. She could be conning you just like Albert did.'

'I know she's a good person, Liz. We met up yesterday and spent a few hours together, and we're meeting up again this morning. You can come, too, if you want. See what Harriet's like for yourself. I'm sure you'll like her.'

'Oh, I'll definitely come. You're not thinking straight, and I need to reassure myself that she's not taking advantage of you.'

'She's not. You'll soon see that she's just like us.'

'Umm.' Liz couldn't hide her scepticism but thought it best not to argue. It was apparent that Sylvie needed to spend time with this woman, and the best thing Liz could do was to go along and meet up with her too.

'But we're not going straight away. I want to open this before we head off.' Sylvie placed a hand on top of the safe box. 'I found it yesterday. Albert had hidden it.'

'Not another one of his secrets.' Liz shook her head. 'I hope you don't find anything awful in there.'

'You and me both.'

'We'll do it together. What's the code?'

'I've no idea. That's why I called Harriet. I've tried every memorable date that I know, so I've asked her to give me a list from her family. She's going to text me, but in the meantime, she suggested I try using the American date format.'

'It might work. Give it a go, you've nothing to lose.'

They spent the next few minutes inputting all of Sylvie's memorable dates in the American format, but none of them worked. And when Harriet's list arrived, they systematically worked their way through those, too, using both British and American formats.

'So you and Harriet are just working together to try to get to the bottom of what Albert was up to?' asked Liz.

'Yes. We figured that with all the lies he told, it's possible that he could have upset the wrong person and got himself killed. And if that's the case, they could come after us. We just need to know we're safe.'

'Of course you do.' Liz reached out and squeezed Sylvie's hand. 'You can count me in. I've got your back. We're not going to let him destroy you,' said Liz. 'Now for starters, let's get this contraption open.' Being someone who was always up for a challenge, she sounded determined.

'What do you suggest?'

'You'll probably think I'm mad, but there's another date that we could try. I'll need to go back to my place first to find out what it is, though. But if that doesn't work then we'll try YouTube. There's video help on there for anything you can think of.'

Almost twenty minutes passed before Liz returned.

'Finally! What took you so long?'

'Sorry, I didn't know what page it was on, but I found it eventually.'

'What on earth are you talking about?'

'It was in one of those Harry Blake books that Albert gave you. The ones you always pass on to me without reading. Anyway, long story short, Harry was a womaniser, and his birthday was mentioned in the first book of the series. I remembered it because it made me chuckle, but I couldn't recall the year his character was supposedly born,' said Liz.

'Why would Albert care about the birthday of a fictional character?'

'I'm not suggesting he would have, but it's sort of relevant to the way he lived his own life, since he couldn't seem to help himself when it came to women,' said Liz. 'Do you want to enter the date?'

Sylvie, who was still sat in front of the safe, nodded.

'Try 140264,' said Liz. She held her breath as Sylvie pressed the relevant buttons on the keypad.

With the date entered, Sylvie turned the knob, which clicked as the locking mechanism was released. 'The fourteenth of February, Saint Valentine's Day. Oh, Albert, you really were one of a kind, choosing the birthday of a fictional character as a memorable code.'

With the box now open they had their first look at the contents.

# CHAPTER 16

Sylvie was starting to realise that throughout the last few days, the revelations of Albert's deception had affected her badly. It wasn't just the case that she had lost her husband in such an unexpected way. It was that being confronted with his massive betrayal had knocked her confidence. It had made her feel naive and stupid.

She hated the thought that people would pity and possibly even laugh at her. She wanted to believe that the people she knew wouldn't be gossiping about her behind her back. But the circumstances she now found herself in were so unusual that it was inevitable that others would talk about her life and her recently revealed sham of a marriage.

It was different with Harriet, as they were in the same boat. Both had believed they were in an exclusive relationship with the man they had married. This meant they both understood the feelings of betrayal upon finding out that their husband was a polygamist, and the growing anger of having been duped by a man who had professed to love them. Then there was a mutual desire to protect their children. A shared lived experience meant they could trust each other. And both women were determined to get to the truth of what had happened so that they could move on with their lives after the inevitable wave of salacious gossip and speculation died down.

Now that Liz appeared to be fully on board with their fact-finding mission it felt as though a weight had been lifted from Sylvie's shoulders. It buoyed Sylvie's mood knowing that she didn't have to be so secretive, and she wished that she'd told her friend about finding the safe box earlier. After all, Liz was the one to figure out Albert's ridiculous security code. She just hoped that Harriet would feel the same way too, as it was possible that Liz's presence could upset the balance.

'It'll be great to go somewhere for breakfast,' said Liz. 'I can't recall the last time I did that.'

'Don't get your hopes up too much.'

'I don't care. It'll just be something different. Which is fine by me. So, what's Harriet really like?'

'She seemed nice enough when we met up yesterday. It sounds weird given the circumstances, but I think we could become friends. I just hope that you two get along.'

Yet again, Harriet was late arriving at the pub. When she eventually arrived, she unceremoniously burst through the door and almost toppled a chair when she knocked it with her oversized handbag. Sylvie and Liz were already tucking into their breakfasts and looked up in surprise.

'Careful there, missus,' said one of the regulars. He'd just finished his second pint and was on his way to the bar for another. 'And they try to make out that I'm unsteady on my feet.' He stifled a burp as he walked away.

Harriet harrumphed and shot him a withering look.

Sylvie waved to attract her attention, and when Harriet spotted her, she headed towards them.

'This is Liz. You met the other day,' she said by way of explanation.

Liz, who was hurriedly chewing a mouthful of pastry, held out a hand, which Harriet shook.

'Hello and thank you. I recall you were kind enough to give up your seat,' said Harriet.

'It was the least I could do. I'm so sorry about everything that's happened. Sylvie's got me up to speed and I'm in. Just tell me what you want me to do, and I'll do it because I want to be one of the gang.'

Both widows stared at her in surprise.

'Oops. That came out wrong. It probably sounded like a bad line from The Famous Five or The Secret Seven. What I meant to say is that I've always fancied myself as an amateur sleuth, and I want to help you get to the bottom of things.'

'Sorry, Harriet,' said Sylvie. 'Liz is just a bit hyper. I think it's all the sugar in those pastries. She's already had three. Go and order your breakfast, we've a lot to discuss.'

'I'm not hyper,' muttered Liz. Harriet was already heading towards the bar to order her food, so she couldn't hear the conversation taking place at the table. 'You know I'm good at solving crimes. I've been at it for years. I've lost count of the number of times I've quizzed Simon. And I've picked up so many useful tips from him. Plus, there isn't an episode of Marple, Poirot, Midsomer Murders or Death in Paradise where I haven't guessed who the killer is, way before their so-called detective has solved the case. It's my thing. You know it is. I'd make a great detective.' Placing the remains of her pastry on the plate she stared at Sylvie defiantly, silently daring her friend to contradict her claim.

'I know you're eager to help. But Harriet doesn't know you, and you came across a bit too full-on. Just rein it in a bit, Liz. You don't need to try so hard. I'm sure we'll all get along.'

Having placed her order and visited the coffee machine, Harriet returned to the table and sat down. 'No full English today?' she asked Sylvie.

'Couldn't face it two days in a row. Thought I'd give the eggs benedict a try. They're nice too.'

Thinking it best to heed Sylvie's advice, Liz bit into her pastry. If she was munching, she couldn't speak. At least until she was spoken to.

'How did it go with the safe box? Did you manage to find the code?'

'I didn't, but—'

'I figured it out,' gushed Liz. Having swallowed the final piece of the Danish pastry there was nothing stopping her from joining in the conversation.

'Oh?' Harriet raised an eyebrow questioningly.

'Yes, in the end it was easy.' Liz looked like the cat that had got the cream as she went on to explain about the Harry Blake books which Albert had liked.

'Patron saint of lovers, eh? It's a wonder he didn't choose Casanova's birthday,' said Harriet, as they collectively erupted into peals of laughter.

'When you get to know her, you'll realise that Liz is very resourceful,' said Sylvie, by way of explanation. 'If she hadn't have walked in when she did, I'd still be sat at the kitchen table tearing my hair out and getting nowhere.'

'Please let me help,' pleaded Liz. 'Pleeease. I've known Albert for almost as long as Sylvie, and I hate what he's done. I'm on your side.'

'I don't see why not. From what you've just said, you certainly seem to think outside the box, and I've a feeling that if we're going to get to the bottom of what our despicable husband was up to and find out who had it in for him, we're going to need all the help we can get.'

'Thank you. Thank you. Thank you,' gushed Liz. 'You won't regret it. I promise I won't let you down.'

'So go on, tell me. What was in the box?' Harriet leaned forward, keen to hear what they had found.

'His will, and a birth certificate.'

Harriet looked surprised. 'Are you sure they're authentic?'

'I've no idea about the birth certificate. After all, it's already been established that he stole people's identities. But as for the will, he made it in the early days of our marriage. Before Annabel was born. It was witnessed by Simon,' said Sylvie.

'My brother's a police officer. He wouldn't put his name to anything that wasn't one hundred per cent above board,' reassured Liz.

'What did it say?'

'I've got it here, if you want to take a look,' said Sylvie. She opened her handbag and extracted the document.

Harriet scanned it. 'There's no mention of any property, but it says any children should get equal shares of the proceeds of his bank and savings accounts.'

'The house was originally my parents', and it's entirely in my name,' said Sylvie. 'At least Annabel, Zara and Leo should get something from their father, after the funeral costs are taken care of.'

'As long as wife number three hasn't taken the money and run,' said Liz. It appeared as though this hadn't occurred to either Harriet or Sylvie, as both women glanced at each other in horror. 'But don't worry about the funeral, I've already told Sylvie that I'll make sure that Dai the Death does it at cost price. He won't go against my wishes, and it's the least he can do.'

'Liz's husband was a funeral director and a partner in Valley View Funeral Home. When he passed, Liz inherited his share of the business,' said Sylvie, by way of explanation. Upon hearing Liz sigh, she squeezed her friend's hand supportively.

'I'm sorry for your loss,' said Harriet. Leaning across the table she reached out for Liz's free hand and gestured for Sylvie's too. 'Seems as though one way or another we're all in the same boat. Guess us widows should stick together.'

'Absolutely,' said Sylvie.

'You mean I'm one of the gang?' asked Liz. It was noticeable that she had perked up at the thought of this.

'Definitely part of the gang,' replied Harriet. She smiled warmly at the others.

'We're like the Three Musketeers,' said Liz. 'All for one and one for all.'

'Hear, hear,' chorused the other two.

Harriet's eggs benedict arrived, and she tucked in eagerly.

'Have you learned anything about the mysterious Tess?' asked Sylvie.

'Not so far. Turns out, Tess Harris isn't an unusual name. I tried the electoral register for that general area, but I didn't come up with anything. It would help enormously if we could find out where they lived. A precise address would be ideal. I can't even find her on social media, and since we've no idea what she looks like we're on a hiding to nothing.'

'I'll talk to Simon,' said Liz. 'I know which buttons to push to get him to spill what he knows. He's never been able to keep a secret from me.'

'You'd do that?' asked Harriet.

'Of course. He's my brother. I know him inside out. And it's not as if I'm just being nosy, pumping him for information. We're real-life detectives now. We're working a case and want answers, so we do what needs to be done. Just leave it with me,' said Liz.

'That's great, because I'm up against it for the next couple of days,' said Harriet.

'Anything we can help with?' asked Sylvie.

'I wish, but no. It's a work thing.'

'Oh, what is it that you do?' asked Liz.

Harriet's cheeks reddened, as embarrassment took hold. 'In the broadest of terms, I guess you could say that I help people.'

'By doing what specifically?' pressed Sylvie. Her interest was piqued, and it was nice to have something that wasn't Albert-related to talk about.

'Well, if I tell you, you both have to swear that you'll keep it a secret.' She looked from one to the other.

'Pinky promise,' said Liz as she crooked her little finger. The others gave her a withering look, but undeterred she continued anyway. 'Well, we're a gang now. A team. All for one, et cetera.' She stared them out.

Sylvie sighed. 'I guess so. Pinky promise it is.'

'Seriously?' asked Harriet. 'It's like I've woken up to find I'm one of the Pink Ladies from *Grease*.'

'And you've a problem with that?' asked Liz.

'Oh, what the heck, I'll let you both in on my secret, but you better not tell anyone else.'

'Pinky promise,' chorused the other two in unison.

Harriet leaned forward and lowered her voice so that it was no more than a whisper. 'I'm Aunt Aggie.'

Both women sat there, wide-eyed, open-mouthed. Liz was the first to recover. 'Oh, I love Aunt Aggie. I never miss reading the problems page. She gives such good advice.' She looked and sounded starstruck.

'Now why am I not surprised at that?' laughed Sylvie.

# CHAPTER 17

Owning and running a small business meant that Sylvie and Liz didn't have the luxury of taking time out without it impacting negatively on their livelihoods. Over the last few days, Liz had done her best to keep things ticking along, knowing that it was too much to expect Sylvie to do her bit. It was easy enough to get people to cover the tearoom. But baking was predominantly Liz's domain, and their stocks were rapidly depleting.

With only so many hours in the day, and an increasing number of orders which needed to be fulfilled, there was a significant amount of preparation and subsequent baking to be done. It was going to be a case of all hands to the pump. As with many small businesses, reputation was everything. And both women knew that if they didn't get on top of things quickly their business would inevitably take a hit.

With that in mind, it had been decided that they would have a change of venue when they met again on the following morning. And the Delicious Desserts Tearoom seemed the best place to reconvene, as it meant that they could bake while they pooled their latest findings. With investigative tasks agreed the women returned home, invigorated with their new-found camaraderie and a common purpose.

Harriet was busier than ever. For someone who was obsessed with efficiency and filled much of her waking time with methodically working through tasks, this latest development in her life was proving a challenge. It was not so much that she was struggling to come to terms with her husband's death. She was used to only spending one week in three with Albert, and if she was honest about it, there had been occasions when she wished she saw him even less. Armed with the knowledge of his infidelity, it was easy now to recognise the fact that he had been keeping her at arm's length. He had made more of an effort at playing the role of the family man while Zara and Leo had lived at home. Since Leo had moved out into student accommodation while he studied Drama, Albert had become less and less attentive, as his mind was clearly elsewhere. Even on the days when he was at home, they had been more like ships passing in the night.

For the first time in a long while Harriet realised that she felt optimistic. It was a strange sensation. Having spent those few hours with Sylvie and Liz, she actually felt relaxed. They'd chatted and laughed, mainly about Albert and what a useless husband he'd been. And strangely, even though she didn't know them well, she knew that these women, who were already lifelong friends, had opened their arms to her and were offering her true friendship.

It wasn't as though Harriet lived her life as a recluse. She had her running buddies, women she met up with day in, day out come rain or shine. They'd shared a fitness routine for years, yet she still only knew them superficially. But in the space of a few hours, she'd learned more about Sylvie and Liz than about any of those women. And perhaps more surprisingly, she'd admitted to them that she was Aunt Aggie. This was something she had always been very secretive about.

The Delicious Desserts Tearoom didn't open to the public until ten o'clock each morning. They had learned early on that unlike town or city centre eateries, there was never sufficient footfall to make it worthwhile opening any earlier.

Following her usual routine, Liz went in at six o'clock to prepare that day's freshly baked cakes, scones, flapjacks and other fancy offerings. She also had two lucrative sidelines on the go. These were special occasion cakes, which meant that there weren't many days when she wasn't fulfilling orders for birthdays or weddings. And then there was an online business for brownies, blondies and cupcakes, which had become an almost overnight success.

At a quarter to seven that Friday morning, Liz heard the bell sound as the door opened.

'It's only me,' called Sylvie. 'Do you want a hand with anything?'

'There's a pile of washing-up needs doing,' said Liz. She knew that there was no point in asking Sylvie to help with preparing the mixtures as baking had never been her strong point. 'Sixteen orders for brownies and blondies came in yesterday. So, I've got to get them off this afternoon. The way it's going I'm starting to think that we're going to have to find separate premises and take someone else on to fulfil these online orders. This kitchen's too small to cope with it.'

'Even I can't make a hash of doing the washing-up,' said Sylvie. 'I don't trust myself to help with the prep, as I'm still distracted.'

'That's unsurprising. I'm just grateful for any input, so if you can start with that lot . . .' she pointed to various mixing bowls, spatulas and spoons, 'I'm just about to get this first batch in the oven, and I've got enough equipment to prep the second batch. But after that I'm stymied until those are ready to use again.'

Sylvie grabbed a freshly laundered apron as she waited for the industrial-sized sink to fill with hot water. Shortly before seven o'clock the doorbell sounded again. This time it was Harriet.

Sylvie stuck her head out into the public area. 'We're in the kitchen, Harriet. Liz has got a huge number of orders to fulfil so help would be appreciated.'

Without further prompting, Harriet took off her jacket, rolled up her sleeves and prepared to get stuck in. 'Just tell me what you need me to do. I'm happy to prep, if you like. I don't often eat cake, too many bad carbs, but I love baking. Find it therapeutic. We can talk as we work.'

The three women quickly adopted an efficient regime, getting through the long list of tasks in a record amount of time. By half past eight, everything that needed to be done had been completed.

'Great teamwork,' said Liz. 'Now, go take the weight off and I'll make us all a nice pot of tea.' She joined them a few minutes later with a tray laden with a selection of flapjacks, scones and crumpets, along with ramekins of jam and cream. Spotting the concerned expression on Harriet's face, she reassured her. 'Try the flapjacks. They're delicious, and oats are supposed to be good for you. Just imagine you're eating porridge, but in a different form.'

Harriet sighed, clearly torn between wanting to indulge, but having to justify this moment of weakness to herself.

'Is this because of Albert?' asked Sylvie. 'Did he keep going on at you about your weight?'

Harriet nodded. 'He was like that from the moment we decided to get married. Kept saying that if I didn't lose a few pounds, I'd regret it when I saw myself in the wedding photos. Then there were the usual digs over the years. Especially when I was trying to lose weight after having each of the kids.'

'Like he was an oil painting,' said Liz. She shook her head in despair. 'But he was consistent. I'll give him that.' She looked at Sylvie, who nodded.

'He was forever having a go at me. I didn't want the aggravation, so I'd always eat healthily whenever he was at home. But I've got a sweet tooth, and the first thing I'd do whenever he left was to head over here and treat myself to a huge piece of chocolate cake. Then I'd drive to the supermarket and buy enough chocolate to last me until he came home.'

'You don't need to please him anymore, Harriet,' said Liz. 'You're a free agent. You can do what you want. Eat what you want, when you want. That goes for you, too, Sylvie. Neither of you need feel guilty.'

'You're right,' said Harriet. She picked up a piece of flapjack and bit into it. 'Ummm, this is sooo good.'

Liz smiled.

'Did you get anywhere with Simon?' asked Sylvie. She was eager to know what Liz had learned.

'He was tight-lipped at first, but I eventually wore him down. Stuck a lemon drizzle cake in front of him and wouldn't allow him to have a piece until he'd spilled the beans.'

They all laughed.

'Turns out that they lived near Bath.'

'Bath! Not local, then. He was certainly broadening his horizons,' said Harriet.

'I've even got their address if you're interested.'

Before leaving the tearoom that morning, a plan was made for the three of them to pay a visit to Bath in three days' time. They had settled on Monday, as the tearoom was closed that day. The only time it was worth opening on a Monday was if it was a bank holiday since tourists flocked to the village on public holidays, keen to do something different and make the most of the day.

# CHAPTER 18

Monday morning arrived, and having agreed upon an early start, Liz knocked on Sylvie's door shortly before half past five. 'You ready?' she asked.

'As I'll ever be. I've had two strong cups of coffee. So, let's do this.' Sylvie set the car's satnav for Harriet's house, and they set off. 'I know it seems ridiculously early, but it's best to get to Bath as soon as we can.'

'I agree. If you're going to speak to Tess, it's best to catch her unawares, because Simon's already said that she has no intention of meeting up with either of you. Apparently, after she gave her statement at the station, she told her FLO that she didn't want any more face-to-face contact. Claims she's finding the whole thing far too traumatic. So, for the time being they're keeping in contact by phone.'

'I can understand her being horrified to discover that there were two more wives, but she can't realistically expect to walk away from this. She was most likely the last person to see him alive, and we need answers to so many questions.'

'I get where you're coming from, but it might not work out the way you think. Just because you and Harriet have worked through your feelings and decided to act in a responsible way, doesn't mean that wife number three will. After all, she doesn't have any kids to think about. Which means she could just decide not to put herself through the stress of this. She could easily cut her losses and walk away. And I doubt there's anything you or Harriet could do about it,' said Liz.

Having collected Harriet, they reset the satnav for Tess's address. It proved a good decision to have set off early, as they missed the worst of the traffic and made it to their destination shortly after seven o'clock. For the last few miles of their journey, the women had sat in silence. Each was lost in their own thoughts.

The property which Albert and Tess had shared was on the edge of a small village a few miles out of Bath. It was set back off the road, hidden behind a well-established copper beech hedge, with a low wooden gate preventing immediate access to a driveway covered in yellowish chippings.

Sylvie pulled up in front of the gates and cut the engine. 'It makes sense to block the gate. No chance of her getting past this,' she said. 'She'll have to talk to us now. Otherwise, I'll just refuse to move.'

'This is your last chance to back out,' said Liz, as she looked from one to the other. 'It's possible this meeting might not go well. I doubt she's going to thank any of us for turning up on her doorstep like this.'

'We're here and we're doing this,' said Harriet. 'We need answers from her, and let's face it, it doesn't seem as though the police are doing anything to make her talk to us.'

'Precisely,' said Sylvie. 'Albert's taken us for a ride all these years, but now he's out of the picture and we're the ones in control. As Harriet's just said, we deserve answers. Tess might not know if Albert had any enemies. But we've talked things over, pooled our information and come up with nothing. So, we need to find out what his latest wife knows.'

'That's right, because if someone did set out to kill him, then what's to say they won't come after us or our kids? If

101

we're going to ensure we're safe, then we need answers, and we need them now. Otherwise, we'll spend the rest of our lives looking over our shoulders wondering if someone's got it in for us too. After all, there's no denying that Albert was good at hiding things from people. Who knows what he could have got us into?' said Harriet.

'Let's get this done,' urged Sylvie. 'I've brought a notebook, so we won't risk forgetting anything.'

'That's so old school,' said Harriet. 'I'm just going to record the entire conversation on my phone.'

Sylvie shrugged, acknowledging that she needed to move with the times. 'That's a good idea. Hadn't thought of that.'

'I use the record facility a lot when I'm out and about,' said Harriet. 'I get ideas at all sorts of odd times, and I find it's best to record them at the time. Otherwise, there's a risk that I'll forget about them.'

'Oh, that's such a good idea,' said Liz. She took out her phone, switched on the record facility and spoke loudly into it. 'Remember to record ideas on the phone.'

The other two chuckled at her enthusiasm. Harriet opened the gate and the three of them squared their shoulders as they marched up the driveway towards the house.

There was a car on the drive and Harriet discreetly snapped a shot of it. 'Might come in handy,' she said.

Liz pressed the doorbell, and they waited. When there was no answer, she pressed it again. Only this time she kept her finger on it. The others looked at her in surprise. 'Well, if she refuses to answer the door when we've been polite, let's see her ignore this.'

Liz's relentless approach seemed to have the desired effect as they soon spotted movement in the door's frosted-glass panel. Moments later, a young man with a harried expression glared out at them. His eyes were hooded and bloodshot. 'That's unbelievably selfish. I've come off a double shift and just dropped off. I'm not interested in whatever it is you want. So please go away and let me get some sleep. Otherwise, I'll be fit for nothing when I go back to the hospital this afternoon.'

'Hospital?' they all chorused.

'Yes, hospital. I work there.'

'That's as may be, but we're here to speak to Tess Harris,' said Harriet.

'Tess Harris? There's no one with that name here. So, you've come to the wrong house and got me out of bed for no . . .' His look of annoyance faded as a thought occurred to him. 'Hold on, I think she was the previous tenant. Moved out at the end of last week. I've only been here since Saturday.'

'Do you know where she went?' asked Sylvie, as it suddenly occurred to her that they were not going to find Tess.

'No, but you could ask my parents. They own this property and rent it out. If I tell you where they live will you go away and let me get some sleep?'

'Absolutely,' said Harriet.

'In that case, turn right out of here, take the second left, then third left after that. They live at number 36 Dragonfly Lane. Their names are Andrew and Claire Bunting. Just tell them that Nate sent you.'

All three women thanked him and headed back to the car.

# CHAPTER 19

Following Nate's directions, the ladies soon found themselves at Dragonfly Lane where the properties were large, well-maintained and clearly expensive.

'Leave this to me,' said Harriet as they got out of the car. They walked up an expansive driveway that could easily accommodate ten cars. Security cameras were visible, and the front door was inaccessible as a locked porch added an additional layer of protection. A sign at eye level secured on a glass panel adjacent to the doorbell stated that cold callers were not welcome. Harriet ignored it, pressed the doorbell, and they waited.

Moments later the inner door was opened by a middle-aged woman dressed in a sky-blue, linen suit. Within the safety of the locked porch, she looked them up and down, and before Harriet had a chance to say anything the woman spoke. Her voice was haughty, as was her expression. 'We don't engage with cold call—'

'Nate sent us,' interjected Harriet.

'Nate?' At the mention of her son's name, her stern tone became hesitant. 'Has something happened?' She reached out and hurriedly unlocked the door, all the while maintaining eye contact with Harriet.

'There's nothing wrong, Mrs Bunting. I take it you are Mrs Bunting?'

'Yes, I am.'

'We went to your rental property to speak to one of your previous tenants. You see, we knew Albert, but as I'm sure you know, he died last week.' Harriet thought it best not to mention Albert's marital circumstances. 'We were hoping to speak to his wife, Tess. Offer our condolences and share some memories with her.'

'Yes, it saddened me to hear about Albert. He was a lovely man and a good tenant. It was such a shock for his poor wife.'

'It was a shock for us all,' said Sylvie. Harriet shot her a warning look, and Sylvie lowered her gaze.

'We were surprised that Tess moved on so quickly after it happened. But I suppose we all react to grief in different ways,' said Harriet.

'Apparently so,' said Claire Bunting.

'You don't happen to have a forwarding address for her, by any chance?' Harriet's tone was sickly sweet. 'It's just that we'd like to offer our support at this most difficult of times.'

'I'm afraid that I don't.'

'But what about forwarding post? Surely you'd have to make provision for that?' Harriet wasn't prepared to give up so easily. If this lead fizzled out, they would have no way of finding Tess. And as they didn't know what she looked like they could have walked past her in the street and not know who she was.

'How do I know that you were Albert's friends? I've not seen you with him. You could be anyone.'

Liz quickly got her phone out. 'I've a photograph here, if you'd like to see it.' She thrust it towards Claire Bunting. The woman took the phone and studied the image. 'There's myself, my brother Simon, Albert and Sylvie. It was taken a few months ago.'

'I've got a photograph of Albert on my phone too. It was taken at a family party,' said Harriet.

Eventually satisfied that these women had known Albert, Claire relented. 'I'm afraid that I don't have a forwarding address for his widow. But I suppose there's no harm in giving you the contact details that Albert gave us when he first rented the property. This person provided him with a glowing reference, and it's possible he might know where Tess has gone. You see, we adhere to a strict vetting policy. We undertook background checks on Albert and obtained references. If you step inside, I'll look up the document for you. My husband, Andrew, deals with our rental portfolio. I'm afraid he's not here at the moment. Had an early round of golf with a business associate.'

They followed Claire Bunting into a home office. There was a shelf packed with labelled ring binders, and a desk with a laptop upon it. 'Now, let me see . . .' She scanned the folders. 'Ah, yes, I believe it's in this one.' She reached up and pulled it down. 'Andrew's fastidious about his record keeping. Has to be when you consider HMRC practically want to know what you've had for breakfast.' As she laughed at her own joke, the three women indulged her by laughing too.

The ring binder contained a series of A4 punched pockets within which were copies of documentary evidence relating to their tenants. Flicking through the pages, Claire soon found what she was after. 'Ahh, this is what I was looking for.' The metal rings clicked as they parted and she removed the relevant section, pulling out the mound of paperwork it contained. 'Now, let me see. There's an address in there somewhere . . .' She began to riffle through the documents when her mobile phone rang. Glancing at the caller ID she sighed. 'I'm sorry, I must take this. I won't be a moment,' and with that she walked out of the room and into another part of the house.

'Quick. Photograph everything,' said Harriet. She split the pile of documents in three and they each raced to capture images of every piece of paper.

'We're like proper spies,' whispered Liz.

'Detectives,' corrected Sylvie.

'Put your phones away, and start talking about cakes or something,' said Harriet as soon as they had finished. 'We don't want her to get suspicious.'

The call took longer than Claire had anticipated. When she returned to the room almost ten minutes later, the three women were discussing whether a scone should have jam on top of cream. Or cream on top of jam. It was proving to be quite a contentious issue.

'What do you think?' asked Liz.

Claire Bunting sighed. 'I'm sorry, I don't have time for this. That phone call has made me late.' She looked at the desk and saw that the paperwork was stacked in the same neat pile as she had left it. Satisfied that these irritating women hadn't touched it, she huffed and puffed as she turned over the pages, looking for the name and address in question. When she found what she was after, she wrote it down and handed it to Harriet.

They thanked her for her trouble and went on their way, armed with far more information about Albert's life with Tess than they had thought possible.

# CHAPTER 20

As they walked from the Buntings' house towards Sylvie's car, they each struggled to keep a lid on their excitement. In the last twenty minutes they had accomplished far more than they had thought possible. It was such a confidence boost. Having used their wits, improvised and worked as a team they had pulled off a coup of major proportions. It felt good. This newly founded group of amateur detectives had just had their first real break-through. It reinforced the idea that they were a team. That if they worked together, they could achieve so much more than by acting alone.

In such a short space of time, Sylvie and Harriet had overcome their initial resentment and distrust of each other. Harriet had been welcomed by both Sylvie and Liz, and felt that she was now part of that friendship group too. If she thought about it too deeply it seemed like a crazy possibility. Yet in the last few days the three of them were getting on like the proverbial house on fire. Harriet realised that she was actually happy. She could laugh, joke and share experiences with these women. Which was something she hadn't done since her teenage years. And it felt good.

'Listen up, no talking or reacting until we've driven away,' ordered Harriet. Having seen how excitable Liz could sometimes become over the most ordinary of things, she didn't trust her to keep a lid on it. Whereas, having years of experience of hiding her professional persona from all and sundry, Harriet was more used to masking her emotions. The last thing they needed right now was for Claire Bunting to suspect that something was up — if she called the police and they examined their phones, the three of them could end up in a lot of trouble.

From the relative safety of the car, Sylvie was the first to speak. 'I vote we find somewhere to have a slap-up breakfast, and while we're waiting for it, we can take a look at what we've found.'

'Seconded,' said Liz. 'All of that talk of scones has made me hungry.'

'In that case, I insist we find somewhere nice. Not a greasy spoon. I don't think my stomach will cope with it. I'm more than happy to have a continental breakfast, some freshly baked pastries and coffee. I'd even be prepared to have something like that eggs benedict again. But please, ladies, no fried food. Think of your arteries,' said Harriet.

Liz and Sylvie both looked at her aghast.

Having parked the car in the centre of Bath, they wandered around until they found what Harriet deemed to be a suitable place to eat. It was a coffee shop cum bakery, and the aroma when they opened the door was heavenly. A huge coffee machine chugged and hissed away making cup after cup of the aromatic beverage. Liz and Sylvie plonked themselves down at a table towards the back of the seating area before Harriet had a chance to change her mind.

'Oh, did you spot those Belgian buns?' asked Sylvie. 'I'm having one of those. They're about twice the size of the ones you make.'

Liz shot her a dirty look. 'It's quality, not quantity, that matters,' she huffed. 'Yes, I saw them, and I agree, they look nice. But I'm going to have a caramel-custard doughnut and an iced bun. What about you, Harriet?'

'Thought I'd have an Eccles cake and possibly a flapjack. I've got a hankering for them after yesterday.'

'You can't beat Liz's flapjacks,' said Sylvie. It was apparent that she was trying to make up for upsetting Liz by commenting on the smaller size of her Belgian buns.

After the waitress came to take their order, they took out their phones to start examining the documents they'd photographed. About ten minutes later they were busily sipping their drinks as they devoured the pastries, looking much like the majority of other customers who also appeared to be addicted to their electronic devices.

'Well, I never!' exclaimed Liz.

Sylvie stopped munching while Harriet put down her cup. They both stared at her, eager to know what she had found.

'I was so busy snapping away back at the house that I wasn't taking notice of what was on the documents. Turns out I've got a copy of both of their passports. They must've needed them for identification purposes.'

'Show us,' said Harriet.

In their eagerness they huddled closer to Liz. As chair legs scraped across the tiled floor, other customers raised their heads and glanced disapprovingly in their direction. But the ladies were oblivious. All they could think of was seeing what was on Liz's screen, and as she enlarged the photograph, they got their first look at the elusive Tess. The photograph was blurred and grainy, but they were able to make out her features.

Sylvie gasped, and her hands shot to her chest. 'She looks so young. Way too young for Albert.'

'She's very attractive,' said Harriet. 'I can see why he wanted to be with her. It must've been quite the ego boost.'

'Surely, the question is, why did she want to be with him?' said Liz. Sensing all eyes were now upon her, she laughed. 'Oh, come off it, you two. I know you both fell for him. But that was a long time ago. Let's face it, a lot's changed in that time. Why would anyone who looks like that want to be with someone who's old enough to be her father? He's balding, not in the best physical shape, and isn't the most interesting of people to spend time with. Surely there can only be one reason why she'd want to marry him.'

'He was never that good in bed,' said Sylvie.

'I don't mean sex.' Liz all but shouted it out and then sighed in frustration. 'She must've thought he had money.'

'But he didn't,' said Harriet.

'We all know that, but it doesn't mean that she did.'

They now had a name, date and place of birth for Tess. The surname Harris was the same as the one stated on Albert's passport. And they were all aware that the chances of this having been her birth name weren't that great. But at least they now knew what she looked like, and they could search the birth records for her town of birth.

As for Albert's passport, it stated that he was Albert Harris and displayed a different date and place of birth than either of his other two passports. It was further proof that he had indeed adopted various identities.

'I've got a document with the name and address of a Ralph Henry Courtenay,' said Harriet. 'Does that name mean anything to either of you?' When they both shook their heads, Harriet continued. 'Apparently, he acted as guarantor when Albert signed the rental agreement.'

'In that case I guess we should check him out,' said Sylvie. 'Where does he live?'

'In the Cotswolds.'

'Guess he would with a name like that. Sounds quite posh,' said Liz.

Harriet did a quick search to see if she could find him online. 'He doesn't appear to have a social media account. But I have found a reference to a Ralph Henry Courtenay who's the CEO at something called Courtenay Creatives. There's no photograph or any other details about him, so there're no guarantees it's the same man.'

'What's Courtenay Creatives when it's at home?' asked Liz.

'I've absolutely no idea, but I say we go and find out,' said Harriet. 'After all, we set aside the entire day to move our investigation along and we've got some leads to follow up. Perhaps for once, we might begin to learn some actual facts about the man we married.'

# CHAPTER 21

After leaving the coffee shop, they headed to a nearby supermarket to pick up provisions for lunch. Liz also managed to sneak in a bag of chocolate limes to share on the journey.

'As it's approaching midday and we've a long drive ahead of us, I'd suggest heading for Ralph's address,' said Sylvie.

'Well, I suppose if he's not there, we could speak to the neighbours and find out if he's a real person. If it turns out that he is, then we could sit outside and wait for him to come home,' said Harriet.

'I hope he's real, and not some made-up person,' said Liz. 'But given Albert's track record, anything's possible.'

'Oh, don't even go there. I can't bear to think that he's created false identities for other people too. We've had to face more than enough lies for an entire lifetime. We need to speak to someone who actually knew Albert, if we're ever going to find out who he really was,' said Sylvie. 'I still can't get my head around the fact that we were both married to him for all those years, yet we didn't know the first thing about him.'

'I know, it's crazy to think that he's the father of our kids, yet we've no idea of his real identity,' said Harriet.

Using the document Harriet had photographed, Sylvie typed Ralph Henry Courtenay's postcode into the satnav.

Moments later the device had suggested the best route for them to follow and calculated an approximate journey time of just over two hours.

With Sylvie concentrating on driving, Liz stared idly out of the window until she remembered the sweets she'd bought. 'Chocolate lime, anyone?' she asked, as she rummaged in the bag. When there were no takers, she shrugged her shoulders and contented herself with unwrapping one and silently sucked on it.

'How do you think we should play this?' asked Harriet. She'd been quiet for the best part of an hour.

'I'm not sure. What do you think?' said Sylvie.

Harriet sighed. 'Well, for starters there are just so many unknowns.' She began counting them off on her fingers. 'Firstly, we don't know if this Ralph guy lives at that address. Secondly, if he does, it doesn't mean that he knew Albert. Let's face it, our wonderful husband was not averse to faking identities, so he'd hardly break sweat at providing documentation from a fake guarantor.'

'But you said that this Ralph exists,' said Sylvie. 'He's the CEO at . . . What did you say it was?'

'Courtenay Creatives. But think about it, just because someone with that name actually exists, it still doesn't mean that he had any connection with Albert. He could have stumbled across his name on the internet, found out a bit about him and faked the document.'

'I hope not, for your sakes,' said Liz.

'What do you mean by that?' chorused Harriet and Sylvie.

'Well, if Albert did that, then this Ralph person could take legal action.'

'But Albert's dead,' said Harriet.

'Yes, but you two were married to him. There might be a way that he could sue you.'

As unlikely as it sounded, they weren't legal experts, and the very suggestion that this might happen caused a glum atmosphere to descend. They all fell silent, lost in their own thoughts, until Liz reached into the bag of chocolate limes once more and asked if anyone wanted one. This time they both craved the comfort it provided.

Sylvie was eventually the one to break the ensuing silence, and it was apparent that Liz's suggestion had been playing on her mind. 'I'm sure we couldn't be held legally responsible for anything Albert did under the name of Albert Harris. He signed up to that tenancy agreement with Tess. We had no idea he was using that identity. So, there's no way anyone could pin it on us.'

'You're probably right,' conceded Liz. 'It was just a thought. So, what are you going to do when we come face to face with Ralph?'

'To start with, I think we should just show him a photograph of Albert and ask if he recognises him,' said Harriet. 'If he doesn't, then we can just walk away without going into specifics about why we think he knows him. But if he does, we can tell him that someone killed Albert and we're trying to find out who did it.'

'Sounds like a reasonable plan,' said Sylvie. 'I just hope that when we get there, we find that Ralph's at home. Otherwise, we could be hanging about for ages.'

'Especially if he's gone away on holiday,' said Liz.

Sylvie glared at her in the rear-view mirror. 'I think we should start calling you Nellie, because for some unfathomable reason you're being really negative.'

'I was only saying,' said Liz. 'Chocolate lime, anyone?'

# CHAPTER 22

The ladies were in for a surprise, as the address they were heading for was no ordinary property. Having travelled along various major roads they eventually left them all behind as they headed through quaint villages. There were thatched-roofed houses, village greens and duck ponds in abundance. The entire area appeared to be picture postcard perfection. A region where tourists would drive through, stop and admire, imagining what their lives could be like, if only . . .

As Sylvie negotiated the latest narrow winding lane, the satnav showed that they would reach their destination within two minutes. Yet it seemed unlikely as they were in the middle of nowhere. The electronic voice announced that in one hundred yards she should take the next left and that they would have arrived at their destination.

'Surely this is wrong? There's nothing here,' said Harriet.

Before Sylvie had a chance to respond she saw a turning up ahead and slowed down to take it. About ten yards further on, a high wall and a set of double gates became visible. A security camera was located near the gate together with an intercom.

'This is obviously another one of Albert's lies,' said Liz.

Sylvie sighed. She had to agree with her friend. It was apparent that Albert's entire life had been based on a series of lies. 'Well, it's taken us long enough to find this place, so we might as well ask if Ralph Courtenay lives here.'

'I agree, we've nothing to lose other than a few minutes of our time,' said Harriet. 'You two stay in the car and I'll press the intercom.' Before either of them responded, she opened the door, walked over to the metal panel, and pressed the buzzer.

Almost instantly the intercom crackled into life and the camera whirred as it focused in on Harriet. 'Please state your business.' This was no electronic voice. It was undoubtedly a real person.

'We're here to speak to Ralph Courtenay.'

'Return to your vehicle, and when the gates have opened ignore any turns and follow the road for approximately a quarter of a mile. When you reach the house, park in one of the spaces to the left of the property. Remain in your vehicle and someone will come out to meet you.'

Harriet walked the few paces back to the car, opened the door and got in.

'Waste of time?' enquired Sylvie.

'No. Seems he's here.' Harriet then relayed the instructions she'd just received.

'Didn't see that coming,' said Sylvie. As the gates opened, she started the engine, put the car into gear and entered the grounds.

They drove slowly and in silence. All three of them were awestruck as they looked around and wondered how on earth Albert had known someone who lived in a place like this. And as the house came into sight it seemed an even more surreal prospect, as it was a grand old building of palatial proportions, surrounded by well-tended grounds. In the distance, to the right was a lake with a folly on the far bank.

'Ralph must be a millionaire to live in a place like this,' said Liz, as she voiced what the other two were thinking.

As Sylvie cut the engine, one of the high double doors of the property opened. A man came out and headed towards them. His appearance suggested that he was in his late fifties. He was slim, tall, with a full head of hair, looking quite the silver fox. 'I understand you wish to speak to me?' He looked at the ladies questioningly.

'Yes, if you're Ralph Courtenay,' said Harriet.

'I am indeed. Now, how can I help?'

'Do you know this man?' asked Liz. She held out her phone and showed him a photograph of Albert.

'Absolutely. That's my brother. Why are you showing me a photograph of Albert? Where is he and what's he done?' His brow furrowed with concern.

'Your brother? In that case I think we need to talk,' said Sylvie. 'There's a lot you need to know, and it's best we all sit down.'

117

# CHAPTER 23

Once inside the house, Ralph led the ladies into a bright, airy sitting room, where it was apparent that no expense had been spared. He directed them towards a large, white sofa covered with oversized cushions of various colours, seating himself on a similar sofa, directly facing theirs.

'Now, I'd like you to tell me what this is all about,' he said. His expression was serious, though his tone remained pleasant and his body language relaxed.

Sylvie leaned forward to narrow the gap between them. Knowing that Ralph was completely unaware of the news she was about to break, her heart went out to him. 'Look, I'm sorry to have to tell you this, but Albert's dead.'

Ralph's brow furrowed as he tried to make sense of what he'd just been told. 'D-dead? N-no, he can't be. When did this happen?' His complexion paled as he listened intently to news of the crash, the car being tampered with, and the fact that the police were treating it as murder.

At first, he appeared shell-shocked, then after a few minutes he eventually spoke. 'I can't believe I'm hearing this. I don't know how I'm going to break the news to Mother.'

'Your mother's still alive?' asked Harriet.

'Yes, why wouldn't she be? I know she's old, but there's plenty of life in the old girl yet.'

'Sorry, I didn't mean to be offensive,' said Harriet. 'But there are still things we haven't told you.'

'Such as?'

'Harriet and I were both married to Albert,' said Sylvie.

'No, you couldn't have been. He'd have told us.' Ralph dismissed this assertion with a shake of the head.

'There's another wife too,' added Liz. 'Though we haven't met her yet.'

'Are you seriously trying to tell me that my brother had three marriages and at least two divorces that he failed to mention?'

'Not exactly,' said Harriet. 'When he died, the police discovered three phones inside his briefcase. Long story short, it seems that your brother was living under three false identities.'

'False identities!' Ralph stiffened and sat forward in the seat. 'Don't be ridiculous. It can't be true. He had everything he could possibly want in life, there was no need for him to do such a thing.'

'We couldn't believe it either. Not until we learned that he was a polygamist, and getting away with it because he was using different identities,' said Sylvie. 'As far as we know, he married me first. Or at least, Albert Franklynn did.'

'He married me about a year and a half later, but I knew him as Albert Joyce,' said Harriet.

'And you're his third wife?' Ralph's question was addressed to Liz.

She laughed and shook her head. 'Absolutely not. I knew your brother as Sylvie's husband. No, it turns out that about eighteen months ago, two wives weren't enough for him, and he married a woman who looks as though she's about the same age as his daughters. Apparently, she's called Tess Harris.'

'Albert had children?' This time, Ralph's voice rose by almost an octave. He placed his head in his hands as he tried to make sense of what he was hearing. 'And in all the time you were married to him he told you nothing of us?'

'That was one thing he was consistent about. He told us that he had no family,' said Harriet.

'We only came here because we learned that he'd lied to us all along. We got your name and address quite by chance, and until you told us that he was your brother, we believed that you were just a friend, or business acquaintance who had agreed to be his guarantor when he took out a lease on a property he was living at with his most recent wife,' said Sylvie.

'But I didn't agree to be his guarantor, and I certainly didn't sign any document to that effect.'

'We have a photograph of it,' said Liz.

Ralph stared at the document in disbelief. 'It's my name and this address, but that's not my signature.'

'I suppose that's hardly surprising, given the circumstances. After all, if Albert had got you to sign that document, you'd have wanted to know why he was calling himself Albert Harris, and not Albert Courtenay.'

Ralph shook his head. 'I must admit, I was sceptical at first, but these revelations change everything. Look, I'm sorry, make yourselves comfortable. We're due to have afternoon tea shortly. I'll arrange for three more places to be set and come straight back. There's someone you need to meet, and it's obvious we've got a lot to talk about.' Standing up abruptly, he walked out of the room without a backwards glance.

'Afternoon tea . . . I like the sound of that,' said Liz. Her expression had taken on a dreamlike quality. 'I wonder what we'll have?' The others ignored her.

'Can you believe that Albert had a brother and a mother that he never mentioned?' said Sylvie.

'Which means that Ralph's our brother-in-law, and he has two nieces and a nephew he didn't know existed. And there's a mother-in-law neither of us have met. Albert certainly had a knack of keeping secrets.'

They were chatting among themselves when the door opened, and Ralph returned. 'I've just told Mother about you and informed her of what's happened to Albert. She's taken the news surprisingly well. Far better than I expected. Then again, she's a tough old bird. She's waiting for us in the orangery, and she's keen to meet you. I take it that you know who she is?' He looked from one to the other and was met with three blank expressions.

'Well, as she's your mother, I guess that she's Mrs Courtenay,' said Liz.

'Not just Mrs Courtenay.' Ralph smiled. 'She's Catherine Amelia Courtenay, which wouldn't necessarily mean anything at all to most people. Which is just as well, as she's a very private person. Though her nom de plume is a different matter. It's known by millions of people worldwide. You see, she's Veronica Dumont.'

'Oh, my goodness! Your mother's Veronica Dumont?' Liz's eyes were wide with surprise, and there was obvious excitement in her tone.

'Yes.'

'Who's Veronica Dumont?' asked Harriet.

'Only this country's new Queen of Crime,' proclaimed Liz. 'First there was Agatha. Now there's Veronica.'

'You've lost me. Who's Agatha?'

'Agatha . . . Agatha Christie.'

'Even I've heard of Veronica Dumont,' said Sylvie.

'I know you have,' gushed Liz. 'Albert kept giving you her books. You weren't interested in reading them, so you kept passing them on to me.'

Sylvie's complexion reddened with embarrassment. 'I've never been a fan of crime fiction, and I had no idea they were his mother's books.'

'You don't need to explain,' said Ralph. 'I can't say that I've read any of the books either. But they weren't all written by mother. As her work gained popularity, she was put under enormous pressure to increase her output. It proved to be impossible, given her age. Which is why she used a ghostwriter.'

Liz's hands shot to her chest. 'Oh, my word! I never knew that.'

'It wasn't made public.'

'You're taking a risk telling us that,' said Sylvie.

'I am indeed, and it's not something that I've done lightly. But under the circumstances you need to know, because Albert was the ghostwriter.'

'Albert? Our Albert?' Harriet slumped into the nearest seat, as she tried to make sense of what she was hearing.

'He only ever spoke about his job in the vaguest of terms,' said Sylvie.

'What did he say?' asked Ralph.

'Just that he was sworn to secrecy. That it was best that we didn't know.'

'I always thought he was some sort of undercover operative,' said Harriet. 'It explained why he spent so much time away from home.'

'Well, I suppose in a sense he was undercover. He's been Mother's ghostwriter for thirty-five years, and he was very good at it too. Of course, Mother still pens the odd standalone novel, but the one who did the lion's share of the work was Albert.'

# CHAPTER 24

For someone approaching their eighty-fourth birthday, Catherine Courtenay was still a force to be reckoned with. As a young wife and mother, her husband had walked out on her when their sons were both of pre-school age. At the time there was a choice to be made. She could either go under, or she could do whatever it took to make a comfortable life for her, young Ralph and Albert.

Catherine's first inclination was to pour herself a large gin and tonic. But after two sips she thought better of it and headed to the kitchen to pour the remainder away. Despite everything her heart was telling her, this was not the time to dull her senses. What she needed more than anything was to keep a clear head. As a pragmatist, she knew that oblivion brought about by alcohol would bring a quick but short-lived relief. It would ultimately solve nothing. And she had her boys to think of, offspring she adored and was fiercely protective of. Appreciating the need to remove the temptation she went to the drinks cabinet and emptied it of every bottle of alcohol, pouring the contents down the drain.

From there, she went upstairs, and looked in on her two little angels, who slept peacefully. Unaware that their father, to whom they had not been close, had walked out on them to start a new life with his mistress. Catherine then went into the bedroom where she collected every item of her husband's clothing and carried them downstairs and into the garden. Less than two hours after he had abandoned them, his clothes and the other possessions he intended to collect at a more convenient time were alight.

Catherine's eyes sparkled as she watched the flames rise and dance. She appreciated that this was a defining moment in her life as she had taken back the control she had previously relinquished to her husband. From this moment she would be everything to her sons. What's more, she would be happier knowing that the cheating wastrel, who for many years had been a weight around her neck, was now someone else's problem.

Having dropped the boys off at school the following morning, she headed to the ironmonger's where she purchased new locks. She could have arranged for someone to change them for her but wanted the satisfaction of doing it herself.

Since before the boys were born, Catherine had been a highly regarded bookkeeper, performing the painstaking task for various local business owners. Her skills were always in demand. This meant that she had enough money to keep her and the boys, without having the worry of making ends meet. She knew that they would be just fine.

Since her teenage years, Catherine had an ambition to write a book. But life had got in the way, and her husband had knocked her confidence. She would never forget the abject humiliation she'd experienced on their honeymoon, when she plucked up the courage to confide in her husband about her literary ambition. He'd laughed in her face, and almost ten years later that laughter still rang in her ears.

Now, at night, with the boys tucked up in their beds, there was nothing holding her back. Catherine was determined to give it a go. She had no idea whether she could write. It was one thing to have ideas, but quite a daunting prospect to turn those ideas into words and create a story that people would want to read. It required planning, commitment and a dogged determination. Even more so back then as there were no computers.

As Catherine had nothing better to do with her evenings she set about the task. Seventeen months later she had a completed, handwritten manuscript. Almost three years to the day that her husband walked out on them, she received a call from a publisher who said he was so impressed with her book that he planned to publish it. When she was asked if she had written anything else, she told them that she had just finished another book featuring the same protagonist, an amateur sleuth named Tilly Taylor.

Catherine's books became an overnight success and went from strength to strength. However, being a private person and not wanting the inevitable drawbacks that fame would bring, she used the pen name Veronica Dumont. It seemed that she couldn't write fast enough, and the royalty cheques kept arriving.

Within a few years, she had more money than she had ever dreamed of, as it became apparent that readers loved Tilly. Reviews claimed that the books were 'More modern than Marple'. Television rights were sold, and a prominent young British actress cast in the role. Weekly episodes were broadcast in a primetime slot, pulling in a huge number of viewers, which resulted in increased book sales. The success of Tilly Taylor earned Veronica Dumont the accolade of Britain's new Queen of Crime.

* * *

'Word to the wise,' said Ralph, as he led the three ladies to the orangery. 'When Mother speaks, she doesn't like to be interrupted. In many respects she's easy-going, but not about that. And believe me, you won't want to get on the wrong side of her.

'This news about Albert has come as a shock. But I guarantee, she'll have a lot of questions for you. And I'm sure you'll learn some things about Albert too.'

The ladies nodded their understanding.

'Oh, and don't be tempted to mention her writing. Above all, Mother has no time for sycophants.' As they reached the doorway to the orangery, Ralph stood aside. 'After you, ladies.'

Two of the three experienced an inevitable wave of nausea at the thought of meeting their mother-in-law for the first time, though perhaps it wasn't such a nerve-wracking experience as it might have been. With Albert dead, and the likelihood that apart from his funeral, this would be the one and only time that they would meet his mother, neither of them were under pressure to try to make Catherine Courtenay like them.

From the moment she had known that they were about to meet her favourite author, Liz was finding it almost impossible to contain her mounting excitement. She kept taking deep breaths as she did her best to keep a lid on things, but instead of relaxing her it was having the opposite effect. She felt light-headed and somewhat unsteady on her feet. She was desperate not to embarrass herself, or anyone else for that matter, but it was as though she was drunk. Suddenly, her lips felt dry, and there was a loud buzzing in her ears. She no longer felt in control of her own body.

Sylvie was surprised to discover that her mother-in-law, despite being more than quarter of a century her senior, could, at first glance have passed for being of a similar age to herself. Indeed, there was hardly a grey hair visible on her stylish tousled pixie cut, which accentuated her cheek bones and emphasised the vibrancy of her dazzling blue eyes.

Catherine, seated in a comfortable chair, reached forward and placed her cup and saucer on a nearby table. She eyed each of the women with shrewd appraisal, then eventually spoke. 'So, which one of you wasn't married to my son?'

Appreciating the fact that she'd just been asked a question by a woman she revered, Liz couldn't help herself. Before she knew it, her hand had shot into the air. 'That'd be me! I'm not your daughter-in-law, but I'm your number one fan. I adore Tilly and I've read every one of your books.'

'I see.' Catherine Courtenay's voice took on a hard edge. Turning her attention to Ralph, she gave him an order. 'Please take this lady to the kitchen. Dulcie can look after her while we discuss family business.'

Sylvie was appalled at Liz being dismissed like this. 'With all due respect, if Liz goes, then we go. She might not have had the misfortune of being married to your son, but she's like a sister to me, and she's also proving to be a good friend to Harriet. Your son ripped our lives apart, and we've only just learned how badly he treated us. Believe me, your literary success and whatever wealth it has brought certainly doesn't impress me. I've never read one of your books in my life, and I have no intention of ever doing so.'

'And your point is?' questioned Catherine. She arched an eyebrow questioningly.

'Sylvie's point is that if you dismiss Liz, we just turn around and walk out of here. Which will be your loss, as there'll be many things about your son that you'll never get to know, and there will be three grandchildren you'll never get to meet.'

Sylvie turned to smile at Harriet, all the while thinking that she couldn't have said it better herself.

'Oh, get over yourselves and sit down. All three of you,' said Catherine. Her expression had changed from that of someone chewing a wasp to someone who looked pleased with herself. 'I like it when women have balls. I find it refreshing. Now, as for you,' she looked directly at Liz, 'let's get this out of the way once and for all. My books are just that.'

Liz looked at her blankly.

'They're just stories that I've made up. Some people like them. Others don't. It makes no difference to me what anyone thinks of them. Back in the day it used to. But that's long stopped being the case. I've made a fortune from my imagination, and it's allowed me to live the way I choose. But just because I'm successful and wealthy, doesn't mean that I want people to treat me as anything special. I don't write under my own name. Though my identity is by no means a secret. I just don't routinely tell people that I'm Veronica Dumont, because I don't want people fawning over me.'

'I can understand that,' said Harriet. 'I have a work persona that few people know about, and in general I've no intention of letting people know my real identity.'

'Umm . . . that's intriguing,' said Catherine. 'Perhaps one day we might speak of it, but for now, we have far more pressing issues to catch up on.'

# CHAPTER 25

Their sleuthing had turned into the most surprising of days. By dogged determination, a little luck and some quick thinking, they had somehow managed to discover Albert's real identity, which he had kept hidden from them throughout their entire relationships. It was something the police had so far failed to do.

'You seem to be coping with the news of Albert's death remarkably well,' said Sylvie.

'Don't let appearances deceive you, my dear,' said Catherine. 'I'm devastated to learn of my son's death, but the truth is I lost him about two years ago when he turned his back on me. His rejection came out of the blue and was callous. I hadn't seen it coming as I'd always believed we were close. I was bereft, but I had to learn to live with it.'

'Only two years ago? You mean that you were in regular contact with him until then?' Harriet sounded surprised.

'Naturally. He worked for me. Had an office here. Turned up Monday to Friday, nine to five, as regular as clockwork. But all that stopped, seemingly without any reason.'

'He was always so cagey about what he did,' said Sylvie. 'He refused to speak about his work.'

'He was quite the mystery man,' said Liz.

Catherine's laugh was hollow, abrupt and unexpected. When she spoke again there was the faintest tremor in her voice. It was apparent to those present that her relatively calm demeanour masked a maelstrom of raw emotion. 'Well, I suppose you could say he was working undercover. After all, he spent thirty-five years as my ghostwriter. Not on the Tilly Taylor series. That was entirely my own.' She sighed. 'No, his creation was Harry Blake, the womanising PI who invariably managed to solve crimes before the police. Of course, he continued to write those books but dealt directly with the publishers. Before that, he always allowed me to read the first draft before it was sent off.'

'I've read all of them,' said Liz. 'They're good, but I'd never have guessed that they weren't written by someone other than you.'

'Oh, my son was a good writer. But it's not enough to be good. Being good doesn't get you a publishing deal. Which is why we decided that the best way forward was to publish them under my name. And it worked too. It was a very successful series.'

'Did you know about us?' asked Harriet.

'Sadly, no. If I had, I would have wanted to meet you. But I suppose it's hardly surprising. You see, Albert was always a very secretive child. He liked to keep things to himself. Which is why he was a perfect ghostwriter.'

'We were both married to him for more than thirty years,' said Sylvie. 'And neither of us guessed that he had another family. He also told us you were dead and didn't mention that he had a brother.'

'Well, I suppose that everything will come out now,' sighed Catherine. 'And Ralph's told me that there's another woman too.' She shook her head and sighed.

'We haven't met her,' said Harriet. 'All we know is that she's named Tess Harris. We found out where they were living and went there this morning. That's when we discovered that

130

she had already moved on, and we stumbled across documentation for a rental agreement.'

'Albert put me down as a guarantor. Which is how they turned up here,' added Ralph by way of explanation.

'His latest conquest didn't waste much time upping sticks,' said Catherine.

'She didn't,' agreed Liz. 'But we're going to do our best to find her.'

'Would you allow me to meet my grandchildren?' asked Catherine. 'I know it's a great deal to ask as we're all strangers. But regardless of the unusual circumstances, we all have Albert in common. Which, in my book, makes us family.'

'They obviously don't know about you yet. We've spoken to them, and they know that there were two families and three wives. But it's a lot for them to come to terms with,' said Harriet.

'All I can say is that Albert obviously lacked a moral code, but you two appear to be exemplary role models. After all, you must both be under an incredible strain to put inevitable resentments aside. But you're doing it remarkably well. I seriously doubt that if I'd found myself in your situation, I would have been able to act with such dignity and resolve,' said Catherine.

'I know this is a selfish request, but at my age, I can't afford to waste time pussyfooting about. What if I play host for the weekend? This place is more than large enough for you all to stay over. We could spend time getting to know each other, and you'd each be free to leave whenever you want if you feel that it's getting too much for you.'

'I'll ask Annabel if she'd be up for it,' said Sylvie. 'She's only just come back from a trip to Brazil, and I'm not sure what her work commitments are like. But I promise I'll ask her.'

'I'll ask Zara and Leo too,' agreed Harriet.

'It might make it easier for them, getting all the meet and greets out of the way in one go,' said Ralph. 'And I'd like to meet them too. It's far too quiet around here most of the time, with only myself, Mother and the staff.'

Catherine regaled them with tales of Albert's youth and insisted that Ralph showed them photographs from their childhood. She was also very keen to see any family snapshots Harriet and Sylvie had on their phones. And her breath caught in her throat as she saw one of Albert and Leo together.

'Oh my, the lad looks the spit of his father,' she said as she wiped a tear from her eye. 'We've all missed out on so much. Years we won't get back.

'I'm sure you'll appreciate that the unexpectedness of these revelations has taken it out of me, and for the sake of my health, I must rest. The offer of you spending the weekend here still stands, and I hope you will take me up on it. The thought of having grandchildren fills me with joy and I would love to have the opportunity to get to know them.'

* * *

As they headed home the car was filled with non-stop chatter. There was so much information to process. Especially with the latest family connection having been revealed in the most unexpected of circumstances. Sylvie and Harriet knew that they and their children would inevitably become the focus of endless speculation and gossip, which is why they thought it was an excellent idea for them all to spend the weekend at Catherine Courtenay's place as it seemed that the only way to come through the inevitable media storm relatively unscathed was to spend time getting to know each other and laying bare every scrap of information about their lives with Albert.

It would inevitably be heart-wrenching to work through the hurt he had caused. But if they could manage to do that and accept — as Sylvie and Harriet so far seemed to be doing — that they had a lot in common, perhaps they could all move forward as friends. Blended families had long since become commonplace. Though, perhaps not those brought together in such an unusual set of circumstances. But anything might be possible if you were able to put resentment aside and look for common ground.

There was no denying that Albert had been a secretive and selfish man. But Catherine was right. There was no point in pussyfooting about. Worrying about what would happen. Or what people would say. Albert had caused this, and he had knowingly broken the law. Whereas Sylvie, Harriet, Tess, and Albert's three children were unwitting victims of his deception. Nothing could change what he had done, and it seemed that they had suddenly acquired an unconventional extended family.

# CHAPTER 26

The following morning there was a knock at the door. Sylvie sipped her coffee as she padded across the hallway. 'Coming!' she called. She opened the door to find Simon standing there.

'How're you doing, Sylve? All right if I come in?' he asked.

'Sure, Si, fancy a coffee?'

'That'd be great,' he replied as he followed her into the kitchen.

'Thought I'd give you an update. We're confident that no one at the garage was responsible for what happened to the brakes on Albert's car.'

Sylvie's brow furrowed. 'How can you be so certain?'

'Because they submitted visual evidence. Apparently, Albert signed a document when he took the car into the garage, allowing them to film the vehicle's service. They were planning on using it for training purposes. The mechanic who carried out the service is supposed to be one of the best in the business. He's got years of experience, and he lectures on the subject.'

'Isn't it unusual to do something like that?'

'It is, but they offered Albert a fifty per cent discount if he agreed to them filming it as it took place,' said Simon.

'If I'm honest, I can imagine Bertie agreeing to something like that. He'd do anything to save a bit of money here and there, and I guess if he knew the mechanic was one of the most experienced, he must've felt there was nothing to lose. And you're sure that everything was done properly?'

'I haven't seen the video myself, but I've been assured by the officers assigned to that part of the investigation that everything was done correctly. So much so that they've ruled out negligence on the part of the garage.'

'Did Bertie collect it from the garage later that day?' asked Sylvie.

'Apparently not. They'd given him a hire car for the day and delivered his car back to the house he shared with Tess. When they dropped it off, they picked up the hire car.'

'So, if someone from the garage drove it back after the service, there couldn't have been anything wrong with the brakes. Otherwise, they'd have crashed.'

'Precisely.'

Sylvie thought out loud. 'And the car would have either been kept on the road or on the drive overnight. And there didn't seem to be any security cameras covering the driveway, which means that someone must have sabotaged the brakes while it was there.' Realising that she'd articulated these thoughts, she averted her gaze, desperately hoping that Simon hadn't picked up on the implications of what she'd just let slip. Her cheeks reddened as she hurriedly picked up the mug of coffee and took another sip.

'You don't need to look so guilty. Liz has already spilled the beans on yesterday's activities,' said Simon. 'She was hyped up about your sleuthing escapade.'

'We didn't do anything wrong.' Sylvie sounded defensive.

'I'm not suggesting you did,' interjected Simon. 'It's remarkable that you found Albert's mother and brother. Our lot have been so focused on trying to establish who's responsible for whatever went wrong with the car that they haven't even discovered his true identity. But you realise that I will have to inform them of your findings?'

'I know.' Sylvie sighed. 'I just can't help feeling sorry for his mother, that's all.'

'It's an awful way to learn about it.'

'Is there any more news on Tess? She moved out of that house very quickly, if you ask me.'

'I suppose everyone's different, and as they didn't have any kids together, there'd be nothing keeping her there,' said Simon.

'Guess not. But presumably she must've been the last person to see Bertie alive?'

'She could very well have been, but as I've said, I'm not assigned to the investigation. My role is purely as your FLO, and I'm only that because I was first on the scene, and I've known you for donkey's years.'

'Umm. Have they made any progress on finding her?' she pressed.

'I've no idea, Sylve. I believe her FLO is in regular contact with her over the phone. So, it's not as if she's done a runner. There'll be officers checking the validity of her alibi. That's all I can say on the matter.'

'Well, Harriet and I need to speak to her.'

'Listen to me. Leave well alone. My understanding of the situation hasn't changed. She's already made it plain that she wants to have nothing to do with you.'

'That's as maybe, but there's Bertie's funeral to consider. She needs to be informed of any arrangements.'

'It'll be a while yet before they release Albert's body. A lot can change in that time. So let the investigation run its course. You need time to grieve, Sylve. It's not down to you, or Harriet for that matter, to do the police's job for them. So do yourself a favour and let it go. You've more than enough on your plate as it is.'

Sylvie appreciated that despite his soft tone Simon was ordering her to stay out of the investigation, which was something she had no intention of doing. If they'd sat back and done nothing they wouldn't have found out about Albert's mother and brother. It seemed obvious that the police would be keen to find the person responsible for tampering with the brakes on Albert's car. After all, it was their job to solve crimes and bring the criminals to justice.

But as Tess was just another of Albert's wives, it seemed the police had no interest in her other than to offer her support if she said she needed it. Yet Sylvie couldn't shake the feeling that something was off with the woman. She could completely understand that Tess would have been devastated by Albert's death. Especially since it seemed that their relationship was comparatively new. And as they'd not had any children it was highly likely that the couple's relationship could have still been in the so-called honeymoon period where they were loved-up.

Sylvie knew from first-hand experience that identifying your husband's body was a traumatic experience. It was something she was certain she would never be able to forget. There was no reason to suspect that it would have been any less distressing for Tess. Then, to find out that the man she loved and trusted had been lying to her, combined with the fact that legally you weren't even his wife, must've been absolutely devastating. Especially since she might have been told that Albert had three children by two other wives. These were families he had no intention of giving up in order to commit exclusively to her.

'Sylvie! Sylve, are you listening to what I'm saying?' Simon squeezed her hand to get her attention. It had been obvious to him that her mind was wandering elsewhere.

Sylvie blinked as her thoughts were disrupted. 'Of course I'm listening.'

'Promise me the three of you will stop meddling in the investigation. It's best all round if you leave things to the police. Albert could have been involved in all sorts of unsavoury things. He was obviously in touch with criminals to be able to get his hands on documentation to create false identities. And believe me, people like that are bad news. They're not the sort you want to have dealings with. Things could get out of hand very quickly if you wind up the wrong person, and none of you are equipped to deal with that kind of danger.'

Sylvie nodded. 'Don't worry, Simon. I've got the message loud and clear. Now, if you don't mind, I've things I should be getting on with.'

# CHAPTER 27

As scary as Simon had made things sound, Sylvie had no intention of sitting back to wait for the police to conduct the investigation, and she knew that Harriet felt the same way. Simon hadn't directly said as much, but it was apparent that they were not going to follow up on Tess. Yet it was likely that the woman had been the last person to have seen Bertie alive.

Simon had only just left when Sylvie's mobile rang. A quick glance at the display told her that it was Harriet. 'I was just about to call you,' said Sylvie.

'Have the police been to see you?'

'Just left. Simon told me that the garage wasn't negligent. They've seen video evidence of the entire vehicle service, and everything was as it should have been.'

'Which can only mean that whoever tampered with those brakes did so when it was back at that property,' said Harriet.

'My thoughts precisely. Did you get warned off about sticking your nose into the investigation?'

'I did, but I've no intention of playing ball.' The determination in Harriet's voice came across loud and clear. 'As far as I'm concerned, we stick to the plan. We made more progress in a few hours than they've made for the entire time.'

'I agree. They're not going to tell us anything about Tess, but we need to know who she is and what she's been up to. I'm just about to make a start on trawling through social media platforms to see if Tess had an online presence.'

'Get you, using all the lingo,' laughed Harriet. 'Though it's not going to be easy as Tess Harris is probably a common name. But it won't do any harm to try. I'm about to follow up on the information we got from her passport. Let me know if by any chance you happen to have a breakthrough. Otherwise, we'll touch base this evening, put our heads together and try to come up with a better way to find her.'

'Absolutely, and good luck,' said Sylvie. She disconnected the call.

For the next few hours Sylvie found herself becoming increasingly frustrated. She had known all along that finding Tess on social media was a long shot. But after the elation of the previous day's unexpected successes, it was such a disappointment not to find anything. When her phone rang, she accepted the call without checking the display and was surprised to discover that it was Harriet.

'You're not going to believe this. I think I'm on to something, and if I'm right, it's another false identity.' She was speaking so fast that her speech was garbled.

Sylvie was having trouble understanding what she was saying as it was difficult to separate individual words. 'Slow down. Breathe.' She heard Harriet inhale deeply.

'I don't think that wife number three is Tess Harris. I became suspicious when I discovered that her birth name was supposedly Tess Harris. It's possible, though unlikely, that you'd marry a man who already has the same surname as you. I've got some more checking to do but I think Tess Harris is another false identity. I'm waiting for the documentary evidence to be sent through to me,' said Harriet. This time she sounded more coherent.

'Seriously?' Sylvie's heart rate increased, and she gripped the edge of the table to steady herself. Even though she was sitting down she could feel her surroundings start to spin. There was one shock after another, and it was beginning to feel as though she was never going to get things back on an even keel.

'I was wondering if you wanted to come over to my place? When the information arrives, I want to make sure that I'm reading it right. The way I'm feeling now there's a real risk that I might just see what I want to see and not look at things objectively. So, I think it'd be better for you to look at it, too, as you might just have a different take on things.'

'Absolutely. I'll get my stuff together and be there soon. We'll go through things together. If you're right about this then we'll have to take it to the police, but we need to be certain. Otherwise, we'll be accused of wasting their time and we'll end up looking like a couple of idiots.'

Sylvie shut down her laptop, stuffed a few things in her handbag and grabbed the car keys. At such a busy time of day it took almost an hour to reach Harriet's house, which added to her frustration as she was keen to delve into this latest development. She pulled up on Harriet's drive, locked the car and headed to the front door. No sooner had she reached it than Harriet opened it and ushered her inside.

'Thought you'd never get here,' she said.

'Traffic was bad.'

'Never mind that. Come and look at this.' Excitement radiated from her as she grabbed Sylvie's hand and all but dragged her towards the back of the house. 'The more I've dug down into things, the more I'm sure that something's up. I'm just wondering what the hell Albert had got himself into, and I hope to God that whatever it was doesn't come back to bite us.'

Sylvie's heart thudded loudly in her chest as Harriet pulled up an extra chair and told her to sit down. The laptop was on the kitchen table. To the side of the screen was a large sheet of paper, crammed full of handwritten notes. Another sheet displayed a partially constructed timeline. It was evident that Harriet had been busy. It was also apparent that she was approaching this task in a methodical way and was being exceptionally thorough.

'What've you got?' asked Sylvie. 'But tell me in simple terms as this looks quite complicated.' She gestured to the paperwork.

Harriet took a deep breath to centre herself. 'I'll explain things slowly, but I want you to check everything I'm saying as I go along. The thing is, at the start I didn't have any doubts that her identity would be anything other than genuine. But the more I delved into things, the more convinced I am that she's not who she says she is. Everything's so messed up and I sort of feel as though I'm going down a rabbit hole. It's like being part of some sort of spy drama, and I'm scared about what we've unwittingly been caught up in.'

'I know how you feel,' said Sylvie. 'Since we found out what he did to us, nothing's been normal. We need to get to the bottom of this. For the sake of our own sanity, if nothing else. So, what have you got? And how did you manage to access these records?'

'I called in favours. Put it this way, a friend of a friend works at the registrar's office where Tess's birth would have been registered. I gave them the information from the passport, and they did the rest. Fortunately, I'd asked if they'd check the death register, too, and that's where they found an entry.'

'You mean she's stolen a dead person's identity?' asked Sylvie.

'I think so. First off, get the image of her passport up, so that you can read the information on there. Then I want you to compare it to these.' Harriet pointed to copies of a birth and death record.

Sylvie studied the three documents, repeatedly glancing from one to the other. 'Looks as though it's genuine. It's got the same date and place of birth.'

'I looked up the location stated as the place of birth,' said Harriet. 'Now take a look at this screen as I've got it on Streetmap. It's an ordinary house. Which suggests it was a home birth.'

'Yes, I'd agree with that.'

'Now look at the name of the father on Tess's birth certificate. He's the one that registered the birth, and his address matches the place of birth.'

'You're right, it does.'

'Now look at the death certificate for a Tess Harris. As you can see, it gives a date of death which would have made her sixteen going on seventeen. It shows the date and place of birth, which matches the passport and the birth certificate.'

'And in section 7, the entry for the name of the informant is the same as the father's name on the birth certificate, and it states that he's the father,' interjected Sylvie.

'Precisely, and it gives his usual address, too, which matches the details in the birth certificate.' added Harriet.

Sylvie swallowed hard, as the implications of what they'd learned sank in. 'We have to take this to the police, Harriet. It's proof that whoever Albert's third wife is, she's certainly not Tess Harris.'

'My guess is that she stole this identity as the original Tess would have been issued with a National Insurance number. Which, in turn, means that she'd be able to use that to make her fake identity more believable.'

'Do you think she was involved in whatever scam Albert was pulling?' asked Sylvie.

'I've no idea. Let's face it, apart from the fact that Albert used false identities to enable him to marry multiple times without raising suspicion, we don't know if he was involved in any other scams. But as this so-called Tess Harris seems to have disappeared, we don't stand a chance of finding her. After all, what's to stop her from stealing another identity and reinventing herself as someone else?'

'You're right. We don't have the time or the resources to track her down. Shall I ring Simon and ask him to come over?'

'I think you should. At least that way, we stand a chance of staying in the loop. If he won't keep us updated, I'd bet Liz would be able to wheedle it out of him.'

# CHAPTER 28

As they waited for Simon to arrive, there was a knock at the door. 'That was quick,' said Harriet as she went to let him in.

'Guess he must've been in the area,' said Sylvie. 'At least we can get this over and done with.'

As Sylvie perused their findings once more, she heard raised voices, one of which sounded like Harriet's. Confused as to why she would be arguing with Simon, she headed to the front of the house. 'What's . . . Harriet, what's happening?'

Something awful must've occurred, though Sylvie had no idea what it could be. All she knew for sure was that the front door was partially open, and Harriet was doing her best to force it shut. As she physically strained to counteract the momentum being applied from outside, her feet kept slipping. As whoever was out there was equally determined to open the door and forcibly enter the property.

Harriet glanced over her shoulder. 'Help me, Sylvie!' she implored. Her voice was high with fear. As she glanced over her shoulder, it was immediately apparent that the colour had drained from her face, and she was crying.

'What's going on?'

'They're trying to get in. Said they're repossessing the house. It doesn't make sense. It's in my name and the mortgage is paid off.'

'Let us in, Mrs Joyce! The bank has already sent you paperwork to tell you this would happen. They've been reasonable and followed procedure to the letter of the law. It's our understanding that you've had plenty of opportunities to comply with the new payment plan to make up the arrears. You were informed in writing that non-payment would result in an inevitable repossession of the property. We'll call the police if we must, but we have a legal right to evict you, and you will be forced to leave the property today.'

'We've already called the police. They're on their way,' shouted Sylvie.

There was a momentary release of pressure on the door, as the bailiff changed position. Harriet capitalised on this unexpected respite and wasted no time shutting then dead-bolting it. She swiftly turned to face Sylvie, and pushed her back against the door, as though her body could prevent anyone from forcing entry if they were determined to do so. 'Ring Simon again. Tell him that these thugs are trying to get in. They're lying about me being in arrears. There's no mortgage on this property. It was paid off years ago.'

A terrible thought crossed Sylvie's mind. 'Is it possible that Albert could have remortgaged the house without you knowing about it?'

'I don't see how. It was solely in my name.'

'You're placing too much trust in him. After all, we've just found out that he was using multiple fake identities.' As she voiced this possibility, an awful thought occurred to Sylvie. What if Albert had done this to her house too? It had never been in his name, but would that have stopped him from stealing it from under her nose? Even after all the dreadful betrayals she'd discovered since his death, this possibility hadn't once crossed her mind. She swallowed hard, as bile rose to her throat.

'Could they be the people who tampered with his brakes?' Harriet's voice had a falsetto resonance, and her eyes were wide with fear, as she imagined the worst. 'If they killed him because he owed them money, they could do that to me too. The bank wouldn't have sent them to evict me. It doesn't make sense.'

'He said that the bank had written to you,' said Sylvie. 'Have you received any correspondence from them?'

'No. I haven't had anything.'

'What about phone calls?'

'No! I'm telling you, whoever's out there is lying. They're not who they say they are. If they get inside, I dread to think what they're going to do to me, and they won't let you walk out of here either. Whatever it is they're planning to do to me, they'll have to do to you too. They won't risk leaving a witness behind.'

Sylvie's mind raced. Even a moment earlier it had seemed like such a ridiculous possibility that whoever was at the door was there to kill Harriet. But then again, nothing had been normal since Albert's death. There had been one shocking revelation after another. It was as though she'd woken up on the morning of the crash only to find that she'd been transported to an alternative universe and was somehow centre stage in a psychological thriller.

Sylvie suddenly became aware of her heart racing as adrenalin flooded her body. As the flight or fight response kicked in, she knew without question which one she'd choose, as Sylvie had never hit anyone in her life. Even during those times when Annabel had been growing up, and was testing the boundaries with some extreme behaviour, Sylvie had never once resorted to smacking her. She abhorred violence of any kind. Confrontation just wasn't in her nature as she was the gentlest of souls.

Sylvie grabbed Harriet's hand and squeezed it to get her attention. 'Harriet, you need to focus. We need to leave — is there another way out of here?'

'Y-yes, there's the back door. It leads to the garden, and the side gate, which will take us onto the drive.'

'But that means we'll still have to head towards the front of the house. Are you sure there's—'

Harriet's scream silenced Sylvie mid-sentence. As she glanced over her shoulder, she saw a man standing not five feet away. In that moment her legs turned to jelly, and she did the only thing she could think of. She began to scream too.

The stranger appeared to be saying something, but as hysteria had taken hold, neither woman was in a fit state to listen to what he was trying to say. There was a repeated thudding on the outer side of the door, and a male voice could be heard shouting something. What it was neither woman could tell as they were both still screaming so loudly that it muffled every other sound.

With nowhere left to go, and no chance of getting past the stranger who now blocked their only route of escape, Harriet turned and fumbled with the locking mechanism of the door. She appreciated that their only realistic possibility of escaping the threat was by forcing their way out of the front of the property while making as much noise as possible to attract the attention of anyone who happened to be passing by. She just hoped that someone would step in to save them.

As the locking mechanism was released, everything happened so quickly. The door opened with force, as whoever was out there pushed themselves against it, propelling Harriet into Sylvie, who was only inches away from her. The women lost their balance and only managed to remain upright as the stranger in the hallway saw what was about to happen and somehow managed to steady them.

Simon and another uniformed officer stepped inside and quickly took control of the situation. Realising that they were safe, Sylvie and Harriet hugged each other tightly as they both wept with relief.

# CHAPTER 29

'Step away from the women, sir,' ordered Simon. His steely tone left no doubt that this was an order, not a request.

The man held up his hands to demonstrate that he posed no threat. He took three steps back, until his heel touched the bottom of the stairs, and he realised that there was nowhere else for him to go. A pile of paperwork was visible in his right hand. 'Officer, I know how this must look, but I have a legal right to be here. If you'll look at this, you'll see.' He slowly held out the documents.

'Take the ladies through to the kitchen and make them a cup of tea. They've obviously had a scare.' Simon addressed the female officer who was standing close by.

'As for you, explain to me why you forced entry to this property and terrified these women.'

'I didn't force entry. I came in through the back door. It was unlocked.'

'That doesn't make it right. You've obviously traumatised them, and I want to know why.'

'I've been sent to serve a notice of eviction for non-payment of the mortgage on this property. I tried to explain this when I initially came to the front door of the property and spoke to one of the occupants. I assure you that all proper procedures have been followed.'

'Let me see the paperwork,' said Simon. He held out a hand.

The man handed it over and Simon scanned the documents. Eventually satisfied that on the face of it, the documentation appeared to be authentic, he addressed the man once more. 'Do you have any identification on you?'

'Yes, it's on a lanyard around my neck.'

'Show it to me.'

The man unzipped his jacket and removed his official identification.

Simon took it and saw that the company name matched that on the bank's documentation. The photograph on the pass was clearly of the man in whose possession it had been. 'And your name is?' he asked.

'Clive Boverton. I've worked for the company for more than a decade. If you give them a bell, they'll vouch for me and tell you that I'm supposed to be here.'

Satisfied that the name on the pass was indeed Clive Boverton, Simon wanted to check out some other things. 'Is that your vehicle on the road outside the property, Mr Boverton?'

'Yes.'

'PC Varney, could you step into the hall for a moment?'

'Sir?'

'I'd like you to remain with Mr Boverton while I make some more enquiries.'

'Very good, sir.' She stood in front of the man, making it all but impossible for him to move. 'I suggest you take a seat on the stairs, sir. This could take a while.'

This comment was directed at Clive Boverton. He sighed, accepting that he was not going anywhere, anytime soon, and sat on one of the steps.

Almost twenty minutes later, Simon walked through the front door. 'I've verified your credentials, Mr Boverton, and I've spoken to both your employers and the bank. We have an ongoing investigation, and this property is now part of that. As such there will be no repossession taking place until our investigation is completed.'

Clive Boverton appeared surprised. He had clearly expected that once the police had verified his claims, they would have allowed him to carry out his task. As he went to speak, Simon held up a hand to interject.

'I suggest you contact your employer to verify what I've just told you. Once you've made that call, I'll escort you from the property, and we'll keep hold of this paperwork for now.'

A few minutes later, Clive left the property, walked to his vehicle and was sent on his way.

Harriet and Sylvie both looked expectantly at Simon as he and PC Varney entered the kitchen.

'Tell me he's gone,' said Harriet. There was no disguising the concern in her voice.

'For now,' said Simon, as he pulled out a chair.

'You mean he's going to come back?'

'That will very much depend on our enquiries.'

'But I own the property outright. I have done for at least fourteen years.'

'And is it solely in your name?'

'Yes. I'd taken out a mortgage a few years before Albert and I got together. Property prices were nowhere near as high as they are now, which meant that I could comfortably make the repayments. Albert's name was never on any mortgage agreement.'

'In that case, do you have the documentation to hand, to show that you now own the property outright?'

'I can get it for you. It's in a safety deposit box at the bank. I always keep it there.'

'And does anyone else have access to this safety deposit box?'

'Thankfully not. It's in my name only.'

'In that case, I suggest we take a trip to the bank, to retrieve those documents,' said Simon.

'Is Albert behind this? Could he have remortgaged the property without Harriet's knowledge?' It was the first time Sylvie had spoken for a while.

'Anything's possible. But for now, we take one step at a time. It's the only way to establish what's happened. Speculating about things isn't going to help. We need cold, hard facts. Now I suggest you go home, Sylvie. There's nothing you can do to help Harriet. PC Varney and I will accompany her to the bank, where hopefully we'll be able to verify her claims.'

Sylvie knew there was no point in arguing with Simon. This was a police matter and as far as they were concerned, she was just a civilian. But she hated to think of Harriet being alone afterwards. 'Come and stay at my house for now,' she said. 'After what's just happened, you're not going to feel safe on your own.'

'Harriet's not in any danger, Sylvie,' said Simon. 'I've made it plain that this property cannot be repossessed while our investigations are ongoing.'

'The offer's there if you want it,' said Sylvie.

'Actually, I would,' said Harriet. 'You're right, I won't get much sleep, if any tonight. Not if I'm alone in this house. I'll see you back at yours later and thank you. I really appreciate the offer.'

'You're welcome. With everything going on, we have to look out for each other. I'm sure you'd do the same for me.' She smiled and reached out to squeeze Harriet's hand.

'Absolutely. We're in this together. Take everything back to your house, Sylvie. I don't want to risk anything going missing,' she gestured to the laptop, and papers they had been looking at before the occurrence of this latest turn of events. Suddenly, it seemed such a long time ago.

# CHAPTER 30

Sylvie arrived home still feeling jittery after the drama of the last few hours. Not wanting to be alone, she made a beeline for the tearoom and quickly filled Liz in on the latest developments. 'I've told Harriet she can sleep at mine tonight,' she added.

'Sounds sensible. If that happened to me, I'd be too scared to be on my own, at least until it gets sorted.'

'We need to push on with the Tess angle of things,' said Sylvie. 'Harriet might not be up for it after everything that's happened to her today. But the longer we leave it, the more chance there is of us never catching up with Tess. Let's face it, she's already done a pretty good job of disappearing.'

'How about a seven o'clock takeout at yours? The tour buses have gone for the day so it's quiet. I'll order it if you like, and we can tally up later?'

'Sounds good to me. Are you asking Simon?'

'Makes sense to. After all, you wanted to tell him about what you'd found, before it all kicked off at Harriet's. Though you know the score. It very much depends on whether he gets to finish his shift on time.'

In the meantime, Simon and PC Varney were accompanying Harriet to the bank. As she was still very shaky, she had taken up the offer of being a passenger in the police car. Once at the bank they had waited until Harriet could speak to the branch manager, a woman she had known for years.

Normally, viewing the contents of a safety deposit box would be the sole privilege of the box's owner. But having explained what had happened, and why Harriet wanted Simon to accompany her, it was eventually agreed that he would be there, together with the bank manager, to inspect the documents.

Harriet couldn't help but breathe a sigh of relief as she removed the documentation from the box. With everything that had happened in the last few days, she wouldn't have put it past Albert to have found a way to access her box and take what was rightfully hers. 'Take a look,' said Harriet. Her hand trembled as she held out the deeds to the property along with the documentation which stated that the mortgage had been paid off in full. 'There can't possibly be a mortgage on the property. This is proof that I own it outright.'

Simon and the branch manager both studied the documentation and agreed that appeared to be precisely as Harriet claimed.

'We need to take a copy of this,' said Simon. 'After that, I suggest that you keep the original locked in the safety deposit box. As things stand, it's the safest place for it. I don't doubt that it's genuine, but a rival bank is claiming that you've defaulted on numerous mortgage payments. So, I'll need to take a statement from you confirming what you've told me, and first thing in the morning, I'll follow up on the possibility that someone, quite possibly Albert, fraudulently remortgaged your home.'

'So, you're saying that this isn't over?' asked Harriet.

'Not until we've established what's happened.'

'I'm not sure how much more I can take,' she said. 'I'm a fool. A stupid, deluded fool. How could I have married that man? How could I have not known that something was off about him?'

Simon gently touched her shoulder. 'I know it's no consolation, but you weren't the only one taken in by him. As you can imagine, I tend to not take people at face value. But he had me fooled too. I thought he was my friend. After all, I'd known him — or rather, thought I'd known him — for more than thirty years, and throughout that time I didn't suspect that anything was off with him. Liz most likely feels the same too. And as for Sylvie, well, in many ways she's in the same boat as you.'

'As far as I'm concerned, meeting Sylvie and Liz is the best thing that's come out of this sorry mess. You'd think Sylvie and I should despise each other, but we've become so close over the last few days. And for her to offer to put me up for the night . . . Well, that just shows how kind she is.'

'You're right. Sylvie is one of the best. She's a loyal friend. If I was up against it, I know she'd be by my side all the way. Look, this issue with your house will get resolved, Harriet. I promise you I'll get to the bottom of it, and I've instructed the relevant parties that they cannot go ahead with the repossession until our investigation is completed, and we've established the legitimacy of their claims.'

'Thank you.'

'You're welcome. I'll drive you home and wait for you to pack a bag. I take it that you're able to drive yourself to Sylvie's?'

'I'll be fine.'

'That's good. Once you're on your way, I'll head back to the station as I've got paperwork to do. But I'll see you at Sylvie's this evening. Liz has messaged me to say that we're all meeting up for a takeout. So perhaps we can talk then, and you can fill me in on why you asked me to call around in the first place.'

A few hours later, Harriet arrived at Sylvie's house to find that Liz was already there. 'Sylvie's told me everything, and I think you need a hug. Just when you think that man can't get any lower . . . Anyway, come here.' She drew Harriet towards her and held her close until she felt her muscles relax.

'Thank you. It's been a stressful, frightening day. I'm just glad that I wasn't on my own when that man turned up. Otherwise, I don't know what I would have done.'

'I've a feeling you'd have done what you needed to.'

'Would I?' asked Harriet. 'I'm not so sure. Until Albert's lies came to light, I'd always thought of myself as capable and strong. But I've quickly come to realise that I've been living a lie for most of my adult life. That house has been my sanctuary. It holds so many memories, good and bad. I'm determined to fight for what's rightfully mine, but I'm dreading whatever other surprises he has in store.'

'Well, you're not alone, Harriet. We'll be right alongside you,' said Sylvie.

Simon arrived a few minutes after the food had been delivered, and the four of them sat around the kitchen table, helping themselves to generous portions of everything on offer. After they'd eaten and the table was cleared, Harriet and Sylvie filled him in on what they had found about the woman calling herself Tess Harris.

'Ever considered becoming detectives?' asked Simon. 'Because you seem to be making more progress than the officers assigned to the case.'

Liz joked, 'We could call ourselves the Wye Valley Widows Detective Agency,' and they all laughed.

'Seriously, though,' said Simon. 'You've done remarkably well, but if this Tess has been living under a stolen identity, chances are she's got something to hide too. It's possible that she could be dangerous, and if that's the case, she's not going to sit back and allow the three of you to meddle in her business. She'll have far too much to lose.'

'Are you telling us to back off and leave it to the police?' asked Sylvie.

'There'd be no point,' said Simon. 'I did my best to warn you off this morning, but I know you and my sister well enough to realise that you wouldn't listen to me, and I sense that Harriet's cut from the same cloth.' He saw all three women share a conspiratorial smile. 'All I'm saying is tread carefully. If you continue to pursue this, you've no idea what you're getting yourself into. So just be careful. Don't get all gung-ho about things. And whatever you do, stay together if you are investigating anything. It's true what they say, there's safety in numbers.'

Over the next few days Sylvie, Harriet and Liz left the detecting to the police. For a group of women who rarely stepped outside their comfort zone they had certainly pushed the boundaries and surprised themselves along the way. But there was no denying that recent events had taken their toll, and they each agreed that it was time to take a step back and collectively consider their next move. They weren't about to give up on their investigation but knew that they needed to have a credible plan if they were going to take things forward.

The weekend visit to Catherine Courtenay's estate came and went. It was a gathering full of expectations, but one which was fraught with simmering resentment. Had it just been the three grandchildren meeting their paternal family for the first time, it might not have been so bad. But despite having learned of the existence of the others, it was a big ask for Annabel, Zara and Leo to play happy families. Especially since they were well and truly past the age where they would play nice because their mothers expected it. Both Annabel and Leo had easy-going natures and discovered that they enjoyed each other's company. However, Zara quickly determined that she wanted nothing to do with Sylvie, Annabel, or her newly discovered grandmother and uncle. Part of the way through dinner on Friday evening, she announced that she was leaving and had no intention of ever returning.

After a weekend of glorious weather, Monday morning turned out to be wet and windy. Sylvie had finished breakfast and was loading the used crockery and cutlery into the dishwasher when her phone rang. It was Harriet and she sounded upset.

'The police have finished looking into what happened with my house. They've confirmed that Albert remortgaged it. He's stolen my home from under me.' She broke down in tears.

Sylvie did her best to console her friend, though it proved difficult. All the while silently thanking her lucky stars that there was no evidence to suggest that Albert had ever tried to steal her own family home. When Harriet eventually stopped crying for a moment, Sylvie spoke. 'I don't understand how that's possible, Harriet. If Albert's name wasn't on the deed, how could he possibly have remortgaged it?'

'Th-they think he knew someone at the bank who helped him.'

'Which is fraud,' said Sylvie.

'I guess it must be.'

'Which means that even though Albert did that to you, they should be able to prove that it was a scam. And if someone from the bank was in on it, there should be no comeback on you, and they shouldn't be able to repossess your house.'

'I suppose. When you put it like that it seems as though I'm worrying unnecessarily.'

'Shall I come over?' asked Sylvie.

'Can I come to yours? I just need to get out of here for a while. Get some perspective. My home feels tainted now.'

'Of course you can come over.'

'Thanks. It'll do me good to get out of here. It doesn't seem like home anymore. Not after what Albert's done.'

'That's understandable. How about we go for lunch in the Monksworthy Arms? They do a mean hotpot. I'll ask Liz to join us, and we can put the world to rights.'

'Sounds good,' said Harriet.

While waiting for Harriet to arrive, Sylvie rang Simon, to find out if the police had made any progress in tracking down the elusive Tess.

'To be honest, Sylvie, the guys are saying that they're not getting anywhere. If it wasn't for you and Harriet discovering the fact that she was using a false identity, they'd have been none the wiser.'

'Your colleagues sound absolutely useless,' said Sylvie.

'That's a bit harsh, but I get where you're coming from. The thing is, they had no reason to suspect that she was anything other than another woman that Albert had conned into believing that he had legitimately married. You must admit that it's not an everyday occurrence to come across someone who created multiple false identities like Albert had. And what are the odds of him marrying someone who had created a false identity too? It's very unusual circumstances.'

'It doesn't give me any confidence in the police,' said Sylvie. 'We've known each other a long time, Simon. I've no doubt that you've got my best interests at heart. But those other officers . . . Well, they're not fit for purpose.'

'I can understand you'd feel that way. As for me, I've absolutely got your back, Sylvie. You only need to pick up the phone any time, day or night, and I'll be there. But you need to understand that I'm not on that investigation. As I keep saying, the only reason I'm acting as your FLO is because I was the first on the scene, and I recognised Albert. But that's as far as it goes. They'd have my badge if they found out I was sticking my nose into any other part of the investigation. All I'm able to do is act like a conduit to keep the information flowing both ways.'

Sylvie sighed. She didn't doubt that Simon would do everything he could for her. But the things he could do were obviously very limited. 'I understand, Si, and I don't want to come across as ungrateful, but it's just so frustrating that the officers running this investigation don't seem to be making much, if any, progress.'

Having ended the call, Sylvie switched the kettle on and while she was waiting for the water to boil, she picked up a notebook and pen and sat at the kitchen table. As Simon had all but told her that it was unlikely the police would be able to track Tess down, it seemed that the only way they were going to get answers to their questions was to find her themselves. They needed to speak to her. But to do that they needed to find out who Tess really was, because all they knew for sure was that this woman had been living under a stolen identity.

It was time to make a to-do list. For much of her life, Sylvie had liked making lists. She didn't so much like seeing a long list of tasks which needed to be completed. But what she — like so many other people — enjoyed was the satisfaction of completing those tasks and being able to cross off each one of them as you progressed. Putting a line through something was such a simple action. Yet somehow it made her feel good and spurred her on to start the next task.

What's more, Sylvie had long since favoured creating subtask lists for complex tasks. She had a cork noticeboard on the wall next to the refrigerator and had used it every day since she'd found out that she was pregnant with Annabel. It had proved itself useful over the years, as there weren't many days when Sylvie either didn't add to or delete from existing lists. It helped to focus her mind and prioritise tasks. This had been especially important as Albert had spent a significant portion of their married life away from home, meaning that almost every responsibility had fallen on her shoulders.

Sylvie appreciated that tracking Tess down would be like no other task she or the others had experience of. They'd got lucky finding the house that Albert had shared with his latest wife. Yet they'd only managed to find that because they'd been given a head start by Liz pumping Simon for information. But during this morning's conversation, Simon had admitted that even the police had no idea where Tess was, and as that was not her real name, it was going to make it even harder for people to find her.

Sylvie's thought process was broken by the sound of the doorbell. Glancing at the clock, she realised that more than ninety minutes had passed since she'd invited Harriet around. She walked down the hallway and opened the door to find Harriet looking far more composed than when they'd spoken on the phone.

'Shall we head straight to the pub?' asked Sylvie.

'Why not? I didn't get much sleep last night, what with Zara acting like a prima donna on the weekend. I tried calling her when I got home, but she's blocked my number. I can't believe she's done that to me. We should be supporting each other, not tearing lumps out of each other.'

'It's a tricky time for all of us. Let's face it, when we first realised what was going on, we didn't feel too kindly towards each other.'

'You're right.' Harriet shrugged her shoulders. 'She's never been easy-going. I suppose she just needs more time to get her head around things.'

'Looking for the positives, did you notice that Annabel and Leo seemed to be getting on like a house on fire? She hated being an only child. Always wanted a younger brother.'

'I did, and I think it's great. Leo's the opposite of his sister. He's a dream. So easy-going. Seems to have the ability to get on with everyone.'

# CHAPTER 32

'This is such a pretty village,' said Harriet, as they walked the short distance to the Monksworthy Arms. 'It must be wonderful living in a place like this.'

'Most of the time it is, but believe me, it has its moments.'

'Are we meeting Liz at the pub?'

'No, I asked, and she would have loved to come, but she's got a dozen orders to get out. She's running herself ragged, taking up the slack because I haven't been pulling my weight. To be honest, I feel bad about it, but my head's all over the place and I don't want to risk messing things up and setting the orders back. There's too much time and money going into that side of the business,' said Sylvie.

'I'm sure Liz understands. Perhaps we could give her a hand after lunch? Help with the basics.'

'Maybe. Look, Harriet, before we go inside the pub, I'd better warn you that they're a nosy lot, but most of them are decent enough. Brendon's the biggest gossip, but I get on well with him. He runs the pub with his husband, Duncan. I haven't been there since Albert's crash, and I guarantee that everyone would have heard about it. News in this village spreads like wildfire. So, are you up to fronting it out?'

'You mean be open about what Albert did?'

'Precisely. Better to face everyone down and have them talking to us rather than about us. At least that way, people won't be making up all sorts of rubbish.'

'Well, that sort of approach will certainly take me out of my comfort zone, as I've a tendency to avoid talking about myself. But what the heck . . . We've nothing to be ashamed of. What Albert did is on him, not us. So, yeah, let's answer any questions thrown our way,' said Harriet.

As usual at this time of day, the Monksworthy Arms was set up for its lunchtime trade. With no coach tours scheduled to call at the village that day, only a few of the tables displayed *RESERVED* signs, which meant there were plenty to choose from. 'Come and say hello to Bren and Duncan,' said Sylvie. She made a beeline for the bar, before Harriet had time to protest.

Duncan was polishing the bar, making sure that everything was just so. Sensing a customer was heading in that direction he glanced up. 'Oh, Sylvie sweetheart, I've been thinking about you. How are you doing? My heart goes out to you, and Annabel, of course. Such a terrible thing to have happened. Bertie cut down in his prime like that. Such a senseless loss of life.' His voice dripped with concern. 'Anything you need, my love, you just let me, or Bren know, and we'll be there for you. Night or day. I mean it.' He placed the cloth he was holding on the bar and held out his hands to her.

'Thanks, Duncan. I appreciate it.' She took his hands, and he squeezed them.

'Did I just hear Sylvie's voice?' Brendon called as he came rushing into the bar. Seeing her standing there, he headed straight to the public side of the counter. 'Sylvie, Sylvie, Sylvie. Let me give you a hug. You must be devastated.' He pulled her towards him, held her close and gently patted her back.

'I'm fine, honestly. We've just called in for some lunch.'

'We! Who's we?' Brendon let go of her and took a step backwards.

'I'd like you both to meet my new friend, Harriet.' Sylvie turned and held out her hand.

It was noticeable that both men exchanged a quick, knowing glance. 'This vision of loveliness, is, I mean was, Bert—' It was as though Brendon's brain had just caught up with his mouth. He stopped speaking mid-sentence, as his jaw dropped.

'That's right. Bertie duped Harriet into believing that he was married to her too,' said Sylvie. 'But we've talked it through, and we're good with it. We've discovered that we have so much more than the obvious in common. We've become friends, and it's going to stay that way,' said Sylvie. Her expression dared anyone to contradict her.

Harriet smiled at both men. 'Well, this is awkward. I suppose all I can say is, hello.'

'Not awkward at all,' reassured Duncan. 'Brendon, that's so unbecoming. Close your mouth, before you swallow any flies.'

Brendon turned to his husband. Realising that he was making a spectacle of himself, he did as he was told.

'Pleased to meet you, Harriet,' said Duncan. He held out his hand. 'Any friend of Sylvie's is a friend of ours.'

'Y-yes, of course, that's right,' echoed Brendon. He managed to recover his composure. 'Where are my manners? What was I thinking?' He held out a hand too. 'Hello, Harriet. I apologise for being so crass. I have a feeling we're going to be firm friends. I must say, I love your sense of style. What label is that? The bias cut is superb, and the colour works wonders with your skin tone.'

'Rein it in, Bren,' said Sylvie.

'You'll scare Harriet off,' said Duncan. He cast his eyes upwards. 'You'll have to forgive my husband. He's a fashionista. In another life he'd have been a model.'

'Too right I would. I'd have brought pizzazz and glamour to any fashion shoot. What with this face, and toned body.' Brendon used his hands to highlight his features.

'Don't worry, you'll get used to him,' said Sylvie. Both women laughed.

'I've a feeling that when we get to know each other better, you and I are going to be besties. Please tell me that you'd be up for us being shopping buddies. It'd be my idea of heaven to hit the high-end boutiques with a kindred spirit. You clearly have impeccable taste, and I'd value your opinion.' Brendon squeezed his eyes shut and clasped his hands as his imagination raced ahead. 'I've given up on Duncan as far as fashion is concerned. He wouldn't care if I was dressed in a sack.'

'As long as it was a reasonably priced sack,' added Duncan with a wry smile.

'And there's the proof.' He flicked his hand dismissively at his husband. 'I'm telling you, he'd darn his socks, if I let him. I've been forced to accept that I'm married to a heathen. You see what I'm up against. I quite literally need you to save me. Without you in my life I'd have to make do with letting my imagination run riot with the likes of *GQ*, *Ape to Gentleman* and *Vogue Man*. But that's merely a superficial fantasy. Glossy pages can't and won't ever nourish the soul.'

Throughout the last few minutes, Harriet had felt the stresses and strains of the last few days leave her body. Following his initial shock, Brendon's subsequent effusive welcome was a tonic. She immediately warmed to him and sensed that they could both enjoy a genuine friendship.

It was odd to think that until recently Harriet had been unaware that Monksworthy existed. Yet she had bonded with Sylvie and Liz and now felt at ease with Brendon and Duncan too. She knew that it was too early to make any rash decisions, but with Albert's betrayal and his unforgivable skulduggery to strip her of her beloved house, she was starting to think that she needed a fresh start in life. And perhaps Monksworthy could provide that. After all, she had already bonded with four of the villagers.

'We'll get something in the diary,' Harriet reassured him.

'You're not just saying that?'

'No. It'd be good to have company. Especially someone with such a discerning eye.'

'Oh, if only I was straight, we'd be a match made in heaven.' Brendon theatrically placed his hands over his heart. 'You, my gorgeous creature, are welcome in this establishment anytime.'

'Now, what can I get you, ladies?' asked Duncan.

Sylvie asked to see the menu and they ordered food.

'Find yourselves a table and I'll bring the drinks over in a jiffy,' said Brendon.

When he arrived at their table, he saw that they were deep in discussion. Sylvie was making notes. 'This looks serious. What are you two up to?' he asked.

'As well as being a fashion obsessive, Bren is also hooked on true crime,' said Sylvie.

'That's absolutely true. Move over Hercule Poirot! If I had been a detective, I'd have given him a run for his money. His fashion sense wouldn't have been a patch on mine. I'd have been the world's best dressed detective.'

Both women laughed, though neither felt inclined to point out the obvious fact that Poirot was a fictional character. Brendon sat at their table and listened, open-mouthed as they told him about Tess and her false identity.

'And the police can't find her?' he eventually asked.

They both shook their heads.

'So, it's possible that she killed him?' His eyes widened. They both nodded.

'Are we talking black widow?' he asked. When they both looked at him blankly, he continued. 'Surely it must've occurred to you. Like in *Arsenic and Old Lace*. Oh . . . my . . . word. Cary Grant! Excuse me while I swoon. Now there's a man I wouldn't have kicked out of bed. Oops,' his hand shot to his mouth, and he looked from one to the other, 'please tell me that I didn't say that out loud.

'You might not have noticed, Harriet, but sometimes I don't seem to have a filter. Before I know it, I've articulated every thought that's just popped into my head. Duncan, bless his cotton socks — the undarned ones, that is — is for ever warning me that it'll get me into trouble one day.'

'Tell us about black widows,' said Harriet.

'Well, what can I say? They target wealthy men and eventually kill them. They do it for money. Mostly they favour using poison.'

'There was no poison involved in Albert's death. The brakes on his car were cut,' said Sylvie.

Brendon was undeterred. 'Tell me everything. And I mean, everything. If we're going to solve this crime, I need details.' He leaned forward and listened intently as they gave him a blow-by-blow account of everything they'd learned. 'The brakes must have been tampered with in the night. Was Albert a light or heavy sleeper?'

'Light,' said Sylvie.

'Absolutely,' confirmed Harriet. 'He'd wake at the slightest sound.'

'Well, I guess she must've slipped him a Mickey.' He slapped both palms on the table, almost spilling Harriet's drink as he did so. 'That'd explain why he heard nothing when she was sabotaging his brakes.'

Harriet quickly picked up her glass, before Brendon's theatricalities wreaked havoc.

'Now, as luck would have it, I also subscribe to a true crime magazine, and I've kept all the back issues. It's a major bugbear for Duncan. But I've told him in no uncertain terms to keep his mitts off them, as you never know when they might come in handy.'

'How will that help?' asked Harriet.

'Because I'm fairly certain that a year or so ago, there was an article on a black widow allegedly operating in Britain.' He arched his eyebrows to emphasise the importance of this statement. 'Now, it might take me a while to find it, but I'll leave you to have your lunch, and I'll see what I can come up with.'

The food eventually arrived, and they ate in peace. As they were about to leave, Brendon reappeared. 'I've found it!'

He held a magazine aloft. 'This is the article I was telling you about. It took me longer to find it, because it's from almost four years ago.'

As Brendon opened the magazine to the relevant page, they realised that Tess Harris was indeed a black widow. The article was actually about a woman named Teresa Clarke, who had married a man named Joshua Harding and had allegedly gone on to kill him. There was a photograph of Joshua and Teresa on their wedding day, and it was the first clear image they had seen of her. It was undoubtedly the same woman who had passed herself off as Tess.

# CHAPTER 33

As their attention focused on the magazine article, it was as though time stood still. Sylvie sat open-mouthed while Harriet broke out in a cold sweat. This revelation was so far removed from any scenario conjured up in their imaginations. Yet the woman in the photograph was the same as the one on the passport. And the headline labelled her a 'black widow'. She had married another man and killed him for his money. Which meant it was almost certain that she had murdered Albert.

Since learning of Albert's constant deception, both women had had to dig deep to come to terms with his betrayal.

Yet this latest revelation in the convoluted existence of Albert Courtenay was perhaps the saddest thing of all. Failing to be satisfied with what he had, he had ramped up his despicable game of happy families and had ended up paying the ultimate price.

'As harrowing as this is, we need to read the article. We have to know what she did to this poor man,' said Harriet.

Sylvie nodded reluctantly.

Brendon had a firm grip on the magazine and showed no sign of letting go.

'Seriously, Bren?' said Sylvie.

'I haven't read this since it first came out, so I've forgotten the nitty-gritty of what happened,' he protested. 'Anyway, if it wasn't for me, you wouldn't even have known about it.' He looked and sounded ashamedly defiant.

Appreciating that there was no point in arguing with him, they scootched up beside Brendon. All three diligently read the article, and every so often their collective silence was broken by gasps of horror and disgust.

Sylvie was the first to recover. 'I need to speak to Simon.' She picked up her phone.

'Do you want a drink? I need a drink.' Brendon's complexion had paled, and beads of sweat had erupted across his brow. 'Duncan! We need some drinks over here.' Having let go of the magazine he held an arm aloft and pointed at their table.

'I don't want a drink,' muttered Sylvie, as she listened to the ringtone.

'Me neither,' said Harriet. 'We need clear heads, not alcohol.'

Simon's phone remained unanswered, and Sylvie left a message. She didn't go into detail. Just asked him to call her as soon as possible.

'That Teresa woman's evil,' said Brendon. 'Poor Bertie. I know he was doing the dirty on both of you, but still, he didn't deserve to get mixed up with a cold-hearted killer.'

'You're right, he didn't. We need to speak to Liz,' said Sylvie. 'Can I take this?' She picked up the magazine. 'We need to show it to the police.'

Brendon nodded. 'You'll keep me informed?'

'Absolutely,' said Harriet.

This was a huge leap forward in identifying Tess, or whatever she was calling herself now. There was no doubt in either of their minds that a black widow had targeted, then murdered Albert.

Reinvigorated with a new sense of urgency they raced to the tearoom. Given Harriet's routine of early morning runs, she thought nothing of it. Sylvie, on the other hand, was sweating and breathing heavily, as they burst through the door like a couple of whirling dervishes.

'Liz! Liz!' yelled Sylvie, as she placed her hands on the counter.

Liz appeared. Her face flushed from the heat generated by the ovens. 'What's happened? Is everything all right?' she asked, looking from one to the other.

'We've had a breakthrough,' said Harriet.

'Great timing, I've just finished the final batch of brownies. They're cooling on a rack.'

'Never mind about that,' said Sylvie. 'We need to sit down and talk this through.' She headed to the nearest table and pulled out a chair. The others followed.

'Well? Don't keep me in suspense,' said Liz.

They filled her in on the latest development, frequently talking over each other in their eagerness to get their friend up to speed.

'This is the article. Look at the photograph.' Sylvie placed the magazine down in front of Liz. 'It's proof that whoever she is, she uses different identities to lure men in before she kills them.'

'So what's the plan?' She looked at them questioningly. 'You must have a plan.'

'I called Simon. There was no answer, so I left a message.'

'It's good you called him. At least we can't be accused of not following his orders. But come on, seriously? We can't just sit back and allow them to run with this. So, I'll ask you again, what are we going to do?' Liz's tone was low, but assertive.

Harriet picked up the magazine and scanned the text. 'I say we find Joshua Harding's sister. According to the article her name's Mary Blythe. It's likely that she knows — or thinks she knows — more than has been printed. But the only way we'll know for sure is by talking to her.'

'How would we go about finding her?' asked Sylvie.

'I've got contacts in the industry, so I'll see what I can do,' said Harriet.

'And if you don't get anywhere following that route, then I'll work on Simon. The police are bound to follow this up. But perhaps not straight away, so they might need a push and Simon's our man on the inside. Don't worry, we'll get her contact details one way or another,' said Liz.

# CHAPTER 34

Sylvie gave Harriet the key to her cottage so that she could make her phone calls in peace. Liz was still busy at the tearoom, and Sylvie set about washing up, cleaning down surfaces and boxing up orders that were ready to go out. It helped to focus on routine things as there was nothing either of them could do to help move the investigation forward.

Meanwhile, Harriet had been given the runaround by various contacts. It had taken almost a dozen phone calls as she was passed from one person to another before she eventually got the information she needed. Many people would have given up long before, but she was tenacious. There was no way she was going to return to the tearoom and admit defeat, and in the end, she came up trumps.

As the time approached six o'clock the ladies were on the road. The satnav told them that they had three miles to go to reach their destination, which was somewhere in Oxfordshire.

On arrival, Sylvie cut the engine, having found a parking space on a residential street where the pavement was wide and tree lined.

'Looks like a nice area,' said Liz, as she got out of the car and stretched. 'What number are we looking for?'

'Sixteen,' said Harriet. She scanned numbers on front doors as she headed off in search of the house.

The others followed, keen to get the introductions out of the way so that they could find out what they needed to know.

The house they were heading for was of large proportions. Stained-glass panels on either side of the black door added vibrant splashes of colour. A polished brass knocker gleamed in the rays of early evening sun, though Harriet chose to ring the doorbell instead. Moments later a willowy woman with lustrous, auburn hair opened the door. At a guess she appeared to be in her late forties and was exceptionally attractive.

'Mary?' asked Harriet.

'Yes.' She gave a welcoming smile.

'I'm Harriet. These are my friends, Sylvie and Liz.'

'Do come in. The others are here and they're keen to meet you.' Mary opened the door to its fullest extent, and they stepped inside.

'What others?' whispered Liz.

Harriet shrugged her shoulders, and they followed Mary along the hallway towards a room at the back of the house. As they walked into a bright and airy sitting room, two men stopped talking and stood up simultaneously. A set of bifold doors were open, allowing a gentle breeze to flood the room, which otherwise might have easily become too warm. The garden beyond was large, colourful and beautifully maintained, suggesting that someone from that household was a keen gardener.

'Ladies, this is Edward Long and Cameron Dawlish. Gentlemen, this is Harriet Joyce, Sylvie Franklynn and Liz Morgan.' With the introductions and handshakes dispensed with, Mary continued. 'Please sit and help yourselves to refreshments. We've a lot to discuss. I've already filled Ed and Cam in on what you told me over the phone, and you know my story as you read the magazine article. So, Ed, perhaps you'd like to go first, and update the ladies?'

Ed sighed, and his shoulders slumped. 'One way or another, all of us, apart from you, Liz, appear to be in the same boat. This woman, who in your case was passing herself off as someone named Tess, murdered my brother. His name was Thomas. He was three years my junior, highly successful, and a very wealthy man. He'd been widowed for the best part of three years before Tamsin Brown came into his life. She met him on a cruise. He was a solo traveller, and they hit it off at a welcome party for single guests.'

Sylvie's breath caught in her throat, as the realisation that there were more victims suddenly hit her. 'And Tamsin was the same woman as the one posing as Teresa Clarke?'

'It took a long time for us to find each other and the connection to be made, but yes, she's the same woman,' said Mary.

'S-sorry, I didn't mean to interrupt. It's just a shock. You see, until this afternoon we only had our suspicions that she was responsible for Albert's death. But when we saw the story in the magazine, we finally put two and two together . . .'

'She murdered my best friend, too,' said Cameron. 'But I'll tell you about that after Ed's finished filling you in about Thomas.'

'And believe me, it's quite a tale, because that woman pulls out all the stops to get away with murder,' said Edward. 'As I said, they met on a cruise, seemingly by chance, and that might very well have been the case. After all, you hear about wealthy singletons being targeted on that sort of holiday.

'All I can say for sure is that since the death of his wife, Thomas hadn't once shown any inclination to have a romantic relationship again. He'd been married to Becky for twenty-four years. They had no children, and they doted on each other. So, you can imagine the shock when out of the blue he announced that he was married. There was no hint of it beforehand.'

'You must've been concerned,' said Harriet.

'I was. Thomas and I had always been close. Best friends as well as brothers. He and Becky only lived a few streets away from my wife and myself. We'd spent our lives in Tewkesbury. Becky and Dawn, that's my wife's name, were the best of pals.

The four of us did everything together. Always in and out of each other's houses. Even after Becky passed, he still came on holiday with us. But on that occasion, he'd decided that it was time for a change. Said he wanted to try something a bit different.

'He was only away for ten days, and in that time, Tamsin got her hooks into him good and proper. When the cruise was over, he came home and all we heard was Tamsin this, Tamsin that. So, we thought it'd be nice to meet her. You know — do things together, as two couples. But no matter what was arranged there was always some last-minute thing that cropped up so that we couldn't get together. At first, we just made a joke out of it. But the longer it went on, the more we began to realise that something wasn't quite right.

'We did our best to find out more about her. And to this day we still don't know where she lived when she met my brother. We never heard of any family or friends. All we knew was that within the space of a few months she'd moved in with him. Got her feet well and truly under the table. And she was a gold-digger. Sponged off him from the start and never had a job in all the time they were together.'

'She targeted him for his money, and you'll soon see that that's the pattern here,' interjected Mary.

'But Albert didn't have any money,' said Sylvie.

'Or at least none that you knew about,' added Liz.

'Given the fact that we now know that he had a foot in three households, it explains why he was always quite frugal,' said Harriet. 'Not that we ever went without things.'

'But it's possible that this woman might have thought he was a man of means,' said Cameron. 'Given the fact that she was just following a pattern of behaviour that she'd found to be lucrative and easy to move on from, the chances are that it would never have entered her head that your Albert was play-ing her too.' Seeing their pained expressions, it occurred to Cameron that he might have overstepped the mark. After all, being only recently bereaved, these women hadn't had time to process what had happened. It was time to apologise. 'I'm sorry. I didn't mean to be insensitive.'

'It's fine,' said Sylvie. 'We've learned the hard way that Bertie was a player. I could easily imagine him spinning her a line. After all, he duped us for years. And apart from the fact that he wasn't a murderer, you could say they were two of a kind. What with using false identities to fool people they got close to.'

'I guess it just didn't occur to either of them that they'd met their match in that respect,' added Liz.

'They would've both believed that they were the one in control,' said Harriet.

'Sixteen months into their marriage she killed him. Of course, it was never proved. They'd gone out walking that day, and he ended up at the bottom of a cliff. Thomas was scared of heights. It was a fear he'd had since childhood. He wouldn't have voluntarily gone anywhere near the edge of a cliff. It's what made us realise that she was responsible,' said Edward. 'That and the money. Thomas had inherited a substantial amount of money from Becky. Her parents were wealthy and as their only child it had all gone to her when they passed.

'Thomas lived comfortably but wasn't extravagant by any means. I know for a fact that before they got married, he had the best part of a million in various accounts. But unbeknown to us he'd changed every one of his accounts to joint accounts. My brother's body hadn't even had a chance to go cold before she cleaned them out. Of course, we didn't know that at the time. She was canny enough to stay around for a few days, playing the grieving widow. But once she realised that we hadn't fallen for the story she'd concocted, she did a moonlight flit, and that was the last anyone saw of her.

'I wondered at the time why she hadn't insisted on the house going into joint ownership. Then I realised that it would have been problematic. After all, if you've been living under a false identity, and someone's rumbled that you've killed your husband, you can't put the house up for sale and hang around waiting for the payday. It'd be a sure way of the police catching up with you. That's why she was only ever after the money in the bank accounts.'

'Couldn't they have traced her through that?' asked Sylvie.

'Believe me, they tried, but she'd set up a series of offshore accounts. It was a complex operation, and there was no way of following the trail. You see, as soon as it arrived in one account it was transferred to another. The best part of a million was untraceable in the blink of an eye.'

'It was more or less the same story with Robert,' said Cameron. 'He'd won a million on the Premium Bonds when he met a woman calling herself Tracey Turner. She targeted him when he was at a posh hotel up in London. Within a couple of months, he'd gone from being one of the lads to turning his back on his mates to spend all of his time with her. Once she'd got her claws into him, it was as though there was no room for anyone else in his life.

'We only learned quite by chance that they got married. Six months later and he was dead. The police reckoned it was a burglary gone wrong. She claimed that they'd come home late at night to find someone had broken into the house. She had some superficial injuries, but nothing that couldn't have been self-inflicted. Whereas Rob, poor sod, received a blow to the head and was a goner.

'We didn't put two and two together at the time. It was only after reading Mary's magazine article that we realised who she was. But that was the best part of a year later. I went to the police. They didn't take me seriously at first. Though I didn't give up and I eventually got someone to check out Rob's bank accounts. That's when they drew a blank as she'd done the same thing with the money. Transferred it through various offshore accounts within twenty-four hours of his death. And by then Tracey was long gone. No doubt living it up under another name.'

# CHAPTER 35

Having learned so much in the last few hours they said their goodbyes and headed home. As they were approaching Monksworthy, Sylvie's phone rang. The earlier fine weather had gone. It was raining, dark and visibility wasn't that great. 'Answer that will you, Liz. I can't afford to get distracted in case we end up in a ditch.'

The caller ID said it was Simon. 'About time. Sylvie left you a message more than six hours ago.'

'What's up, sis? Why are you answering Sylvie's phone? Is she all right?'

'She's fine, and it's a long story. More to the point, why has it taken you so long to return her call?'

'I can't go into specifics. Let's just say it was police business and leave it at that.' Simon's curt tone left Liz in no doubt that no amount of cajoling was going to get him to answer that particular question. 'What did Sylvie want? She said it was urgent but didn't say why.'

'It's too late to get into that now, Si. It's been a long day and we're all exhausted. Are you able to call around to Sylvie's first thing tomorrow?'

'Sure. I'll be there eight o'clock sharp.'

Sylvie gave Liz the thumbs-up to indicate that she was happy with the arrangement. When the call ended, Sylvie spoke. 'Are you both up for staying at mine tonight? We need a plan if we're going to track Tess down. She's already got a head start and is probably grooming her next target.'

'I agree. No matter how badly Albert treated us, he didn't deserve to die like that. The woman's a serial killer and we need to make sure that she's arrested. She has to pay for what she's done, for everyone's sake,' said Harriet.

'We also need to get Simon on board, or at least fill him in on our suspicions,' said Liz. 'A serial killer is a police matter, and I just don't understand why they aren't taking it seriously. Let's face it, even if we managed to track her down, we can't just stroll up to her and make a citizen's arrest. We're out of our depth. She's dangerous. How could we stand up to someone like that?'

'Are you suggesting that we shouldn't try to track her down?' asked Sylvie.

'No. We should, we absolutely should,' said Liz. 'I'm just saying that we need to think about our own safety too.' It was a reasonable point to make and the others knew it. Each of them wanted to do everything possible to find this woman, but they certainly weren't equipped to do anything other than that. And given Tess's propensity for disappearing and reinventing herself under another identity — seemingly at the drop of a hat — they couldn't afford to give her the opportunity to slip through their fingers. The woman was a sharp and ruthless operator, who had demonstrated on numerous occasions that she had no problem killing people to get what she wanted. They were under no illusion that she would be anything other than a formidable opponent.

They sat around Sylvie's kitchen table into the early hours, munching sandwiches and cakes, washed down with mugs of strong filter coffee. They all agreed it was not such a good idea to have caffeine at so late an hour as it would undoubtedly make it difficult for them to sleep. But they knew that for the time being they needed it to stay alert.

'This reminds me of my student days. Staying up all night. Cramming for exams,' said Harriet.

'We'll pay for it tomorrow,' said Liz. 'Someone will probably find me face down in a mixing bowl, snoring my head off. I'll be fit for nothing.'

'You don't have to stay,' said Sylvie. 'Go and get your head down for a while.'

'Are you kidding? You know I'm obsessed with crime fiction. I live and breathe it, and now by some strange quirk of fate we're on the trail of a real-life serial killer. This is huge! If we can track her down, we can make a real difference. Do something the police have failed to do. And if we find her in time, we've got a chance of saving her next victim.'

Sylvie rummaged through a drawer. 'OK, I suggest we go old school. I've got three large pieces of paper, a stack of different coloured Post-it notes, pens and highlighters. Write a single fact on the Post-it, stick it on the paper and keep going until you've got every bit of information recorded. It doesn't matter if something seems silly or pointless, write it down anyway. Then rearrange your Post-its into chronological order. Liz, you concentrate on what Mary said. Harriet, you take Edward, and I'll take Cameron. We'll each have a different colour so as not to confuse things. Come on, ladies, let's do this,' she said.

The room fell silent as they each concentrated on dredging their memories to retrieve the facts. Half an hour later there were three sheets of previously empty white paper. But now one had an array of yellow patches. Another, green. And the third, pink.

Harriet was the first of the group to speak. 'I can't remember the last time I used a pen for such a prolonged period. It almost felt like an exam, and it's made my hand ache.' She made a fist then stretched out her fingers as she tried to relieve the tension in her digits.

'I know what you mean,' agreed Sylvie. 'But at least we've got a lot of facts recorded, so we can work with that. We've still got to do the same thing for Albert, but that should be easier because it's virtually all we've thought about since we learned what happened. Bertie can have orange Post-its.'

It was approaching two o'clock by the time they had finished, and everyone was exhausted.

'Let's call it a night,' said Sylvie. 'I'll set my alarm for six.'

'That should give us time to have a quick breakfast and then we can get back to these fact sheets and see if we can find any patterns,' said Liz. 'Detectives look for patterns of behaviour.'

'Makes sense. After all, they say you can predict future behaviour by studying what a person has already done,' said Harriet.

# CHAPTER 36

Having managed only a few hours' sleep, the six o'clock alarm was loud and unwelcome. But determined to push on with the task of finding Tess, Sylvie struggled out of bed. She yawned loudly as she shuffled to the bathroom, feet barely capable of clearing the floor. Her eyes were bleary, her thoughts fuzzy and her body felt almost too heavy to move. Having reached the sink, she splashed copious amounts of cold water on her face until it had the desired effect.

Eventually feeling wide awake, she heard voices downstairs. And as she headed towards the kitchen, she got her first smell of coffee and warm pastries. Liz and Harriet were already at the table, plates littered with crumbs.

'I thought I'd be the first one up,' said Sylvie.

'Hardly. Apparently, we're both early risers. Don't need the alarm,' said Liz. 'I've been out and called at the tearoom. Collected a selection of goodies.'

'And they were delicious, too,' added Harriet, as she wiped the remaining crumbs from the corner of her mouth. 'Don't worry, there's still some left, and there's coffee in the pot.'

'I thought you preferred a healthy breakfast,' said Sylvie.

'I usually do, but I'm trying to be more flexible, and those pastries were particularly tasty.' She gave Liz an appreciative smile, then immediately turned her attention back to Sylvie. 'Anyway, I'm sure it won't hurt me having the odd treat here and there, and it's especially welcome when we've got a long day ahead of us and we're running on so little sleep,' said Harriet. 'Shall we make a start reviewing last night's efforts?'

Liz nodded enthusiastically. 'I'll just clear the table first, so we can spread everything out on there.' She picked up the plate of pastries just as Sylvie was about to reach for one.

'Hey, I thought those were for me,' she groaned. She'd only been up for a matter of minutes and was already feeling as though the house was no longer hers.

'They are yours,' reassured Liz. 'But we need the table. We've still got a lot to do, and we want to be ready for when Simon calls.'

'But he's not due for ages yet,' said Sylvie.

'That's not the point. I don't want to come across as bossy, but so far, we haven't managed to get the police to take our concerns seriously. These new facts are our best chance of getting them on board. They already seem to think that we're interfering busybodies. Which means we have to prove them wrong. But we'll only have one shot at this, so we need to get organised,' said Harriet.

'OK, I get it. I'll eat while we work,' said Sylvie. The other two smiled, and as Sylvie poured herself some coffee then helped herself to the pastries, they set out the four sheets of paper littered with their respective Post-it notes. The data they'd collected took a lot of rearranging. Then again, they were approaching this task in the old-school way.

Finally, when everything was laid out in chronological order and the lists compared, a pattern emerged. However, they were forced to acknowledge that they had no actual evidence of what Albert's relationship with Tess had been like. As such, all they could do was presume that Tess had followed a similar pattern as she endeavoured to pull him into her web.

'She moves around a lot,' said Liz.

'Guess she'd have to, so as not to get caught. It'd be very risky to operate in a small geographical area. Someone might recognise her,' said Harriet.

'Looks as though she picks up her victims at hotels,' Sylvie pointed out.

'Well, she targeted one on a cruise ship,' said Liz.

'Which is basically a floating hotel,' countered Harriet.

'Guess so,' conceded Liz.

'I wonder if she found Bertie at a hotel? And if so, where was it?'

'I doubt we'll ever know,' said Harriet.

'Have you noticed that she selects men in a certain age range?' asked Liz. 'Plus each of them was single, with no dependants.'

'Not in Bertie's case,' said Sylvie.

'But she wouldn't have known that. He would have made out that he was single,' said Harriet.

'You're right,' sighed Sylvie.

'And from what we were told yesterday, she does everything she can to isolate them from any friends or siblings,' said Liz.

'Less chance of anyone asking awkward questions once she's killed them,' said Sylvie, 'which explains why she took off like a bat out of hell the moment she realised that Bertie wasn't the man she thought he was. I doubt she'd have touched him with a barge pole if she realised that he was a polygamist. She'd have known that if it ever came out, she'd find herself in the middle of a police investigation.'

'And for someone who operates in the shadows, that would be a risk she'd never want to take,' added Liz.

'The weddings all seem to have been low-key events,' said Harriet. 'Having had the conversations at Mary's house yesterday, it's safe to say that none of the other victims' friends or families had been invited or even heard about the weddings before they happened. They've all been small registry office events. Yet the men she married could have afforded to go all out, no expense spared. Surely that should have set some alarm bells ringing with the potential grooms?'

'Don't see why. It's usually us women who like the big occasion,' said Liz. 'Blokes are more likely to want to tone it down a bit to save the pennies, so that they can spend their money on other things. If anything, I would have thought they'd see it as a refreshing approach. It might even make her more appealing in their eyes. Reinforcing the idea that this woman genuinely cares about them, instead of their bank balance.'

'You're right,' said Sylvie. 'It's possible they'd be stupid enough to fall for that. And it'd be a huge ego boost to have a younger woman who seemingly wants you for you.' She sighed. 'Truth is, I could imagine Bertie falling for that. Couldn't you, Harriet?'

'Unfortunately, I could. I can picture it playing out in front of my eyes. Albie would have been flattered. He was always flirtatious. Had an eye for a pretty face. And since he'd been playing us successfully for all those years, he'd most likely think that he could pull it off again, without anyone being any the wiser.'

Sylvie slapped her hand on the table, making everyone jump. 'We forgot about Barney! We know that she only goes for wealthy, single men of a certain age. He fits the criteria.'

Harriet's brow furrowed, as she tried to make sense of what Sylvie had said.

'You're right. We have to warn him,' said Liz. 'He's been away for the last few weeks, so he might not have heard about Albert. Though I think he came back the day before yesterday.'

'I've no idea who you're talking about,' said Harriet. She looked and sounded perplexed.

'That's because you haven't met Sir Barnaby Cavendish-Mortimer yet,' said Liz. 'She'd see him as a perfect target. He's not bad looking. He's single. A hopeless romantic. And he's as rich as he sounds.'

184

# CHAPTER 37

The front door was unlocked. 'It's only me,' called Simon as he walked into the house at eight o'clock sharp. 'Sorry I didn't get back to you yesterday, but I spent the entire shift chasing my tail. As I've already told Liz, I can't go into specifics, but it was busy.'

'Take the weight off and have a cuppa,' said Sylvie.

'There's some pastries there too,' added Liz. 'I know you're partial to them.'

Simon sat at the table and tucked in.

'Has there been any progress on the case?' asked Harriet.

Simon nodded as he munched. Every eye was upon him, anticipating his response. He held up his hand as he chewed then eventually swallowed. 'It's been established that there were traces of a strong sedative in Bertie's system.'

'Sedative! In all the years we were together, Bertie never took anything stronger than an aspirin,' said Sylvie.

'I agree. That woman obviously drugged him so that she wouldn't realise that she was tampering with the brakes on his car,' said Harriet.

'You both knew him better than anyone, and I appreciate that you might think that Tess drugged him. All I can say is

185

that on a personal level I think you're probably right. But I'm afraid that we can't go on hunches or feelings. We only deal in cold hard facts and so far, we can't be certain that Bertie didn't take that sedative himself.'

'Has any progress been made on locating Tess?' asked Liz. She could see that both Harriet and Sylvie were upset by the news of the sedative.

'Not so far. First off, her FLO has been suspended pending investigation. Though that's no consolation at this stage. As for locating Tess, there are officers looking into it, but she's done a good job of covering her tracks. I know this is upsetting and frustrating, but resources have been allocated to track her down. All I can say is that in cases like this, there aren't any short cuts,' said Simon.

'Cases like this! What do you mean "cases like this"? The woman's nothing but a cold-blooded serial killer, Simon. And as far as I can see, the police are twiddling their thumbs instead of going all out to find her.' Sylvie's eyes blazed with contempt.

'I appreciate that emotions are high, but you don't know that she's a serial killer,' said Simon.

'Yes, we do!' Sylvie struggled to control her frustration and pounded the table with her fist. It seemed inconceivable that Simon was seemingly refusing to see what was so blindingly obvious to the rest of them. Did he know something that they weren't aware of? Or was he purposely being obtuse? Whatever his reasons, it wasn't helping them find the woman.

Sylvie was resolute as she tried to make him see sense. There was no way she was prepared to back down or to give up so easily. 'You have to listen to what we're saying, and you need to take it seriously. We know that Bertie was her fourth victim, as we've already spoken to the families of three other men she murdered. We're all absolutely convinced that she's the same woman and she's using different names.'

'You spoke to family members of other victims?' Simon's voice had risen. 'Right, consider this a warning. The three of you need to back off.' He looked at each of them in turn. 'I'm serious. You have no investigative authority. You don't know anything about these people that you've spoken to. It could land you in all sorts of trouble. I'm telling you; you can't go around doing things like this.'

'Why can't we?' demanded Liz. 'It's not as if the police are doing anything to move this investigation along.'

'You've no idea what's going on behind the scenes,' countered Simon. 'That's the way investigations work, Liz. So, stop playing Miss bloody Marple and leave it to the professionals before you find yourselves in a dangerous situation which you have no control over. Acting all gung-ho and blundering around is how people end up getting hurt!'

'These families have approached the police on numerous occasions, but the police have refused to examine any links between the cases. They've got a blinkered approach and are treating each of the murders as separate cases,' said Sylvie.

'Apart from this area, we're talking about three other police forces here, Si,' said Liz. 'I'm telling you, you need to start taking this seriously, because this woman has probably already got her sights on her next victim. And if you choose to ignore what we're saying, and she kills another man, then you'll have to live with the fact that you might have been able to save his life if you'd followed up on this information.' Her tone was deadly serious, and she stared him down to emphasise the point.

Simon knew that his sister believed what she was saying. Liz was someone he trusted implicitly. They always had each other's back, no matter what. 'Fine,' he sighed and held up his hands in defeat. 'Give me their names and contact details. I'll pass it on to someone further up the chain of command.'

'And you'll see to it that they'll take it forward?' asked Sylvie.

'I'll do everything I can, but I can't force them to follow it up. It doesn't work like that,' said Simon. 'I'm only a lowly sergeant. They don't listen to the likes of me. I don't have any sway over anyone of a higher rank.'

187

By the time Simon left the house, the three women still weren't convinced that the police would investigate the allegations or even speak to the relatives of the other men.

'Well, I guess we shouldn't hold our breath,' said Sylvie. 'Looks as though it's down to us. If Tess is going to be found, we'll have to track her down.'

'I agree,' said Liz. 'I know Si's my brother, and I love him to bits, but sometimes I just want to shake him.'

The others nodded in agreement.

'It's odds on she's going to kill again,' said Sylvie. 'She's got a taste for it now and won't be able to help herself. Especially since she slipped up with Bertie. She must be furious about that. And I don't want some other man's death on my conscience. Which it would be if we don't do everything possible to track her down and stop her.'

'So where does this Sir Barnaby whatshisname live?' asked Harriet.

# CHAPTER 38

For centuries, Sir Barnaby's family had owned the Cavendish-Mortimer Estate. And being the only child, he inherited his birthright upon the death of his father.

Sir Barnaby, or Barney as he insisted his friends call him, was in his late fifties. He was a manly man. Quick-witted, personable, and easy on the eye. At over six feet tall, he cut a dashing figure. With a full head of dark wavy hair, which in recent years had become flecked with the occasional strand of grey, he appeared far younger than his years. It helped that he kept himself in shape, drank only moderately, and was careful not to overload himself with the dreaded carbs.

With the passage of time, it was looking increasingly likely that the Cavendish-Mortimer lineage might end with Sir Barnaby, as he proved either incapable of, or perhaps unwilling to commit to a long-term relationship. For a man who was in love with the idea of romance, he had an uncanny knack of forming passionate relationships with women with whom he had little in common. Almost invariably falling head over heels in love with the object of his desire, he'd come on too strong, try too hard and be devastated when his clumsy, ostentatious attempts at wooing his latest belle were not enthusiastically reciprocated. It was an inevitable recipe for disaster. Yet a lesson he failed to learn.

Admittedly, the path to finding true love was fraught with other difficulties for Barney. In fact, far more so than for most people. His family estate included a home of palatial proportions, together with a variety of successful business interests. This made Barney one of the country's most eligible bachelors. And there were plenty of gold-diggers out there who were drawn to what Barney had to offer. Without complete anonymity, it was almost impossible to ignore the fact that he was a man of means. Consequently, the odds of him finding that elusive happy ever after were most definitely stacked against him.

Sylvie and Liz had been friends with Barney for as long as they could remember. They'd hung out since their pre-teenage years, during the long school holidays when the young Barney had returned from boarding school. Barney's parents hadn't made a secret of the fact that they were less than pleased their son and heir was spending so much time with a couple of village girls. Especially as they got older, and they dreaded him getting one of the locals pregnant. This had caused a great deal of hilarity among the three teenagers as their relationship was friendship, pure and simple. There had never been any hint of physical attraction between them.

The first thing Sylvie did when Simon left her house that morning was to text Barney and ask if they could pop along for a chat. As he had so many business ventures on the go, it was easier to send a text message. There was always the chance that he could be in the middle of some time-sensitive business deal.

They barely had time to clear the paperwork from the kitchen table when Sylvie's phone pinged. It was Barney, confirming that he had a few hours free that morning and could see them straight away.

As they reached the Cavendish-Mortimer Estate, Harriet whistled. 'I clearly underestimated your friend's wealth.'

190

'Oh, he's rich all right, and a big employer in these parts,' said Sylvie. 'There's no denying that Barney's hopeless in the love stakes, but when it comes to being an astute businessman, I doubt there are many that could better him.'

'Sounds just like the sort of guy that Tess would target,' said Harriet. 'I hope for his sake that she hasn't got him in her sights.'

'Well, at least we can fill him in on what we know. Especially as he wears his heart on his sleeve. Forewarned is forearmed, and all that,' said Liz.

'Absolutely,' agreed Sylvie. 'Barney's the most eligible bachelor in these parts, and he's just the sort of man who would fall for her guff, so we need to protect him.'

'Come on in, ladies,' said Barney, as he opened the door to them. 'Sylvie, I'm so sorry to hear about Bertie. The man was a fool and a love rat. He wasn't worthy to kiss the ground you walk on.' Placing a hand on each of her shoulders he looked her squarely in the eyes. 'You'll let me know if there's anything I can do? As always, I'm here for you.'

'Thanks, Barney. That means a lot,' said Sylvie. She smiled and nodded her appreciation.

'Hello. I don't believe I've had the pleasure?' Barney raised an eyebrow questioningly at Harriet.

'This is our newest friend, Harriet,' said Liz. 'Harriet, this is Sir Barnaby Cavendish-Mortimer.'

'I'm very pleased to meet you,' said Harriet as they shook hands.

'So how do you know these lovely ladies?' asked Barney.

'Ah, now that's a long story. I think it might be best if we all sat down,' said Sylvie, before Harriet had the opportunity to say anything.

'Well, you know me, I love a good story. Come in and make yourselves at home. You know the way.' He gestured for Liz to lead them through to the sitting room. 'I take it you'd all like a cup of tea?' Everyone answered in the affirmative. 'In that case, I'll instruct Eliza to put the kettle on and ensure she rustles up a packet or two of Jammie Dodgers.'

Liz and Sylvie both smiled.

'What's with the Jammie Dodgers?' asked Harriet, as they waited for Barney to reappear.

'It's our thing,' said Liz. She went on to explain it was a long-standing tradition among the three of them. Throughout their childhood, they'd hang out in various places on the Cavendish-Mortimer Estate, and the girls would take it in turns to bring a packet of Jammie Dodgers so that they could munch something if they got hungry. The biscuit, which was not the usual sort of fare on offer to Barney, quickly became his favourite. And as adults, whenever either or both visited him, Barney always produced a packet. It was a simple reminder of the past they shared and the resilience of their friendship over the years.

'Refreshments are on their way,' said Barney as he strode back into the room and flopped down on an oversized chair. 'Now, let's not waste any more time. I'm clearly at a disadvantage as I know nothing about Harriet.'

'Harriet was also Bertie's wife,' said Sylvie.

It was apparent to everyone that Barney hadn't expected this news. It was one of the few times in his life that he found himself lost for words, and his jaw dropped as he stared first at Sylvie, then at Harriet. Eventually he cleared his throat, then shook his head as he tried to make sense of what he'd been told. They waited in silence until he eventually spoke.

'Wow! Just wow! I can't get my head around the fact that you've both instantly come to terms with what that philandering scoundrel has done. I know that I wouldn't have, if I were in your shoes.'

'It hasn't been easy,' said Sylvie. 'Our lives have been turned upside down, and there was the natural kneejerk reaction to finding out about what Bertie had done.' She looked at Harriet for confirmation.

'Absolutely,' said Harriet. 'But we quickly realised that the only person to blame was Albie. He duped us both. Sylvie and I both believed we were in a monogamous relationship with our husband. And then there's our kids to think of. It's bad enough they've lost their father, but if we don't set the example of behaving in a reasonable way, what hope is there for them?'

'I must say, the way in which you're supporting each other is impressive, though thoroughly bewildering,' said Barney. He fell silent as the door opened and the housekeeper wheeled in a trolley containing the refreshments.

'Would you like me to pour, sir?' she asked, as she waited for instructions.

'Thank you, Eliza, but that won't be necessary,' said Barney. 'Please close the door on the way out.'

'I'll be mother,' said Liz, as she picked up the teapot.

'There's a reason we asked to see you, Barney,' said Sylvie. 'Bertie didn't just die in a traffic collision. He was murdered.'

'Murdered! You can't be serious.' Barney's complexion paled. 'Do the police know who did it?'

'Well, we know who killed him,' said Sylvie.

'And we've told the police, but we don't have any confidence that they're taking us seriously,' added Harriet.

'We're talking about a serial killer,' said Liz. 'A black widow. Albert's her fourth victim, but there could be more.'

Barney whistled in a protracted manner. 'Well, ladies, they're not going to ignore you any longer. I absolutely will not allow it. I'm a friend of the Chief Constable. I've done him numerous favours, and he owes me. This will be partial payback. Now, eat up, drink up, we've work to do, because I need to be fully apprised of the facts.'

# CHAPTER 39

Liz had only just finished pouring the tea when Barney stood up.

'Ladies, please excuse me. I just need five minutes to get Beatrice to cancel my appointments for the rest of the day.' Beatrice Cornish was Sir Barnaby's personal assistant, a role she'd performed for fifteen years. With his fingers in many so-called business pies, she was used to her employer informing her of last-minute changes to various arrangements. And as she oversaw his diary, it was she who kept on top of such matters.

Sir Barnaby returned to find that the ladies had demolished the refreshments, though Liz had placed three of the biscuits on his plate, as she knew they were his favourite. With his tea already cooled, he picked up the cup and drained it quickly. Only then did he reach for one of the biscuits. But before he took a bite, he spoke.

'Given the importance of this issue, I've cleared my diary for the rest of the day. So, talk me through what you know. I'll have one shot at this, so don't leave anything out. And it's best if I record this, as I don't want to risk forgetting something important when I speak to Andy. The Chief Constable, that is,' he added, by way of explanation.

Liz sat back, allowing Sylvie and Harriet to tell their story. It seemed only fitting, as they were the ones who knew Albert best. And as Sir Barnaby learned more about what had happened, his usually serene expression changed to reflect the seriousness of what he was being told.

'We've constructed visual aids for each of her victims,' said Harriet. 'We've already photographed them so you can have the originals to show the Chief Constable.'

'Do you have them on you?' asked Barney.

'Yes.' Harriet opened her oversized bag and extracted them, carefully unrolling and laying them on the floor so that Barney could have a clear view of all the information.

Sir Barnaby stood up and looked down at each of the sheets, studying them intently. He rested an elbow on the wrist of his other arm placed across his midriff and repeatedly tapped his thumbnail on his lower incisors. While he did this, no one spoke as it was evident that he was deep in thought.

Barnaby was the first person who seemed to be taking their concerns seriously. Not that he was in any position to investigate their findings. But still, this appeared to be their one and only chance of getting the police to act.

Sylvie was so tense that she was aware of the pulse pounding in her ears. She was silently willing her long-time friend to come good and champion their cause. Barney had the ear of those in positions of influence, the sort of people that the likes of ordinary citizens would never encounter. There was so much riding on this moment that the tension in the room was palpable as they waited for his response.

Eventually, Barney spoke. 'Impressive, ladies. As you know, I'm no detective but you've convinced me. It's just inconceivable that no one on the force has taken this seriously and linked these cases. They could easily check the validity of these claims by speaking to the family members. Even I can see that this woman uses variations of the same modus operandi. It's frankly terrifying to know that there's such a woman on the loose. After all, I'm the sort of man she'd have in her sights.'

'That's precisely what we thought,' said Liz. 'Which is why we wanted to warn you. We know you're a sucker for the ladies, Barney, and we'd hate for anything bad to happen to you.'

'And I appreciate your concern. It's touching.' Barney placed a hand over his heart. 'We'll always look out for each other. True friends to the end, ladies. True friends to the end.

'Anyway, enough of the sentimentality. It's not going to achieve anything. We need action. And to that end, do you have a photograph of this hideous creature?' asked Barney.

'We do indeed,' said Harriet, as she pulled Brendon's true crime magazine out of her bag. 'This is the clearest image we have of her.'

'May I?' asked Barney. He reached out and took the magazine. 'For starters I'll get Beatrice to run off a hundred copies of this. That should do for now.'

'A hundred? That's a lot of copies.' Liz sounded surprised.

'It's just a starter. We'll probably need more. If we're to stand any chance of finding and stopping her we're going to have to think big,' said Barney.

'But you can't risk going public on this as it'll let her know we're on to her. In which case she'll either stop all together or move abroad and start again,' said Harriet.

'We're not going public on this. We just need to get the word out there to the sort of people who might be in the cross hairs. I'm going to give everyone on my workforce a copy. If she sets foot on my estate I want to know about it. Plus, I regularly socialise with just the sort of men she'd prey on. And let's not forget, I have a wide network of old school chums.'

'Can you make some copies for us too?' asked Sylvie. 'I think we should give them to Ralph. After all, he's rich and single, and I wouldn't be at all surprised if he knows other men she's likely to target.'

'Ralph?' asked Barney. He raised an eyebrow questioningly.

Sylvie quickly filled him in on their recent discovery of Bertie's family.

'Absolutely, how many do you need?' said Barney. 'The more we spread the word in the right circles, the better. For her to have done this at least four times it can't be purely about the money. I'd hazard a guess she's already got more than enough money to be comfortably off for the rest of her life. And that amount of wealth gives her real choices. She could take herself off in the blink of an eye and reinvent herself half-way across the world. Somewhere where there was no risk of anyone finding her. Yet instead, she chooses to groom a new victim shortly after killing her last. It's a compulsion. She's playing a deadly game and getting a kick out of it. It seems to me that she's not going to stop until she's caught.'

'If you ask me, it's time this spider got caught in a web of her own making,' said Liz.

'My thought precisely,' said Barney. 'We must get things up and running immediately. Now there's a lot to do, so once the copies are ready, we'll go our separate ways, and touch base this evening. I just hope that we're not too late.'

# CHAPTER 40

This new-found glimmer of hope lightened the mood as they headed back to the village. In reality, they were no closer to finding Tess. But with the realisation that Barney had the ear of the Chief Constable came the understanding that soon they might have a powerful ally in their corner.

Over the years, Sylvie and Liz had witnessed many examples of Barney's tenacity. He might very well be hopeless in love, but he was an impressive man who wouldn't allow their concerns to be ignored. He'd insist his mate, Andy, treat them seriously, and demand that an immediate and thorough investigation commence. The vast swathes of ordinary folk had no sway over the police. But there were a few individuals, such as Barney, who had the power and influence to make things happen.

For the first time since it became apparent that Tess was a black widow, it felt as though they were not alone in their mission to find and bring her to justice.

'I know you two are planning to speak to Ralph,' said Liz. 'But I've so much to get on with at the tearoom. Would you mind if I left you to it?'

'That's fine, Liz. Best you get on with things. I know I've dropped you in it as I'm not pulling my weight, and I'm really grateful for everything you're doing to pick up the slack. I just wish I could help more, but my head's not in the right space, and I know I won't be able to settle back into a routine until we've done everything possible to find this woman,' said Sylvie.

Liz squeezed her friend's hand. 'Go do what you need to do, and don't worry about the business. I've got things under control.'

While Sylvie and Liz were chatting, Harriet used the time to phone Ralph. She filled him in on recent developments and asked if he'd like to meet up, so that they could give him a stack of photographs of Tess. He agreed, as just like Barney he knew many wealthy single men who could quite easily be targeted by the woman who had recently murdered his brother.

Ralph explained that he was about to go into a meeting at a venue located about an hour's drive from Monksworthy. The meeting was scheduled to last no more than an hour and they agreed to meet up with him at a nearby pub as soon as he was finished.

When the two women arrived at the meeting point, there was no sign of Ralph. It was a typical country pub, quaint, with low ceilings, beams that could quite easily be hazardous for unwary taller persons, and an inglenook fireplace which, given the pleasant temperature, was unlit. As it was early, the place was reasonably quiet. It was too late for those wanting lunch, and too early for the after-work crowd. They chose a table close to one of the windows, as it overlooked the car park. They would undoubtedly spot Ralph when he arrived.

Harriet was at the bar, ordering them both a lime and soda, when Sylvie's phone rang. The sound took her by surprise, and caused her to flinch. Rummaging through her bag she located it moments before it went to answerphone. The caller ID said it was Barney. Sylvie's stomach lurched in anticipation of what she was about to be told.

'I hope I haven't caught you at a bad time?' asked Barney.

'No, it's fine. We're in a pub, waiting for Bertie's brother to arrive.'

'Just wanted to let you know that things are moving apace at this end.'

'Why, what's happened?' Sylvie's voice was suddenly shrill.

Harriet, who was on her way back from the bar, looked at her questioningly. When Sylvie ignored her, she placed the drinks on the table and sat down to listen to Sylvie's side of the conversation.

'I think you might just have saved my life,' said Barney. 'Which means that as well as my friendship, you now have my eternal gratitude.'

'What do you mean, saved your life?' Sylvie's heart began to race.

'After you left, I placed a call to Andy, the Chief Constable. As usual, he was in the middle of something, and his secretary said she'd get him to return my call. Not wanting to waste any time, I headed over to the spa. Which, as you know, has a relatively select clientele.'

'You mean that most ordinary people have better things to spend their money on,' interjected Sylvie.

'Harsh assessment, but possibly fair,' said Barney. 'Anyway, I digress. My thought process was that it was just the sort of place that someone like this Tess would probably use. Either on the off chance of making a connection with a possible next target, or merely to unwind.'

'And?' pressed Sylvie. 'Oh, c'mon, Barney. You're stringing this out. What happened?'

Barney sighed. 'Very well. To cut a long story short, I took some copies of Tess's photograph over to the spa, and a couple of the staff recognised her.'

'Is she one of the regulars?' There was no escaping the impatience in Sylvie's voice.

'No. From what I was able to ascertain, she's only been there on one occasion. The day Bertie died.'

Sylvie gasped. 'Poor Bertie wasn't even cold, and she was already looking for her next victim.'

'Either that, or it was an attempt to give herself some sort of alibi,' said Barney.

'She would've travelled a fair distance to get to your spa. She'd come from just outside Bath. Oh, Barney, I'm so glad you were away on a business trip. Otherwise, you might have bumped into her. One thing could have led to another, and you could have been her next victim. You fit the profile of the men she targets, and since Bertie had lied to everyone about his identity, she would have had no idea of his connection to the area.'

Barney cleared his throat. When he next spoke, there was a noticeable wobble to his voice. 'Best not to dwell on what might have been. I haven't told you the best bit, yet.'

'Go on,' said Sylvie.

'I checked the security footage and the guest register. She didn't check in as Tess Harris. Apparently, she was Thea Robinson. She paid by debit card, and the external cameras show her arriving and leaving. Which means we have the make, model and number plate of the vehicle she was driving. Anyway, Andy's popping around shortly. And I'll be passing on all the information we have.'

Sylvie squealed with delight. 'Oh, Barney, how can I ever thank you? You really are the best.'

'No thanks needed, Sylvie. As I've already said, I think it's highly likely that you've saved my life.'

'One more thing, Barney, could you text me the details of her vehicle? I think it's wise for us to pass that on to Ralph. Just in case.'

Sylvie disconnected the call and turned to Harriet, who was all but champing at the bit to discover what Barney had been saying. As she updated her, Sylvie's phone pinged. It was a text message from Barney, relaying details of Thea Robinson's vehicle.

# CHAPTER 41

Harriet and Sylvie were deep in conversation when Ralph arrived. They'd chosen to sit by the window to enable them to spot his car as it pulled into the car park, but they were so engrossed with discussing Barney's update that they hadn't once looked out of the window.

'Sorry I'm late. The meeting overran. Justin Delaney is such a windbag. So full of his self-importance. It's hard to get a word in edgeways.'

'No matter. You're here now,' said Harriet.

'Can I get you both another drink?' asked Ralph. He pointed at their almost empty glasses.

'Yes, please. Lime and soda,' said Sylvie.

'Me too,' echoed Harriet.

Ralph placed his coat and briefcase on one of the free chairs and headed to the bar. He returned a few moments later. 'The barman said he'll bring them over.' He pulled out a chair and sat down. 'So, let's see this photograph. I hope it's clearer than the one you showed me the other day. Frankly it was impossible to get much of an idea of what she looked like.'

'This is much better,' said Harriet. 'Of course, she could have changed her hairstyle, or the colour of it. So, it's possible she doesn't look quite the same now. But at least it should give you a better idea of what she might look like.' She handed him one of the photographs.

Ralph studied it closely. 'So, this is the woman who killed my brother.' He sighed and shook his head. 'What the hell was he thinking? She's young enough to have been his daughter. But I suppose it would've been quite the ego boost.'

'Precisely,' said Sylvie. 'Bertie was asking for trouble, deceiving us the way he did, but still . . . He didn't deserve to die like that. None of them did.'

'Are you saying that this woman's killed more men?' Ralph looked from one to the other, as they both nodded.

'That photograph's from a true crime magazine article. It was taken way before she killed Albie,' said Harriet. 'I called in favours and got the contact details for the woman who approached the magazine about her brother's murder. We went to see her the other day.'

'That's when we discovered that Thea had already killed three men, possibly even more, before she killed Bertie,' said Sylvie.

The barman arrived with their drinks, and they fell silent until he was out of earshot.

'Thea? I thought you said her name was Tess,' said Ralph.

'Bertie knew her as Tess, but we've just learned that on the day she murdered him, she was already passing herself off as someone named Thea Robinson.'

'I'm sorry, I need a moment to get my head around this,' said Ralph. He picked up his glass and gulped some orange juice. 'Just as well I'm teetotal, eh?' he said with a wry smile. 'This is enough to drive anyone to drink.'

'We know how you feel,' sympathised Harriet. 'The more we find out the worse it gets.'

'Are you saying she's a serial killer?'

'Yes. She's what's known as a black widow,' said Sylvie. 'From what we've learned, she targets wealthy older men. Marries them, then kills them for their money.'

'And just like Albie, she reinvents herself under a new identity. To a certain extent they were two of a kind. Both con artists. The only difference between them was that I don't believe that Albie set out to intentionally hurt anyone. Though I recently discovered that he remortgaged my house without my knowledge, and the property wasn't even in his name. That aside, she's all about the money, and she murders the men she sets out to con,' said Harriet.

'My God, until you told me about this, I didn't think things could get any worse. This really is a case where truth is stranger than fiction. I'd even go as far as to say that it's more outrageous than any plot in Mother's novels.'

'We've also just established what car she drives, and we have the vehicle's registration number,' said Sylvie. 'Though it's conceivable she might have sold it on and got herself another one by now.'

'We're hoping that you can put the word out. Let's face it, you move in different circles to us, so chances are you might know rich, single, older men that she might hit on. One of our friends is wealthy and well connected, and he's contacting men in his social circle who might be vulnerable to someone like her. But as we've no idea where she's moved to, we were wondering if you'd do the same? We just don't want her to kill anyone else. We've brought along a stack of photographs so that you could hand them out to anyone who might need them.'

'Absolutely, but first tell me everything you know,' said Ralph. 'You see, a close friend of mine runs a dating site for single, wealthy older gentlemen. It's a very select service. You have to supply proof of your financial worth before you're granted membership. I think I might just give him a call and let him know about this. After all, if this diabolical woman gets wind of it, she might think it's worth the risk. Let's face it, she missed out on any payday she was expecting to get from Albert. Which makes it likely she'll want to make the next one count. What better way to do that than target someone who is extremely wealthy?'

204

They continued their discussions for a while and Ralph assured them that he'd stay in regular contact and keep them informed of any developments at his end. When Harriet and Sylvie headed back to Monksworthy they were confident that they had done everything possible to cover all the bases. Whatever happened now was out of their hands.

# CHAPTER 42

Time passed and it was almost a month since Albert's death. Barney had been true to his word. He'd come up trumps and called in a massive favour from the Chief Constable. Yet despite the police now taking their claims seriously and actively searching for Tess, Thea, or whatever it was she might have subsequently decided to call herself, they had no luck in finding her. It seemed likely that she had either gone to ground in another part of the country or relocated somewhere abroad. Possibly somewhere that didn't have an extradition treaty, so that she could live out her life without the ever-present fear of being arrested and forcibly returned to Britain to stand trial for her alleged crimes.

Not a day went by when Barney didn't speak to Sylvie, either on the phone or in person. Discovering that this woman had visited his spa on the very day that she had murdered Sylvie's husband affected Barney deeply. Especially when he learned that she was a black widow who targeted rich, lonely men. He'd always been a hopeless romantic, and this made it impossible for him to ignore the fact that he might very well have succumbed to her charms and, in effect, sealed his own death warrant. It was a possibility he didn't want to dwell on, but he appreciated that he'd had a lucky escape. If he hadn't been on an extended business trip at the time, then he might have popped across to the spa and things could have played out very differently.

Barney reassured Sylvie and Harriet that he was in regular contact with the Chief Constable. He was determined to keep up the pressure to ensure that finding Albert's killer remained high on Andy's agenda.

As those weeks had passed by, it seemed that life was beginning to get back to normal. Well, as normal as it could since they had still not been able to have Albert's funeral. Following the post-mortem, his body had eventually been released, but as usual there was a backlog at the crematorium, which resulted in a long wait for the funeral.

Much to Liz's relief, Sylvie had resumed work at the tearoom. She was the first to admit that she wasn't fully up to speed. Unsurprisingly, in quieter moments her thoughts were still preoccupied with Bertie's betrayal and the woman responsible for his death. Still, she acknowledged that it helped to keep busy. And the tearoom was the perfect place to surround herself with people. The sound of chatter and laughter, combined with the aroma of baked goods, was guaranteed to stimulate the endorphins and lighten the mood.

Harriet was back in her usual routine too. She was still worried about the house, as it was proving not to be a straightforward case of accepting that Albert had fraudulently taken out a mortgage on a property that, although he had lived there for many years, he didn't legally own.

She remained in daily contact with both Sylvie and Liz. Through their shared experience, their friendship had deepened, and it was a connection all three women were determined to maintain. Despite being in limbo until the legalities over her own property were sorted out, Harriet was determined to sell the place eventually, as it no longer held the appeal it once had. She hadn't yet said anything to the others, but she hoped to buy a cottage in Monksworthy as she had become fond of the village. In recent weeks she was spending an increasing amount of time there. Sylvie even kept a bed made up for her in one of the spare rooms, for the occasions she stayed over.

That Thursday evening, Harriet was heading to the village. It was the Monksworthy Arms pub quiz, and she was the latest addition to the long-standing team comprising Sylvie, Liz, Simon and Barney. It was a weekly event that they tried to maintain ever since Duncan had set up quiz night.

At the start they had agonised over the team's name. Liz had suggested they call themselves 'Watching the Detectives' as they all liked Elvis Costello, and she also watched a lot of TV crime drama. Simon had objected as he didn't want their team's name to remind him of work. There were a couple of other suggestions that they couldn't agree on. Then eventually they reached a consensus when Sylvie suggested they call themselves 'The Yabadabadoos'. It was a reference to their childhood, as back in the day they had given Barney the nickname Barney Rubble since he was a fan of *The Flintstones*.

Apart from Harriet, who was already seated at their regular table, the rest of The Yabadabadoos were cutting it fine. She'd paid the quiz entry fee, collected the numbered answer sheet and written their name at the top of the page. Sylvie and Liz arrived with minutes to spare, though there was still no sign of Barney or Simon.

'Thought we'd be late,' said Liz, as she draped her coat over the back of the chair and sat down.

'Mad rush, I'm afraid,' said Sylvie. 'Had a couple of customers who just wouldn't take the hint. Thought they'd never go.'

'And I've just had a text from Simon to say that he can't make it,' said Liz.

'What about Barney, anyone heard from him?' asked Harriet. Liz and Sylvie shook their heads. 'Oh well, just the three of us then. We'll have to bring our A-games if we're to stand any chance of winning it. The Doom Raiders are a full complement tonight, so I don't fancy our chances.'

'I see that The Detectorists are looking chipper too,' said Sylvie.

She nodded in the direction of a small group of locals, whose team name reflected the fact that they obsessively spent their spare time scouring the area with their metal detectors, convinced that, hundreds of years ago, treasure had been buried somewhere in the Wye Valley. Their dedication to their cause was admirable, though quite baffling. Come rain or shine, they slowly walked up and down fields and woodland in search of their elusive prize.

'Don't forget to switch your phones off. We don't want to be accused of cheating,' said Harriet.

'Oh, you're such a goody two shoes,' laughed Liz.

'Don't worry, I've already done mine,' said Sylvie.

As usual on quiz night, the Monksworthy Arms was busy. It was a popular event, with teams from outside the area regularly taking part. As people settled down, Duncan switched on the microphone, causing everyone to wince as it squealed.

'One, two. One, two.' He tapped the microphone with two of his fingers. 'Can everyone hear me?'

'Course we can. Just get on with it, Duncan!' yelled someone from a table on the far side of the room.

'Right, you know the rules. No phones. No cheating. Here we go. Question one . . .'

About twenty minutes into the quiz, the door opened, and Barney entered the pub. Scanning the room, he spotted his teammates huddled together at their usual table and made a beeline in that direction. 'Don't you lot ever put your phones on?' he said, as he sat down heavily on one of the two remaining seats at their table.

'Shhh!' hissed one of The Doom Raiders.

Barney flicked his hand dismissively, without turning around. This caused a chorus of tutting from numerous tables.

'Forget the quiz. There's been a development. We need to get out of here,' he said.

Harriet dropped the pencil she was holding, and it clattered to the floor. It was as though the temperature in the room had dropped to a sub-zero level.

# CHAPTER 43

With the collective tutting and muttering getting louder, it was apparent that loyal quiz enthusiasts were fast becoming annoyed by the disruption. Sensing that he was losing control of the situation, Duncan made an announcement. 'Time to break with convention and have a short pause. Get your next round in, and we'll continue with the questions in ten minutes.'

'Come on,' urged Barney. 'There's no time to lose. I think she's changed her name again, and I believe I know who her next target is. We need a plan. But we can't talk here. It's far too public.' His voice was low and urgent.

They each grabbed their belongings, and as Sylvie's house was closest to the pub, they headed there. Liz fell behind as she texted Simon to let him know that something was up.

'C'mon, spill,' demanded Sylvie.

'Spill what?' asked Barney. He clearly had no idea what that meant.

'Oh, Barney!' Harriet huffed. 'She means tell us what you know.' There was no mistaking the irritation in her voice.

'What've I missed?' asked Liz as she rushed into the kitchen.

'As you know, I've put a great deal of effort into connecting with my old school chums,' said Barney. 'It's not been easy. You know what it's like. Time passes. Life gets in the way, and you lose contact with people.'

They all nodded in agreement.

'Anyway, long story short. I'd managed to contact all but three on my list. I discovered that one had emigrated to Australia a few decades ago. Another was dead, natural causes. But I've failed to get in touch with Percy Cloverdale. I never socialised with him. In my opinion he was a feckless waster. Traded on family money and connections, but unlike me he had no drive or ambition.'

'What makes you think he's in danger?' asked Harriet.

'Put it this way, he's seriously wealthy. Moneywise he's way out of my league, which makes him a target. Add to that the fact that it's rumoured he's had some sort of whirlwind romance and is about to get married. But apparently, it's all hush-hush, and there's talk of them eloping.'

'I don't like the sound of this,' said Liz.

'Me neither,' added Sylvie. 'It doesn't make sense. Why would someone of that age, and with that amount of money, elope?'

'Precisely. If he wanted a private ceremony he could afford to hire a small island, somewhere in the Caribbean, or anywhere, come to that. He could buy anything he wants without batting an eyelid,' said Barney.

'But that's not quite everything. I didn't turn up for the quiz because I was on the phone to Angus Roth. He's an odious specimen and best avoided. But he kept in touch with Percy over the years. Anyway, according to Angus, Percy's very cagey about his bride-to-be. Not shown her off to anyone. But after a great deal of persistence, Angus managed to ferret out her name. It's Taylor Smith.'

Sylvie's hands shot to her chest. 'It's got to be her. She always chooses a first name beginning with T. She's reinvented herself.'

'She must've got spooked, when she realised that Albie played her,' said Harriet. 'She probably has readily available documentation for multiple false identities.'

'Sounds reasonable. I'm sure someone like her would do that,' agreed Liz. As she spoke, the front door opened.

'Sorry I'm late,' called Simon. 'Got held up on shift. So, what have I missed?' He looked at the four worried faces, all turned in his direction. Then held up his hands as they all started talking at once.

'Stop!' he ordered. 'One at a time, please. Otherwise, it's just a wall of sound and I can't make sense of what's being said.'

'You've done the groundwork, Barney. It's best you explain,' said Harriet.

Simon pulled out a seat and sat down. He placed his notebook on the table. Listened attentively and made copious notes while Barney went through his findings once more. Occasionally, he asked Barney to pause and answer some pertinent questions as his exposition unfolded.

'So?' asked Liz. 'What are we going to do?'

'There's no "we". You're not going to do anything,' said Simon. His tone was firm. 'The best I can promise is that I'll pass this information up the chain of command.'

'I'll give Andy a call,' said Barney. 'The Chief Constable to you,' he said, as he nodded in Simon's direction.

'I might not move in your social circles, but I know who he is, Barney.' He sighed. 'Fine. Give him a call. But I'm sure that he'll say that as yet, there's no evidence that a crime is about to be committed. For all we know, this could just be a coincidence.'

'But it fits the profile,' said Sylvie.

'First off, you've only got . . .' Simon, flicked through his notes, 'Angus Roth's word for it. He could have made it up.'

'Why on earth would he do that?' Barney interjected.

'I've no idea,' said Simon. 'He might be telling the truth. Then again, he might not. You've already said that you don't trust the man. There could be all sorts of reasons why he would make something like this up.'

'Like what?' asked Harriet.

'I don't know. All I'm saying is that it needs to be checked out before anyone goes jumping in feet first.'

Liz went to say something, but Simon stopped her. 'Enough! If — and I stress the word *if* — this information is correct, it's possible that this woman could be Bertie's killer. But it's also possible that it's just a complete coincidence and this Taylor Smith is an ordinary, law-abiding person. She and Percy could genuinely want to have a low-key wedding. And if that's the case it really is no one's business, as they're not breaking any laws.'

Since Simon's arrival, his uncompromising attitude had dampened their enthusiasm. There was no mistaking the fact that the mood around the table had soured. The women and Barney had all hoped that he would either pick up the phone or head back to the station to immediately take this latest information forward. But it was apparent that there was no way this would happen. At least not tonight, and there was no point in trying to coerce him into doing their bidding.

As Simon yawned and stretched, he failed to spot a collective glance whereby the other four people at that table arrived at an unspoken decision. They each appreciated that even if Barney called the Chief Constable about this latest information, his officers wouldn't do anything about it tonight.

'Any food going spare?' asked Simon.

'No, sorry. We've already eaten,' said Sylvie. She experienced a pang of guilt as she lied to Simon. 'And the cupboards are bare. What with everything going on, I haven't got around to doing a food shop.'

'In that case, I best head home,' said Simon. 'I'm starving.' He got up and they said their goodbyes. 'I promise to pass the info on when I go back on shift. Though I can't guarantee how quickly anyone will follow it up,' he told them as he headed towards the front door.

# CHAPTER 44

Sylvie followed Simon to the door and locked it as soon as he left. She didn't usually lock the door until she went to bed, as unlike many towns and cities, Monksworthy was a safe place to live. But on this occasion, she didn't want Simon to turn around in a few minutes and walk straight in again. 'He's gone,' she called, as she headed back to the kitchen.

'So, are we doing this?' asked Harriet.

'Absolutely,' said Liz.

'Not until I've eaten,' said Barney. 'I've spent hours on the phone today. Eliza prepared food for me but I was so focused on what I was doing that I didn't stop to have anything.' His stomach growled loudly, as though to emphasise the point he was making.

'Don't worry, there's plenty here,' said Sylvie. 'We dropped the leftovers off before we went to the pub. There're also sausage rolls and a few pasties in the fridge. I was saving them for later in the week, but I can stick them in the microwave. I've got crisps and nuts too.'

'Sounds completely unhealthy but welcome all the same,' said Barney. 'I think better on a full stomach.'

'And we've plenty of cake,' added Liz.

'Let's get on with it. The sooner we head out the better,' said Barney.

Sylvie set about heating things in the microwave as Liz took plates out of the cupboard and Harriet made a pot of tea. Within minutes the aroma of sausage rolls and pasties filled the air. Soon they were all tucking in as though they were ravenous.

With tea brewed, poured and now steaming in mugs, they each selected a cake. Now the initial pangs of hunger had abated, everyone was more relaxed and clear-headed, which allowed them the opportunity to discuss their next move.

'If we're all in agreement, I think we should pay Percy Cloverdale a visit,' said Sylvie.

'Definitely. We need to track him down straight away,' said Harriet.

'I think Simon had a point,' said Liz. Her cheeks coloured when she saw the others glare at her. 'Well, I'm only saying that he could be right. We don't know for certain that the woman this Percy's marrying is the black widow.'

'I agree that there's an element of doubt,' said Barney. 'Which is why we need to establish the facts one way or the other. And I think we should do that tonight. If we've got it wrong, the worst that could happen is that we've made fools of ourselves. But if we're right, we could save a man's life. It doesn't matter that I've never really liked Percy. It's the right thing to do.

'And don't forget, that vile woman visited my spa. If I'd come face to face with her, she'd have played me like a fiddle. That means that I came this close to becoming one of her victims.' Barney held his thumb and forefinger millimetres apart to emphasise his point. 'It terrifies me to think that if events had transpired differently, you could have been planning my funeral . . .' Barney's voice faltered.

Sylvie hugged her friend tightly and whispered in his ear. 'We've got your back. Now, man up and stop with all the histrionics. You're here. You're safe. We've a killer to catch and you're the only one who can lead us to Percy Cloverdale.'

As Sylvie released him, Barney's moment of weakness dissipated, as it suddenly occurred to him that both of his childhood friends knew and accepted him for what he was — weaknesses and all. But Harriet was a recent addition to their group, and he was uncertain about what she might think of him. And there was something about Harriet that he quite liked. A feeling which, once all this awfulness had been put to bed, might evolve into something that transcended the bounds of friendship.

Barney cleared his throat. 'Profound apologies for my momentary wobble. I'm just so far out of my comfort zone that I don't know what came over me.'

'Don't worry about it,' said Harriet. 'Since learning about what happened with Albie, I'm sure we've all had wobbles. I, for one, have most definitely experienced moments when I've felt vulnerable. But what I've also learned is that we're stronger as a group, and even if we don't end up stopping this woman, we have something she'll never have. We have true friendship.'

'Absolutely,' said Liz. 'All for one . . .'

'And one for all!' chorused the others.

'Right, ladies, it's time we set off,' said Barney. 'We've a long drive ahead of us and the clock's ticking. We'll take my car. It'll help me focus and we might as well make the journey in comfort.'

As it turned out, the journey took more than three hours despite much of it being on open roads with little traffic. Midnight was approaching as they reached Percy Cloverdale's home. Yet again it was one of grand proportions, set in acres of English countryside. This didn't come as a surprise as he had been a pupil at the exclusive private school Barney had also attended. Whether or not he'd gone on to carve out a successful career, this was a man who lived a privileged life.

As they approached the main residence, movement sensors activated a series of security lights. For ten yards or so from the perimeter of the manor house the area was transformed from what had been almost absolute darkness to what now resembled a floodlit stage. The shock of being caught out in such a way would undoubtedly be the perfect deterrent for any would-be burglars. But for the four occupants of the vehicle, it wasn't an issue. They wanted Percy Cloverdale to know they were there, because the sooner they got to speak to him the better.

Liz gasped the moment she got her first look at the imposing Gothic manor house. Being a creative person, it was natural for her imagination to run wild with all sorts of off-the-wall thoughts entering her head. The residence appeared more creepy than homely. With mullioned windows, and oversized front entrance it was quite easy for her to imagine the worst, as she pictured various Hammer House of Horror productions that could conceivably be playing out for real inside this building.

# CHAPTER 45

Barney opened the driver's window to its full extent and cut the engine moments before the property's front door opened with an ominously loud squeal. Every eye was on the rotund, middle-aged man who stepped outside brandishing a shotgun. He was clad in a paisley dressing gown, and striped pyjama trousers, ending above the ankles.

'I'm armed and prepared to use it!' Pointing the weapon upward he fired a warning shot in the air. As well as succeeding in making everyone in the car jump, the noise startled nearby roosting birds. The result was a cacophony of panicked squawks and frantic flapping as they took flight.

'We should go,' cried Liz. Her voice was no more than a high-pitched squeak of desperation as her life flashed before her eyes. 'We can always come back in the morning.'

'Not bloody likely,' said Barney. 'Don't worry, ladies. Leave this to me. I know what I'm doing. You're in my world now.'

'Whoever you are, I'm warning you, I've alerted the authorities. They'll be here shortly. Now either state your business or get off my land!' Percy Cloverdale was doing his best to exude bravado, but despite holding a weapon a tremor was noticeable in his voice.

218

Turning his head sideways, Barney shouted as loudly as possible to enable his voice to be heard above the panicked wildlife. *'Boars together! Boars together! Sniffle, snaffle, snuffle, truffle!'*

'Good God,' muttered Percy. 'Did I hear you correctly?'

'You did, Cloverdale! Remember the Truffle Club oath each of us swore to abide by all those years ago,' shouted Barney. He then repeated himself. *'Boars together! Boars together! Sniffle, snaffle, snuffle, truffle!'*

It was apparent that Percy Cloverdale hadn't anticipated this strange mantra. But whatever it meant, it had the desired effect of defusing what only moments earlier appeared to be an inevitable confrontation. Removing his finger from the trigger, he lowered the shotgun to his side, and shouted, *'Stand on one leg! Turn around . . .'*

At which point Barney joined in with the remainder of the rhyme and both men continued. *'Open your mouth and swallow it down.'*

Suddenly, Harriet, Liz, and Sylvie felt as though they'd been transported to an alternative universe.

'Reveal yourself, brother!' ordered Percy. He then went on to emit a series of deep throaty sounds which sounded something like, *'uk-uk-uk-uk-uk.'*

Barney slowly opened the car door, and as he stepped out of the vehicle, he raised his head and responded to the strange call, with a volley of ear-splitting, high-pitched squeals. 'Gu-gu-gu-gu-gu.'

'Now that's an unexpected blast from the past,' proclaimed Percy. 'Welcome, brother. What brings a fellow member of the revered Truffle Club to my humble abode?'

'There's no denying that our appearances have changed over the years, Percy. I don't know if you remember me, I'm Barnaby . . .'

Percy, who had closed the gap between them, leaned forward to get a closer look and squinted, as he stared at Barney's face. 'Well, I never . . . it's Cavendish-Mortimer, if I'm not mistaken,' he interjected.

219

'Got it in one, old bean,' said Barney. 'Look here old chap, I've brought along some lady friends, and it's imperative we talk to you.'

'What, at this time of night?' He yawned.

'I'm afraid so, Percy. This is absolutely a life-and-death situation. It's far too important to wait, and it's in your best interest to hear us out.'

'In that case, you'd better come in. Though I can't imagine what could be so important. Come on, out you get.' He opened the closest rear door of the car and, spotting three females each sporting an uneasy expression, did his utmost to reassure them. 'Don't worry, ladies. You have my word that I won't shoot you.'

An audible sigh of relief came from inside the vehicle.

'At least until I can see the whites of your eyes,' he added, and laughed at his joke before turning to head back to the house.

Liz's expression suggested she was puzzled. 'What do you reckon they put in their mouths?' she whispered. Seeing the other two staring at her blankly she elaborated. 'They said, "open your mouth and swallow it down". I was just wondering what it could be.'

'Best not to think about it,' said Harriet, as she wrinkled her nose in disgust. They followed Percy into his labyrinthine home. His eclectic choice of décor and artwork spanned the ages and seemed somewhat incongruous with the exterior of the building, which was surely listed.

'Come through to the den, but keep your voices down until we arrive there,' he said. 'My fiancée's asleep upstairs, though it's conceivable the gunshot might have disturbed her.'

'Your fiancée?' asked Barney.

'Yes. Just between us, we're getting married in a couple of weeks,' he whispered. 'I'm in the process of selling up. We're moving abroad.'

Harriet, Liz and Sylvie shared a knowing look. Barney, however, kept a poker face, and refused to look at his companions.

The den turned out to be a room as large as the entire ground floor of Sylvie's house. It oozed testosterone. Dark wood panelling covering three walls leached light from the central chandelier. Four well-worn Chesterfield sofas added to the manly feel. As did the full-size snooker table, a pinball machine, and a two-lane bowling alley.

'Impressive, Percy,' said Barney. He pursed his lips and nodded his approval.

'This is my pride and joy. I'll be sorry to leave it behind. But I'm open to offers should you wish to purchase any of the items. I expect a fair price, of course.'

'Naturally. I'll bear it in mind,' said Barney.

'Please, sit. Now tell me what this is all about,' said Percy. He gestured towards two of the sofas as he plonked himself down on what was presumably his favourite.

'I heard on the grapevine about your impending nuptials,' said Barney.

'Your point is?' Percy's body language changed. He sat forward in the seat and his eyes narrowed.

'Bear with me, as this is a long story. One that will require the input of at least two of these lovely ladies.'

Percy's head turned in their direction, and it was immediately apparent to all three of the women that he was no longer relaxed.

Sensing that it was in everyone's interests that they get to the point, Harriet decided to take control of the situation. 'Firstly, I apologise profusely if we've got this wrong. But please understand, we are telling you this with the best of intentions.'

Percy listened in silence as they collectively told him their sorry tale. When he eventually spoke, his tone was calm. 'I can understand why you might have thought that I was in danger. And it's touching that you care, but I assure you that in my case, you've made a mistake. I agree that I fit the victim profile, but that's as far as your theory goes. You see, I'm marrying the most wonderful woman ever to grace this earth. Her name's Taylor Smith. She's an American heiress. Her papa, God rest his soul, was an oil magnate. Believe me, she's no black widow.'

'And you're absolutely certain your fiancée's not this woman?' Sylvie held out a copy of the image printed in the magazine.

'I'm—' Percy stopped speaking as the door to the den opened, and a woman appeared. She was clearly of a similar age to everyone else present. Her hair was naturally grey, and her eyes sparkled with intelligence. 'Sorry, darling. Did we wake you?' Percy stood up and headed towards his wife-to-be.

'I didn't hear you get up, so when I turned and saw you'd gone I wondered where you were.' She spoke with a Texan drawl, and was so obviously not Tess, or Thea, or whoever she now claimed to be.

With introductions out of the way, they apologised for disturbing the couple and wished them well. As they were leaving, Percy called Barney to one side.

'What you've just told me has got me thinking. I know four other single chaps who could be susceptible to that woman's charms. Give me your email address. I'll look out their contact details and forward them on. I'd make some enquiries myself, but as you can see, I'm up against it. What with upping sticks and the impending nuptials.'

\* \* \*

The sun was coming up when they eventually arrived back in Monksworthy. It had been many years since any of them had voluntarily pulled an all-nighter, and everyone was exhausted.

Having set out with a reasonable level of optimism they now felt like failures. They had done everything they could to locate her, but their attempts had failed. They now had no idea how to take things forward.

Having set off with the best of intentions to save a man's life and bring Albert's killer to justice, they had reached a dead end. Perhaps it was time to finally accept that it might never happen. After all, this was real life. Not some generic movie where the good guys track down the killer and ensure that justice was served. It wasn't as though they could visit every wealthy eligible bachelor in the country and warn them to be on the lookout for a black widow.

'I guess we could approach the mainstream media and try to get them to run the story,' said Harriet. 'I've got some contacts and could get the ball rolling.'

'There's social media too,' added Liz.

'Won't it just increase the likelihood of her skipping the country?' asked Sylvie. 'And if she does that then we'll have no hope of finding her. She'll just start again somewhere else.'

'I agree with Sylvie. It's not a good idea to go public on this. At least not yet, as it could have unintended consequences. I suggest we leave it a day or two,' said Barney. 'Bringing this woman to justice has consumed our thoughts and some distance might do us the world of good. We're exhausted. Not thinking clearly. I can't tell you what to do, but I intend to get my head down for a few hours, then focus on my work commitments for a while, as there are other things that need my attention.

'It's best not to make any rash decisions. We've struck out tonight. So, let's see what develops over the next forty-eight hours. We'll have re-energised by then. And who knows, maybe the police might have made some headway in finding her. If not, perhaps we can come up with a more effective plan.'

'In that case, I suggest we meet at my house in two days' time,' said Sylvie.

They all nodded in agreement.

# CHAPTER 46

As it turned out, their investigation was soon to take a huge leap forward, and it occurred in the most unexpected way.

Harriet was summoned to Worcester to attend a meeting at the head office of one of the magazines she was contracted to. It was something that had been on the cards for a while but had been postponed due to Albert's death. As the meeting, scheduled to last an hour, was due to take place on Monday morning, Sylvie and Liz went along for the ride. It meant that all three could enjoy the remainder of the day, have a leisurely lunch and mooch around the city centre.

True to form, Sylvie and Liz sat at a table outside a café, soaking up the sunshine while they shared a pot of tea and a selection of pastries. Harriet was due to join them after her meeting finished, but she was already more than an hour late.

Sylvie sighed as she checked her watch for the umpteenth time. 'This is ridiculous. Where could she have got to?'

'They must've had a lot to talk about. Oh, speak of the devil, here she comes now,' said Liz. 'And it looks like something's up.'

Sylvie turned and saw their friend racing towards them as though all the hounds of hell were in pursuit. 'Hope she doesn't lose her footing in those heels. She could break her ankle,' she said.

Moments later, Harriet arrived at their table. 'I've seen her,' she declared. There was no need to ask who she was referring to.

'Where?' asked Liz. 'In Worcester, today?'

Sylvie's heart skipped a beat at the unexpected possibility that Albert's killer might be found and apprehended.

Harriet shook her head and grabbed Sylvie's half-finished cup of tea, gulping it down. 'Sorry. My mouth's so dry. I tried calling both of you. Left messages on your phones. Why didn't you pick up?'

Sylvie and Liz each rummaged through their bags. Liz's was large and crammed full of detritus. Pushing the now empty cup and saucer into the middle of the table, she extracted handfuls of rubbish and unceremoniously dumped it on the freed-up space in front of her. It was apparent to the others that when it came to personal matters, Liz was not the most organised of people. There were numerous letters, flyers, sweet wrappers, two lipsticks and an unusual looking key ring, which had the word Brazil emblazoned on it.

'My battery's dead,' said Sylvie as she fiddled with her phone. 'I guess I must've forgotten to charge it.'

Having finally managed to locate her phone among all the rubbish, Liz's cheeks flushed with embarrassment. 'Oops, mine's on silent,' she said.

'Seriously? With everything that's going on, you both need to always be contactable,' said Harriet. There was no disguising a note of frustration in her voice. 'Luckily for you, I've a power bank and cable in my bag. Plug your phone in while I order another pot of tea. Then I'll fill you in on what's happened.' She handed Sylvie the device and cable before heading into the café.

'Did Annabel get you that key ring?' asked Sylvie. 'She mentioned she'd got you a little something.'

'Yes, it was so thoughtful of her. It's not just a key ring, it's a corkscrew too. Though I'm not a big drinker, so I can't imagine when I'll use it for anything other than my keys. But I suppose you never know . . .' She picked up the key ring and pushed the central part to reveal a corkscrew.

'I've not seen one like that before. It's quite a novel idea,' said Sylvie.

Harriet returned to the table a few minutes later. She was carrying a plastic bottle of chilled water, and the container was damp with condensation. 'They'll bring the tea out when they have a chance,' she said as she wiped the bottle before decanting its contents into a thermal metal sports bottle.

'Never mind that. What have you found out?' asked Sylvie.

'Well, after the meeting finished, some of them asked me about Albie. I suppose it's only to be expected. They were sympathetic but curious. So, I explained what had happened. My initial reaction was to keep things vague. But then I thought, to hell with it. It's not as if I've anything to feel guilty about, and you can guarantee that the whole sorry mess is going to make its way into the public domain sooner or later.'

'Did you tell them that he was murdered?' asked Sylvie.

'I didn't set out to, but I've known them for years, so once they promised not to print anything I started talking, and it all came tumbling out. I told them everything we've learned about Tess. The fact that she reinvents herself using false identities, and I even showed them the photograph of her from the magazine article. That's when it all kicked off. You see, someone recognised her. Not only that, but it looks as though we were right. She's already got her claws into her next victim!'

Sylvie gasped. 'Who is he? Where are they?' Despite wanting this moment to happen so that there was a chance of finally catching Albert's killer, the news filled her with dread. This wasn't just about finding Tess and ensuring that she was arrested. The stakes were far higher, as there was the real possibility that she posed an imminent threat to another man's life.

'His name's Edmund Bainbridge. He's the CEO of a publishing house that is about to be sold to one of the big players. Word is that the deal's due to be signed tomorrow. And when it is, he'll get a payday of millions,' said Harriet.

'That doesn't sound good for his long-term chances of survival,' said Liz.

'Precisely.'

'We need to warn him. Do you have his contact details?' asked Sylvie.

'No. Though I'm hopeful someone will pass them on to me. You see, he's not linked to the magazine. More a friend of a friend of the Editor-in-Chief. Apparently, there was a huge industry bash a couple of days ago, where Bainbridge turned up with this younger woman in tow, whom he introduces as his fiancée, Thea Robinson.'

'Isn't that the name she used when she visited Barney's spa?' asked Liz.

'Yes,' Harriet nodded. 'Anyway, there're always photographers at these industry events, but Thea's camera-shy to the extreme, and Bainbridge was very protective of her privacy. But privacy is never going to happen at a shindig like that. Apparently, she didn't even finish her first drink before bailing on Bainbridge. Made her excuses about having a migraine.'

Sylvie and Liz looked at her questioningly.

'Well, you know what it's like with the paparazzi. You'd have more luck waving a red rag at a bull than ordering that lot to back off and put their cameras away. They're nothing if not creative, devious and downright determined. Long story short, a cleverly placed camera on a timer and voila! No one's any the wiser and a couple of those illicit shots made their way to the magazine. Turns out, one of the sub-editors is in a relationship with the guy who took the photos.'

'And you're absolutely certain it was her?' asked Sylvie.

'Positive.'

'Has anyone alerted this Bainbridge guy to the danger he's in?' asked Liz.

'That's what they were attempting to do when I left the building, though I doubt that anyone will be able to contact him quickly. As I said, he's not linked to that magazine, and no one at his publishing house was answering the phone. Hardly surprising they're not taking cold calls. Their focus will be on the up-and-coming merger.

'As luck would have it, the magazine's editor-in-chief is dealing with some sort of family emergency and left instructions he's not to be disturbed. So, it looks as though they'll have to jump through hoops to get contact details for Bainbridge. And even if they get lucky, you can guarantee they're not going to be able to contact him directly.'

'In that case, I'll see if I can get hold of Barney,' said Sylvie. 'Unless you've already spoken to him about this?' she asked.

'I don't have his number,' said Harriet, as she slipped the sports bottle into her bag.

'It's best we tell him. He can alert the Chief Constable. People of that rank must talk to each other if there's an imminent threat in another force. Once I've got hold of him, I'll pass the phone over to you. It'll speed things up.'

The pot of tea arrived as Sylvie spoke to Barney, and she passed the phone to Harriet who updated him on recent developments. He reassured her that he would pass the information on immediately.

The initial excitement eventually petered out, as they realised that there was nothing more they could do. Having no idea of where to find Albert's killer, it was completely out of their hands. They just had to hope that the police would act swiftly to locate Edmund Bainbridge and arrest his fiancée before she had a chance to slip away.

They were all on tenterhooks, collectively willing the phone to ring to inform them that an arrest had been made. Although, they knew it was unlikely to happen quickly, if at all. And having finished the latest pot of tea, they decided to revert to the original plan for the day and indulged in a spot of retail therapy followed by a leisurely lunch.

\* \* \*

Later that afternoon when they reached the car, Harriet changed her footwear, as she preferred to drive in training shoes. Their journey home was painfully slow. Lanes of traffic crawled along, initially hampered by a broken-down vehicle, and subsequently by roadworks on the M5. Sylvie's phone pinged to alert her that she'd received a text. It was from Barney, to say that he'd spoken to the Chief Constable and informed him of the latest developments.

As they approached the sign for a motorway service station, Liz asked Harriet to pull over as she needed to use the bathroom, and they all agreed it was a good idea. After parking up, they headed towards to the building, chatting as they went.

About ten yards from the entrance Liz stopped. 'You two go on ahead. I'll catch you up in a moment. I think I've got a stone in my shoe.' She took it off and shook it, balancing adeptly on one leg.

Sylvie and Harriet continued without her. As the automatic doors opened, a woman who was heading out to the car park collided with them, and Sylvie almost lost her balance.

The woman showed no sign of remorse. An expensive handbag was draped from the crook of her elbow, while she held a takeaway coffee. She had clearly not been paying attention to her immediate surroundings as she was staring at her phone. Despite being the one at fault she was quick to lay the blame at the older women. 'Why don't you watch where you're going? You almost tipped my coffee over me!' she snapped.

As she glanced up and glared defiantly at them, Sylvie and Harriet got their first look at the woman who had killed Albert.

It took a moment for Sylvie to realise who she was, but when she did, she couldn't help herself. Everything else faded into the background. 'Murderer!' She screamed the accusation so loudly that other people stopped in their tracks to see what was going on. Sylvie reached out to restrain her husband's killer, but the younger woman's reactions were too quick for her.

Being outnumbered and caught on the hop, all she could do was to put as much distance between them as quickly as possible. As such, all Sylvie manged to get hold of was a clump of the Black Widow's hair, torn from the scalp as the younger woman made her escape. Tess, Thea or whoever she really was yelped and dropped her takeaway coffee as she raced towards her car.

Sylvie was momentarily frozen to the spot, aghast at what she had done. It was the only time she had attacked anybody in her life, and she stared at the clump of hair she now found herself holding.

Harriet had already set off in pursuit of the Black Widow. Glancing over her shoulder she saw that Sylvie was yet to move. 'C'mon, Sylvie, I can't do this without you! We've got to stop her before she gets away!'

Her friend's plea shook Sylvie out of her reverie, and she set off in pursuit of the Black Widow too. Appreciating that this could be their one and only chance to apprehend the woman who had killed Albert, meant that they couldn't afford to allow her to slip away.

Liz, who had not yet caught up with her friends, was confused to see them both race away from the building. To be fair, Sylvie wasn't moving that fast, but Harriet was running flat out. For a split second she wondered what on earth was happening. But then she saw who they were pursuing.

Instead of immediately joining the chase, Liz dialled the emergency services. It was only as the ringtone sounded that she set off after the others, walking as quickly as she could until she had spoken to the operator and requested assistance.

Sylvie soon appreciated that running through the car park was a hazardous affair. With moving vehicles and pedestrians, there was a potential for an accident to occur. Yet Sylvie, Harriet and the woman they were pursuing were all moving quickly and erratically.

The weekly group exercise class was the only thing Sylvie did to keep her body in shape. But even that was merely a gentle workout. Actively chasing Albert's killer was stressing her body in ways she couldn't have imagined. With blood pounding in her ears, she winced as a sharp pain shot up her leg, telling her that she had pulled a muscle.

Sylvie felt like Mary Beth Lacey. Though that fictional New York detective had merely performed for the cameras, whereas Sylvie was slap bang in the middle of a real-life situation. This was the most dangerous thing she had ever done. Which made it both exhilarating yet terrifying at the same time.

There was no doubt in Sylvie's mind that physically she was no match for the younger woman. Even in her younger days she hadn't been a sporty type. And as her attitude hadn't changed throughout her adult life it was unsurprising that she lacked speed and agility. But for once in her life, she was determined to push her body to the limit if needs be, as she wanted to play a significant role in bringing an end to this woman's murderous ways. 'C'mon Sylve. You can do this,' she growled, as she reinforced her self-resolve to end this woman's reign of terror.

Having set off a few paces behind Harriet, Sylvie had the sense to take a slightly different direction. After all, it was pointless following in Harriet's wake. She'd never be able to catch up, and they could cover more ground by separating. Which ultimately would narrow the options for the woman they were determined to catch.

Though the Black Widow proved fleet of foot as she deftly weaved her way through lines of parked vehicles, regularly changing direction to wrongfoot her pursuers. For much of the time she managed to avoid moving obstacles, that is until she bumped into a young child, who was small enough to be out of her line of sight and sent him clattering to the floor. The child wailed. The boy's mother screamed, and nearby people shouted their disapproval.

Harriet was the first to spot the black widow's car, as a remote sounded and lights flashed to indicate that it had just been unlocked. 'It's over here! Quick Sylve, we can't let her get away.' She held up her hand and pointed in the direction of the vehicle.

Appreciating that the women were closing in on her from different directions, the Black Widow realised that it wasn't going to be easy to reach the vehicle and make a quick getaway. In her peripheral vision she sensed them closing in on her, and quickly assessed that the shorter, plump one posed less of a threat. Their persistence had left her no choice, she had to go on the attack. If she threatened to harm one of them hopefully the other would back off and allow her to escape. Without a second thought she turned and charged at Sylvie.

Sylvie's scream died in her throat as in an almost seamless move the Black Widow held her in a vice like grip. They were so close that apart from the obvious difference in clothing, it was difficult to tell where one body ended and the other began.

'See how you like your hair being ripped out,' she snarled as she grabbed Sylvie's hair, pulled the head backwards exposing her throat which she swiftly covered with her arm.

'Come any closer and I'll kill her!' she yelled, as specks of spittle flew from her mouth.

Harriet's blood ran cold as she was close enough to see the fear in Sylvie's eyes. In a matter of seconds, the tables had been turned and there was no doubt in anyone's mind that the Black Widow would make good on her threat.

Harriet held up her hands to try to placate her. 'I'll back off. Just don't hurt her.'

'Which one of you has your car keys?' shouted the Black Widow.

'I do, they're in my bag,' said Harriet.

'Take them out slowly and hold them up so that I can see them.'

Harriet did as she was told.

'Good, now toss them over here.'

Harriet did as she was told.

As the keys landed on the ground a few yards from the Black Widow, she shuffled herself and Sylvie towards them, until she was close enough to kick them beneath a parked vehicle.

'This is how it's going to go. You're going to stay back, while your little friend accompanies me to my car. If you play nice and you let me leave, I won't hurt her. It's in everyone's interest that I go. No one else needs to get hurt.'

Harriet knew that she had to agree to the Black Widow's demands. With Sylvie's life hanging in the balance there was no other option.

'Are you going to be sensible about this?' Having regained the upper hand, Albert's killer sounded almost gleeful.

'Yes, you won't get any trouble from me,' said Harriet.

'In that case, walk back towards the building, and don't stop until you reach it.'

'You'll be OK Sylvie. Try not to worry,' said Harriet, doing her best to make her friend believe that everything would be all right. As she turned, she was surprised that there was no sign of Liz. Which made no sense as she must have known what was happening.

Harriet heard the black widow's car being remotely unlocked once again. Swallowing hard she wiped a tear from her eye, knowing they had been so close yet so far. She prayed that Sylvie would be unharmed, but there was nothing she could do to help her friend. She just had to hope this woman would be true to her word and not hurt her.

As these thoughts raced through her mind she was startled by the sound of a piercing scream. Harriet spun around to see Sylvie and Liz struggling with the Black Widow. Though even with it being two against one it appeared that the younger woman still had the upper hand.

Harriet set off at a pace faster than she ever imagined possible. As she bounded towards them, she reached into her bag and grabbed the sports bottle. Skidding to a halt she saw that Albert's killer had blood pouring from her upper arm. However, it was obvious that the injury had not incapacitated her.

As Liz and Sylvie struggled to restrain the woman, Harriet gripped the bottle and raised her arm as she took the last few steps to close the gap between them. Without any hesitation she brought the bottle down on the Black Widow's head. It was over. Albert's killer was down and out for the count.

'Are you both OK?' asked Harriet.

'Never better,' said Liz.

'I think I could do with a strong cup of tea,' said Sylvie. 'I'm shaking like a leaf.'

'Where were you and why is her arm bleeding?' asked Harriet.

'First off, I called the police. Then I used my key ring,' said Liz. 'The one Annabel gave me. It's got a corkscrew attachment. When I spotted her car lights flash, I headed over here to disable it. I punctured the tyres. I think I did a good job of it as they look quite flat now. She wouldn't have got very far.'

'Brilliant quick thinking,' said Harriet.

'I thought so. That horrible woman was concentrating so hard on you and Sylvie, that I don't think she realised I was there. So, when she reached the car, I took her by surprise and jabbed the corkscrew into her arm. It worked too, as she let go of Sylvie.'

'You saved my life, Liz.' Sylvie's eyes streamed with tears of gratitude.

'Well, there was no way I was going to let her hurt my oldest friend.'

'It's safe to say we make a formidable team,' declared Harriet, as the three friends hugged each other.

# EPILOGUE

Almost two months after his death, the morning of Albert Henry Aloysius Courtenay's funeral arrived. Those weeks had been a tumultuous time. Relationships had ended. New friendships were forged. Families extended in surprising ways. And a killer, who had got away with her crimes for many years, was now behind bars.

At the best of times, Tobias Daniels, the vicar of Monksworthy village church was accustomed to preaching to only a handful of people. Yet given the controversy around Albert's life, which had only become apparent following his death, Tobias was certain that this funeral service would be well attended.

Truth be told, the thought of having so many eyes fixed upon him and so many people listening to what he had to say was a worrying prospect. He was recovering from a bout of laryngitis and hoped his voice would project sufficiently. He'd suggested that another vicar could conduct the funeral, but Sylvie was adamant that no one else would do, and Tobias felt obliged to carry out her wishes. The last time he'd felt this apprehensive was a case of first night nerves when he'd played Romeo in a university am-dram production.

Unable to face even the most basic of breakfasts, Tobias left the vicarage a full two hours before the service was due to begin. He wanted to ensure that everything was set up at the church. Not that there was much, if anything, for him to do other than a few last-minute touches as his wife and a few of the other villagers had already seen to the flower arrangements and ensured that the church's interior was in a state of tip-top cleanliness.

No sooner had Tobias turned the corner to head down the lane towards the church than he stopped abruptly. His jaw dropped as he stared at a queue of people, snaking its way along the path and through the rickety lych-gate that always squealed in protest at the slightest of movement.

Despite Tobias's imagination having run wild over thoughts of how this morning would pan out, he realised that he had underestimated the public interest. He had known that there had never been a chance of keeping things secret. Mainstream and social media had seen to that.

He didn't recognise any of these people. And as he passed one after another, nodding and repeatedly saying, 'Good morning,' he could feel a palpable energy emanating from the crowd. This wasn't the usual sombre, respectful gathering of mourners. It was more like a reality TV show. A news crew had already set up their equipment and were interviewing people who most likely had no connection with Albert or his loved ones.

'Excuse me! Coming through!' called Tobias. He spoke with an air of authority as he made his way through the crowd towards the main door of the church. When a reporter tried to start a conversation with him, he held up his hand to silence her. Having reached the entrance to the church he turned and addressed the crowd.

'Your presence here is inappropriate. Please show some respect and remove yourselves from the church grounds. This is the House of God, and the service later this morning is to mark the passing of a life. I would ask everyone to be respectful and remember that there will be grieving family members present.'

There was no way that he wanted Albert's family to be upset more than necessary. After all, Sylvie had been one of the first to welcome him to the village. He had also christened Annabel and watched her grow up. And in recent weeks he had met and got to know Harriet too. This was a close-knit community where life and friendships would continue long after this undignified kerfuffle died down, and he intended to care for every villager, regardless of whether they attended his church services.

Tobias stood a bit taller as he unlocked the door to the church. He had an important role to perform, and nothing was going to prevent him from doing it. Glancing at his watch he reassured himself that he had an hour before Sir Barnaby and Simon arrived to act as ushers for the funeral guests. They were to show mourners to their allocated seats, hand out copies of the Order of Service supplied by the funeral director and ensure that no uninvited person got into the church. This was to be a private service for family and close friends only. But even so, that number would inevitably be far larger than those who had attended any service he had conducted so far.

Within the hour, copies of the Order of Service had arrived, and a single candle lit to represent the life lost. Later, with the church almost full, Tobias's wife, Elsie, caught his eye and signalled the arrival of the cortege. Moments later she switched on the music for the coffin to be brought into the church.

Mourners stood in unison and all heads turned to watch the coffin and the family enter the church. The funeral director, David Pritchard, or Dai the Death, as he was more commonly known, was completely focused as he led the way. His cane tapped the floor as he strode sombrely in front of the coffin, top hat held to his chest in a mark of respect. Six pall-bearers carried the coffin, while Albert's family walked dutifully behind. Sylvie and Harriet proceeded either side of their newly discovered mother-in-law. Each of the three women had chosen to wear oversized sunglasses, to obscure their faces from any overzealous photographers milling around outside.

As the coffin was set in place, a simple wreath of lilies was laid upon it, along with a framed photograph of Albert, chosen by his mother. The service commenced and followed the specially produced order of service. At the appropriate juncture, Tobias called upon both Sylvie and Harriet to give the eulogy, as in a show of unity and friendship they had opted to do this together.

Albert's offspring had been given the task of choosing a hymn. It was another attempt by Harriet and Sylvie to force them to communicate and help the siblings bond. What should have been a straightforward task had led to much discussion and numerous disagreements.

With only a day to go until the funeral, Annabel, Leo and Zara had finally settled upon a hymn, which they all agreed was their father's favourite. The decision came much to the relief of David Pritchard, as the company responsible for printing the order of service was pushing him for an answer. The hymn they had chosen was 'All Things Bright and Beautiful'.

'Please stand to sing the hymn printed in the Order of Service, which I believe was one of Albert's favourites,' said Tobias.

As the congregation stood and the music played, all eyes turned to the printed words. Sylvie was the first to spot the error and gasped. Harriet stifled a laugh. While Annabel, Leo and Zara showed no restraint and guffawed loudly.

As the hymn choice had been a last-minute decision, it had been rushed through to the printers, and it appeared that David Pritchard hadn't checked the returned proof as thoroughly as he should. As a result, instead of the phrase 'All Things Bright and Beautiful', the wording read, 'All Thongs Bright and Beautiful'. Just depressing one letter to the right of the other on the keyboard had resulted in an entirely different meaning.

'Oh . . . my . . . word!' exclaimed Tobias. He felt his cheeks burn and lowered his head in embarrassment. 'I-I'm so sorry about this. Words fail me.'

'Don't worry about it, vicar,' chuckled Ralph. 'I assure you; my brother would have appreciated it.'

Catherine Courtenay spoke for the first time since entering the church. Despite her obvious grief, there was no mistaking her amusement. 'My son had many failings, but one of his strengths was that he possessed a wicked sense of humour. If he was here now, I know he'd be splitting his sides with laughter at this typo. Given the recent revelations about Albert and the way he chose to live his life, he'd be the first to agree that this error is amusingly apposite.'

## THE END

# ACKNOWLEDGEMENTS

This book wouldn't have been written without Steve's unwavering support and encouragement.

My gratitude to Steph Carey for initially commissioning my Jemima Huxley series and latterly this one. Thank you so much for believing in me, loving my characters as much as I do, and championing my work. Your support means the world to me.

Jasmine Callaghan also deserves a special thank you. Having taken over from Steph, you've always been there to help me when needed.

A huge thank you to Jon Appleton, Tara Loder and Elizabeth Hinks. Their meticulous attention to detail throughout the editing process has been very much appreciated.

Many thanks to Jasper and everyone at Joffe Books, especially Kate Ballard. A thoroughly professional team and an author's delight to work with. It really is a dream come true to be one of your authors.

Last but not least, my gratitude to everyone who has taken the time to read some or all of my books. This series is so different from the darkness Jemima and her team encounter and is an absolute joy to write. I hope I've succeeded in whisking you away from your day-to-day reality for a while. Harriet, Liz and Sylvie are my fictional friends, and I hope they've become yours too.

Finally, if you've enjoyed reading this book, please take some time to rate and possibly review it. And perhaps even recommend it to a friend or two.

Thank you so much.

# THE JOFFE BOOKS STORY

We began in 2014 when Jasper agreed to publish his mum's much-rejected romance novel and it became a bestseller.

Since then we've grown into the largest independent publisher in the UK. We're extremely proud to publish some of the very best writers in the world, including Joy Ellis, Faith Martin, Caro Ramsay, Helen Forrester, Simon Brett and Robert Goddard. Everyone at Joffe Books loves reading and we never forget that it all begins with the magic of an author telling a story.

We are proud to publish talented first-time authors, as well as established writers whose books we love introducing to a new generation of readers.

We won Trade Publisher of the Year at the Independent Publishing Awards in 2023 and Best Publisher Award in 2024 at the People's Book Prize. We have been shortlisted for Independent Publisher of the Year at the British Book Awards for the last five years, and were shortlisted for the Diversity and Inclusivity Award at the 2022 Independent Publishing Awards. In 2023 we were shortlisted for Publisher of the Year at the RNA Industry Awards, and in 2024 we were shortlisted at the CWA Daggers for the Best Crime and Mystery Publisher.

We built this company with your help, and we love to hear from you, so please email us about absolutely anything bookish at feedback@joffebooks.com.

If you want to receive free books every Friday and hear about all our new releases, join our mailing list here: www.joffebooks.com/freebooks.

And when you tell your friends about us, just remember: it's pronounced Joffe as in coffee or toffee!

www.ingramcontent.com/pod-product-compliance
Lightning Source LLC
Chambersburg PA
CBHW011454170626
46814CB00009B/3053